TRIGGER

TRIGGER

Faith Underwood

ISBN: 978-0-9989562-0-6

10 9 8 7 6 5 4 3 2   0 7 0 6 1 7

Printed in the United States of America

∞This paper meets the requirements of ANSI/NISO Z39.48-1992 (Permanence of Paper)

For my coach and number-one fan, Mom.

"Believe in yourself as if you are a religion."

Acknowledgments

To my paw, donators, readers, and publishing staff—
thank you for supporting my dream.

Chapter 1

Lena stood over her stove, stirring a pot of rice and wondering what she would wear tomorrow. She'd spent too many mornings rummaging through her closet looking for an outfit. Those extra minutes spent rummaging had caused her to leave late and rush to work more days than she was comfortable with.

She slowly rocked her shoulders to the soft R&B softly playing from her stereo system in the living room. A few candles were lit, and all the lights were turned off except for in the kitchen. She walked to her room, bouncing her shoulders to the slow, drumming beat. Her blue flip-flops flopped all the way down her narrow hallway, clapping her feet with every step. Once in her room, she picked up a few pairs of shoes and put them away in her closet. *I need to give away some of these clothes*, she thought.

As she sorted through her work clothes that she'd worn earlier in the week, she ran across a pair of old jeans she had taken from her mom's house the weekend before. She held them up to herself in the floor-length mirror in her room. *I used to look so good in these.* She remembered where she bought them and everything about that period—fresh out of college, optimistic, and on the hunt for a job to start her career. She always received some type of flirtatious greeting from a guy in the store when in those jeans. It never failed. *I should wear them tonight.*

Everyone who knew Lena knew she wouldn't be caught in denim walking around her apartment unless she was one, heading out, or two, just getting in. She put them on anyway, thinking that Lonnie, her boyfriend, was probably tired of seeing her in sweats. She tugged the tight jeans over her hips and jumped up and down a few times to secure them around her waist. *I thought the fresh-man fifteen was a killer. Damn.* She danced to the music and twirled around in the mirror to check how they fit, then rubbed the stressed denim that covered her thighs. *Who was I talking to back then? Cameron? Yes, Cameron! He was pretty cool.* Her thoughts were interrupted by the sound of the front door to her apartment opening.

She rushed down the hall to see Alonzo barreling in the door with his duffel bags. His tired shoulders filled the cream-colored doorframe. His arms were stretched and strained, but looked firm carrying the bags under his grease-stained shirt. His skin, which was usually brown, shiny, and smooth, appeared chapped from dried sweat. Alonzo had clearly had a hard day of work.

"What's up, babe?" Alonzo said while walking through the door. She walked up to him and kissed his cheek as he bent over to place his bags on the floor.

"Hey, Lonnie." She smiled then returned to her pots on the stove.

"Aww man, you're cooking? Something told me to stop and get something while I was on the way."

"Hmph." She quietly laughed. "Don't come in here starting with me."

He chuckled and started to pull some clothes from one of his bags and toss them in the hamper by the door. He pulled his shoes off, walked past the flickering candles on the table, and stood next to the bar. "So, how was work today?" he asked.

She turned from the stove to face him. "My day was good, could've been better."

He walked over to her and placed a small kiss on her cheek. "What happened today? Did you have another bad panel interview?"

Lena was a human-resources manager for Power Communications, a small yet growing local telecommunications company. Two weeks earlier, she sat in on a panel interview in which two of the five interviewers were totally unprepared. One of the unprepared interviewers was a department head. Unfortunately, someone ended up losing their job that day. That was one of her worst days ever.

She checked her chicken that was sautéing. "No. *Thank God.* I was running late today. Rushed to work, and it just set the tone for an unnerved day. Lunch with Tammy calmed me down a bit."

Walking toward the laundry basket, he said, "Glad it got a little better."

He stripped out of his work clothes and tossed his greasy pants and shirt in the basket. Lena watched as he walked from the laundry basket, past her, and down the hallway.

He yelled from the back, "I'm going to hop in the shower."

Before she could yell back "Okay," he doubled back to the kitchen. "One more thing."

"Yes?"

He walked up behind her smelling like musk and patted her on her butt. "I like those jeans, girl."

She bit her bottom lip and smiled.

He walked back down the hall and said, "Don't burn the chicken this time!"

"That was one time!" *Well, maybe it was two.*

As she was preparing his plate, she noticed a small, oily-looking fingerprint on her white counter. She hated how Lonnie tracked grease everywhere. She'd started placing the basket by the door on days that he'd come over, because his clothes were so greasy from working at Automotive Works. She was sure that a few of her blouses were ruined because of his clothes in the wash, and because of that she told him to wash his clothes at his house or a laundromat; he insisted that that was too much work, as there were no laundromats near her apartment in Ballantyne, a posh neighborhood in the city of Charlotte, North Carolina. He usually stayed a few days whenever he came over, so he needed to wash the clothes he had on to wear them within the week. She wiped the counter off, removing the grease spot, as her phone rang.

"Hey, girl."

"Hey! What are you doing?" Sheree nearly sang. Lena could tell that Sheree was probably leaving work.

"Trying not to break up with Lonnie. He's over here talking about my cooking!" She laughed. "You must be leaving work? You sound ecstatic."

"Girl, stop playing!" Sheree's voice shot up an octave. Lena could hear Sheree's grin through the phone. "You know you're about to be Mrs. Alonzo Thompson before it is all said and done."

Lena cringed. "So, you're going to ignore my question? And can you stop with the Mrs. A-lon-zo!" Lena wasn't fond of Lonnie's real name. In fact, that's how he received his nickname, Lonnie. She had always told him that he wouldn't have any chance with her if he wasn't so charming and good looking. It was a little vain, but everyone was sometimes.

Two minutes passed.

"Hello?" Sheree said. "Lena, are you there? You must be in the Lena Zone . . ." She sighed.

Lena was indeed in the zone. She was triggered.

She immediately saw herself and Alonzo on the couch at his old place on Lily Green Court. She remembered the conversation occurring after they had known each other for almost a year. He was eating salt-and-vinegar chips and said something to her, but in that moment, all she could comment on was his tangy breath. She joked about it, saying that his breath made her eyes water. He laughed out loud and attempted to kiss her. She fought him off, laughing.

He stopped tussling with her and scooted away. "Whatever, girl. You know you love you some Alonzo!"

"Not as much as you do, A-LON-ZO!" she said while still giggling. "And just so you know, if we ever get married, you're not allowed to have a junior. Your name kind of bothers me . . . a lot."

He paused for a few seconds and looked at her in wonderment. "Married?" He paused again. "Oh, so you want to marry a brother? Say what you want about my name, you still love you some Alonzo!"

She blushed . . .

"I AM GOING TO HANG UP!" Sheree said, snapping Lena out of the zone.

Lena cleared her throat. "I'm here!"

Sheree snapped back, "No, you weren't! Where were you?"

"I was here, and what do you mean, before it's all said and done?"

"I mean, before it's over, you two will be married. You'll leave Selena Harris behind and become Mrs. Selena Thompson. It has a nice ring to it."

"And all I'm wishing for is a nice ring."

"I hope he lets me tag along to help pick it out. I know what you like, girl!"

"Yeah, you do. We should figure out a way to set that up." Lena laughed. "Let me go, he just got out of the shower. I have to feed him, ask him how his day went, and all that other good-girlfriend stuff." They ended their call.

Lonnie walked into the kitchen smelling clean, dressed in a light-gray T-shirt and some black sweatpants. "Let's eat! It better not be burnt!"

"Hush now!" she said while rinsing off the rice. Holding his plate, she loaded it with rice, poured some gravy on top, added two chicken breasts, and forked some salad in the corner. He probably could've used more salad, but she knew he was big on meat. Lastly, she handed him a beer in his favorite koozie.

Chapter 2

Alonzo rubbed her thigh as he flipped through the channels. They had nestled on the couch, and he was looking for a movie to watch before bed.

He stretched his arm around her shoulder. "So, I had lunch with Mike today."

She could sense the seriousness in his tone. "And?"

He explained to her that Mike, his boss, was seriously considering opening another shop. Mike possibly wanted Alonzo to manage the new one while he continued to run the Concord franchise. He even mentioned maybe proposing a small partnership between the two of them.

He squeezed her closer. "What do you think?"

"I think you should sound more excited and not so worried. I think it's a great idea. You've worked with him forever and already practically run the place. Yes, you will have more responsibility, especially with owning a percentage of the company, but you'll also be getting compensated for it. It's really a great opportunity, Lonnie!"

Alonzo had worked at Automotive Works since high school. He started off as an aid to the other mechanics. Mike Carruthers Jr., the owner, was a thirty-something, all-around good guy and had taken a liking to Alonzo's work ethic. He started showing him the ins and outs to the business side of the shop as well. He had promised Alonzo that if he finished college or tech school, he'd give him a job at the shop. He even gave him a little scholarship of sorts.

Mike had worked with his dad, Mike Sr., and ran Automotive Works in Greensboro after his father retired, but he had always wanted to open up his own shop somewhere else. He never did out of respect for his father, who had chimed, "Don't mess up a good thing, son!" Their shop was in good standing and had plenty of valued customers in the community.

Mike's suggestion to Alonzo seemed like fate, because it had perfect timing. Mike's dad had passed a few months before his proposition to Alonzo, and he had already decided that he would open a shop somewhere close to Charlotte. He handed over the Greensboro location to his little brother, Josh, who was in his late twenties, and decided that he would manage it part time. So, while Mike was relocating to Concord, Alonzo was attending Guilford Technical Community College from home and working part time at the shop. He didn't enjoy it as much because Josh was nothing like Mike. He even came off a little rude at times, but he knew that all he had to do was be a good employee and collect his check for a year or two. He had to show and prove because his loyalty was to Mike, and Mike had promised him a job. He had obtained his associate's degree in automotive-systems technology and relocated with Mike's assistance to Concord, North Carolina. He felt so accomplished and his mom, Ray, who had supported him through it all, had been so proud.

He sighed. "I guess you're right. I should be more excited."

"So, why aren't you?"

"I don't know!" he said in a frustrated voice. "He's been giving me more responsibility, which I don't mind, but our receptionist—and, I guess, account manager— is messing up, and I keep late evenings clearing up her messes. It gets on my nerves."

"Well, maybe you can bring it to his attention."

"How can I? It's his mother-in-law."

Lena burst out laughing. "Ms. Susan needs to retire, huh?"

"Yes!" He shook his head. "She's pretty out of it. It's almost like she's dyslexic, but with accounts instead of letters and numbers. Yesterday, she charged Mr. Walton's account for a tune-up. Now, granted, we do have at least four Walton accounts, but he was the wrong one. He was one of our very first customers in Concord and has recommended us to a lot of people around there."

Her laughing calmed into a smile. "Well, baby, I think that you can break it to Mike easy. There is no way that you can let her or fear keep you away from taking what is yours. You were offered a partnership. Man up, take his offer, and make your suggestion for changes. He respects your opinion. If he didn't, we wouldn't be having this conversation."

He looked at her. In fact, he stared at her and didn't take his eyes off of her. "You know, if it wasn't for Mike and his shop, I probably would've never met you."

"Yeah . . ." She nodded and smiled and drifted off to a bar in downtown Charlotte. She was triggered.

It was her and Alonzo's first meeting. She was out with Sheree and one of Sheree's friends, Cynthia. They were sitting at the bar, enjoying their drinks. Lena was working on margarita number two when Alonzo and two of his buddies approached the bar. One of his friends shook hands with the bartender. Sheree was sitting closest to where they were standing and nudged Lena with her elbow.

"I see them!" Lena whispered loudly to Sheree. Cynt laughed at both of them. The guys got their drinks and walked to the area where the pool tables were located.

"All of them were fine," Sheree chimed.

Cynt nodded her head and agreed. "I like the one with the blue shirt."

No one knew that the guy with the blue shirt would become Lena's man. Later that night, Sheree, Lena, and Cynt made their way to the sectionals near the dance floor. Sheree and Lena had taken a shot of tequila and were dancing in front of the sofa that they had been sitting on. Cynt was still sitting and probably a little irritated because she was now the designated driver, when Sheree had been the one to volunteer for it before they went out. Some guy eventually came over and sat with her. All was well then.

Sheree and Lena continued to dance and sing with each other. Next's "Butter Love" started fading in and Lena sat down.

Sheree, who was still standing, looked down at her. "What are you doing? I love this song."

Lena laughed and looked down at her phone. "I'm not dancing with you to this." She didn't know why she looked at her phone. It was Saturday night and she knew that she wouldn't have any missed calls or texts. She wasn't dating anyone, and she was out with her one friend that she talked to on a daily basis. She was just about to sit back when the guy in the blue shirt walked up to Sheree. Lena and Cynt were both looking him over. He had on a navy and light-blue plaid button-down with dark-blue jeans and what looked to be dark-brown Cole Haans. Lena smiled, thinking, *She got her one.* Cynt, however, didn't look so happy.

He looked like he stood at about six foot two and was leaning over, talking in Sheree's ear. She saw Sheree laugh. Lena stood up. It had been about forty-five minutes since her last hair-and-face check, so she decided to do that while the other two ladies were canoodling with their new club friends. As she took her first step, Sheree grabbed her arm. "Where are you going, Lena?"

Lena looked at her and him with a confused face. "To the ladies' room. Is that okay?"

Alonzo laughed. Sheree held her hand toward him. "This is Alonzo. It seems that he was enjoying our show and would like to see more . . . starring you."

Alonzo laughed again. He flashed her a bright smile and held his hand out. Lena couldn't help but smile back, maybe a little too hard, as she shook his hand. *This damn tequila.* He laughed again.

Cynt got up and brushed Lena as she walked off toward the ladies' room.

This heifer. Lena's eyes followed her then went back to Alonzo, who was still smiling. "Are you going with her?"

"No, I was just going to check my hair."

"It looks fine," Sheree and Alonzo both said in unison.

"I like him, Lena!" Sheree exclaimed.

Lena shook her head and blushed. Alonzo blushed too, then said, "My friend and I were wondering if we could get you two a drink."

"What friend?" Sheree asked inquisitively, gawking with her already big, round eyes.

Alonzo turned around and pointed at a guy standing by the pool table. "That's my boy, Tony."

"That's cool," Sheree answered before Lena could get a word out. "Two margaritas!"

Alonzo laughed again and looked at Lena. "Is that okay, Lena?"

Lena was looking good that night. She was dressed in a black, high-waist, fitted skirt and an army fatigue–green crop top. The top was cut just low enough to show the cleavage of her C cups. The skirt made her hips look wider than they were and went up far, but not so far as to cover some of the skin from her small waist. She completed the outfit with black stilettos. Her hair was pulled up into a bun.

Sheree interjected, "Look at him. Checking to make sure you're satisfied already. Yep! I like him."

"Sheree!" Lena yelped. She was clearly embarrassed.

Sheree stepped back. "My bad."

The three of them walked to the bar. Tony joined them. They chatted and laughed. Alonzo noticed Lena rocking to the music and asked her to dance. Lena usually never danced, but she was feeling his vibe—thanks in part to her drinks. She was definitely dancing that night.

"I'm going to dance. Are you going to check on Cynt? She's probably upset."

"She's grown! And that's her fault. She could enjoy herself instead of bumping into people. I'm enjoying my drink and talking to Tony. She can't go anywhere. I have the keys!" She sipped her drink. "This is the last time she's coming out with me."

Lena laughed as Alonzo held her hand and guided her to the dance floor. Lena was into him, and he was into her. There was no denial. They talked every day after that night. They were in a relationship within a year.

"Lena. Lena. Lena . . ." Alonzo said in a singsong voice. "Come back to me."

"I'm here." She laughed. "That should make you want to accept this offer even more."

"It does. I'm happy that you're back."

"Hush." She apologized for her brief absence. "But you know what to do. Plus, you need to pray about it."

They finished letting the TV watch them talk and fall asleep and called it a night around ten p.m. She nudged him to wake him from his sleep and led him to her bed-room.

"Dang, girl, to the bedroom already?"

"Yes, but I only want you to lie next to me. I don't know if you're ready for me in any other way."

He whispered in her ear, "Oh, I'm ready."

"I guess that's why you were snoring and drooling." She laughed.

They climbed into bed. They kissed each other good night and drifted off to sleep. That night, he dreamed of them together, and she dreamed of a man from her past, Danen Wimbush.

Chapter 3

Having already picked out an outfit the night before, Lena was ready to get her day started. Alonzo had gotten up, showered, and left her in bed around six thirty a.m. He had a fifty-something-minute drive to Concord, depending on the traffic. She rested well. She always slept soundly when Alonzo was there. She snoozed her alarm only once, which was good compared to her normal three snoozes, and checked her phone before hopping in the shower.

Alonzo: *Have a great day, baby. I'm glad that we talked last night. I'm talking with Mike today. TTYL.* She smiled as she read the text from Alonzo and then sent him an emoji blowing kisses.

There was another text from Tammy: *I'm stopping by our coffee shop. Do you want anything?*

Lena replied: *Cream-cheese cinnamon roll, please!*

She hopped in the shower, applied her makeup, and then put on a dark-gray, tweed skirt suit with a navy-blue blouse. She looked over her shoes for a few minutes, then decided on her dark-gray—so dark that they were almost black—pumps. Lena hurried to the kitchen and poured her hot tea in her mug. Then, she was off with her travel mug in hand.

Beep, beep. Lena unlocked her car. She loved her Acura. It was a champagne color, drove so smoothly, and was classy just like her. She laughed at the conversations from her local radio hosts playing through her speakers. Twenty minutes later, she was pulling up in the parking lot at Powers. She gathered her tea, purse, and workbag, shuffling them in her hands and arms until they were comfortable to tote. Finally, she was heading to the employees' entrance, where she swiped her key card and entered the building. Two big, burly security guards sat at the front desk. She would often bring them pastries in the morning. They greeted her with a smile and nodded as they normally did. She smiled back. "Good morning, Larry, Pete!"

"It's always a good morning when we see you," Larry responded. Larry was always more talkative than Pete. Larry had to be over six feet and weighed at least 270 pounds. He had a shaved head and a long biker beard. Tattoos covered his right arm. He looked big and mean, but she could tell he was a big teddy bear by his big smile.

Pete laughed. "Ditto."

She laughed with them, then headed to the elevator. She waited for a few seconds and rode it up to floor three. Once she was in her office, she unloaded her things, sat down at her desk, looked out of her small window, and took a breath.

Knock, knock.

"Come in."

"One cream cheese–frosted cinnamon roll!" Tammy grinned as she sashayed in. She had a natural glow to her ivory skin, and you could barely catch her without a smile. Tammy was a brunette with hair hanging to the middle of her back, but she normally wore it in a low bun.

Lena's mouth was watering. "Girl, thanks! I owe you big time."

"As many times as you've bought me drinks? C'mon, Lena. I'm still trying to catch up."

"Well, you know I like my after-work beverages." Lena chuckled.

"I like them, too!"

Tammy sat down in one of Lena's chairs. "Oh yeah, I can't find my Powers flash drive. It's one of those blue ones. Have you seen it?"

Lena thought *flash drive* to herself and suddenly found herself triggered and in a room with Danen. She thought deeply, then remembered. *Oh my gosh! I dreamed about Danen last night!*

Tammy got up. "Let me know if you see it. I need to pick up my copies from the copy room before someone takes them. Want to do lunch today?"

"Sure, will do, and thanks again for breakfast." Lena was flustered at the thought of Danen. *What's going on with me?*

She stared at her computer screen. If someone was in the room, they'd think that she was reading intently, but she was in her zone. She was triggered by something as simple as a flash drive.

She remembered being in class with Danen when he showed her the small memory device during second period. They were saving their papers and she had forgotten her floppy disk. He had offered to let her save her paper on his flash drive. She was skeptical but gave in.

High school. Things were so different back then. She had no idea what a "gig" was back in the day. He probably had more along the lines of twenty-five megabytes on that thing, but there he was with his deep-brown eyes, saving the day as usual. Nice smile, broad shoulders, low haircut, sandy tan skin, a football player—someone who all the girls wanted, but he was hers. Always and forever, they thought. They dated for two years in high school, junior and senior year, and even lasted two years through college with a few minor breakups. They were in a long-distance relationship, but not by much. She attended the University of North Carolina in Chapel Hill, while he attended North Carolina State University in Raleigh. They were about forty minutes away from each other. He played football and crossed in a fraternity. She couldn't handle all of the groupies and missed time. He also admitted to not being able to handle them and their long distance himself. They ended and didn't talk for about a year. They saw each other back at home a few times and decided to keep in touch. Besides, they had been friends first before they were anything else. *His lips,* she thought.

A window popped up on her computer screen to notify her of a new message. It slightly pulled her back to reality, but wasn't enough to pull her away from her thoughts of Danen. Her phone ringing definitely was enough to pull her back. She shook herself out of her daze while reaching for her ringing phone. It was from office number twelve, her boss. "Good morning, Mr. Edwards," she said, wiping crumbs from her mouth.

"Good morning, Selena, hope your morning is off to a good start. I ran into Greg from tech support. Two of his technicians are having problems with their new-hire packets. Normally, I'd tell him to help out, but he'll be out of the office for a couple of days working on-site. Find someone to help them for me."

She jotted down notes on her sticky pad. "No problem. I'll help them myself."

She could've gotten Tammy to talk to them, but she didn't really cover benefits. They were still looking for someone to help them on that end. She hoped they would find someone soon. Mr. Edwards planned on hiring at least twenty or thirty people within the next six months.

"One more thing, Selena," Mr. Edwards added. "My sister has been bothering me about my nephew. He's in school and needs some work experience. I told him to apply. Flag his app when it comes in and give him a call." He went on to explain that he wanted Lena to go through the whole interview and hiring process, but he did not want her to hire him immediately. He advised her to let his nephew wait for a week or two, and then she could set him up to shadow an accountant.

Lena listened to all of his requests and answered, "Will do." She hung up and thought, *Must be nice.*

She grabbed her cell phone and started to compose a text: *You will never guess* . . . She stared at the cursor for a couple of seconds, then erased it. She started again: *Danen.* She hesitated, then hit send.

Chapter 4

Lena and Tammy's lunch hour seemed like it took forever to come around, but when it did, they were out the door and on the way to a bistro. Lena was all about warm foods. No cold salads or sandwiches, just stomach-sticking stews, soups, and home-cooked platters. They were seated in a booth near the front windows. The restaurant was chilly, but the warmth from the sun glaring through the windows warmed Lena up. Tammy casually flirted with their server, Wayne. Wayne had a creamy, latte complexion and pretty, gray eyes. Tammy batted her eyes, patted her hair, and placed the loose strands behind her ear while she ordered her french-dip hoagie. Lena decided on a bowl of chicken-and-dumpling soup and damn near avoided eye contact. She thought Tammy was flirty enough for the both of them. *With eyes like that, he must rack up tips.*

"Did you find your flash drive?" Lena asked.

"I sure did. It was in the copy room. To be honest, I'm not quite sure how it got there. I never take it from my desk, unless it's on my lanyard. Anyway, did Lonnie come over yesterday?"

"Yeah, he did. We didn't do anything. Just ate and watched TV."

"Well, that's all you need sometimes."

Lena smiled. "I missed his face. He's been keeping late nights at work and hasn't felt like coming over. I volunteer to go to his place, but I think he's too exhausted on those nights and just tells me, 'Next time.' It bothered me at first, but he needs his rest. He works hard." She smiled hard, thinking about how his hard work was paying off.

"Late nights, huh?" Tammy teased.

"Yeah. Are you concerned?"

"No." Tammy chuckled. "Not at all. You two are the cutest lovebirds, and you are a keeper, honey. I honestly doubt he'd do anything to mess this up!"

"Yeah, but what if?"

"Well, don't let your mind wander. If he does mess up, then you'd have a decision to make." She sipped her sweet tea. "Jason messed up. He has messed up big, but I thought it was something that I could forgive him for and that we could work through. It took some time, but we worked through it."

"I don't know."

"Well, you never know until you're put in a situation."

Lena nodded in agreement and, in an attempt to change the subject from her and Alonzo, asked, "How did your little Lisa do at her recital?" She then realized that it was a bad attempt. She wanted to have a family. She wished she had her own little ballerina to talk about. She wondered when she would be able to have her own proud-parent moments.

Tammy jumped to answer the question. "Oh! She was excellent! The best six-year-old there. I cannot believe that I didn't send you the picture of her in her tutu!" Lena smiled while Tammy dug through her huge designer purse looking for her cell phone. "I wish I'd brought my tablet." She kept searching. "Found it." She started swiping through her photos then held her phone toward Lena's face.

Lena backed up a bit. "Oh, she looks so sweet! If I had a daughter, I would definitely put her in ballet."

Amused by Lena's comment, Tammy chuckled. "Making plans, are we?"

Lena laughed and sarcastically stated, "Of course—not!" But deep down, she wanted to. Lena was a year from thirty and felt like she had no idea what the next few years, or even the next year, would bring. She used to be so sure of Alonzo, but for certain reasons, she wasn't anymore. She remembered how anxious she was to start at Powers, but the zeal had subsided. She felt like she was just . . . there.

The waiter was approaching the table with their orders when Lena felt her phone vibrate in her purse. Wayne sat Tammy's dish on the table. Lena eyed Tammy's sandwich. It looked so good. She thought, *I should've ordered that.* He set her salad, soup, and roll on the empty table before her. She had so much food. She might as well have asked for a to-go box to come out with her food.

"Does everything look okay, ladies?" Wayne directed most of his attention toward Lena.

"Yes," Tammy said while smiling at him. "How about yours, Selena?"

"Oh yeah, I'm fine. It's kind of hard to mess up chicken and dumplings."

Wayne smiled at her this time, but Lena was looking down at her phone and unlocking it. He then told them, "Let me know if you need anything else," then returned to the server's station.

"He sure had eyes for you." Tammy started pouring ketchup over her piping-hot french fries while Lena looked back at her phone.

Lena looked up for a second. "Huh? I didn't see that." She was sure that Mr. Edwards was sending her more e-mails concerned with his family—something that was well below her pay grade.

"My apologies. I forget you only have eyes for Alonzo." Tammy tossed a fry into her mouth.

"Oh my gosh. Whatever. Do I seem that head over heels?" Lena placed her phone in her lap and was in her purse again, looking for her hand sanitizer.

"Yes, you do." Tammy started munching away at her french-dip sandwich.

Without interruption, Lena finally had a chance to view her text messages. Danen responded to her text from earlier.

Danen: *Yes, Lena Harris? Wait, did you mean to text me?*

She laughed to herself.

Lena: *Yes, I meant to text you.*

His response came in moments later.

Danen: *Oh. Did your boyfriend tell you that you could talk to me?*

Lena: *I don't need permission.*

Danen: *Better not get caught.*

Lena: *Enough with your jokes!*

He sent a smiley emoji.

Danen: *Lighten up Lena, lol. What's up?*

Lena: *Not your whack-ass jokes.*

Danen: *lol! Still feisty, I see.*

Tammy looked up and saw that Lena was still texting. "Your soup is getting cold, Miss Chicken and Dumplings. That must be that man. Tell Lonnie that I said hey!"

"You're right, it is getting cold." She placed her phone back in her purse, started eating her food—beginning with her soup—and chatted with Tammy. She never responded to Danen's last text.

The rest of the day went by pretty fast. She scheduled a few interviews for the following week. She was especially excited about one prospect. He had mostly all of the experience that she was looking for, and the other skills he lacked could be taught easily. Mr. Edwards had left early and would be out until the next Wednesday. She was very happy about that, and she had two Internet workshops on federal and state compliance that would block off some of her time. She was looking forward to her next work week but knew that she'd be putting other duties off. She needed to update some applications and job descriptions for the company's career website as well as make a new presentation for the new hires' orientation. She'd chosen to work in human resources because she knew it was a safe field to be in. Jobs would always be available. Plus, she'd figured it would be easy, but her work was proving to be tedious and, overall, uninteresting.

Lena started packing up as she wrapped up the last of the work that she was completing. Tammy came in and proposed that they have an after-work date at the bookstore next week. Lena thought it was a good idea because it had been a while since she had last purchased a book for pleasure reading. Lena told her she agreed.

Tammy said, "Great! We can sit, drink coffee, and watch all of the hot, metro guys walk around."

Lena almost burst out laughing. "You're a mess. I don't want to look at any 'metro' guys."

I just want to take my mind off things.

Chapter 5

"I'm so happy to be off, Momma. It's Friday!" Lena had left work thirty minutes early and was driving home with her mom on speakerphone.

"You say that as if you're going out or something. You know Alonzo ain't having that." Her mom laughed to herself.

"I don't need his permission. Why is it that people feel like he runs me lately?"

"Who else agrees with me?"

"No one."

"You're not making sense, girly. You know . . ." Lena could hear her mom crunching on something. "You know, I saw Danen the other day. He was at the grocery store with his niece. Have you talked to him? How is he doing?"

"Fine, I guess. We text."

"Oh. Have you talked to Dougie?"

"No ma'am. What's he done?"

"Why do you ask that like my son is always in trouble? I have a good boy."

"Yeah right, Mom." Lena laughed.

"He's working now. Did you know that?"

"Nope. The last time we talked, he told me that he was failing trig."

"What?" her mom shouted.

Lena always teased her mom when it came to Doug Jr. He was her little golden child. The baby of the family. She could remember a time when Dougie could do no wrong, and if Lena laid one finger on him, she'd be on phone punishment for a week. Dougie was spoiled rotten. Not so much by their dad, but by their mom, though times had changed. Dougie had actually grown up to be a nice twenty-year-old and was attending North Carolina A & T.

Although Dougie had once told her that he was having a hard time with his college trigonometry, she reassured her mom that she was kidding around. She knew her mom wouldn't spare a minute and ride to Greensboro in a minute to see or check on him. Her mom wrapped up their conversation, mentioning that she had a head to do in about an hour. Lena, surprised that her mom was doing hair so late on a Friday, asked who the client was. It was her aunt, who was as usual doing something last minute— getting her hair done for a program she would be in the next day. She sent her love to her aunt and told her mom that she loved her.

Lena got home, undressed, and hung up her clothes. She threw on a white undershirt and brown, velour pants. She sat on the sofa, turned on the TV, and sipped on one of the beers that she had bought for Lonnie. *Peace.* Oh, how she loved the peace and quiet. *What to do?* She knew Lonnie was coming over tonight. *Maybe I'll just rest until he gets here.* She lay back, feeling slightly buzzed from her beer, and closed her eyes. Her phone started ringing. *Never fails.*

It was Alonzo. He was on the way to her place from work and wanted to know what she wanted to do that evening. It didn't matter to her; she gave him the responsibility and urged him to pick something for them to do. She had no idea what he'd want to do. She honestly wanted to do nothing, but it had been a few weeks since they'd spent quality time together. So, she would do whatever his heart desired. With almost three hours to burn, she texted Sheree.

Lena: *TGIF.*

Sheree responded a few minutes later.

Sheree: *IKR!!!! I'm ready to go. Are you going out tonight?*

Lena knew she wouldn't be able to hang out with Sheree, but sent *I don't know* anyway.

She sat her phone down and lay across her couch. About twenty minutes went by when her phone buzzed again. Another text came in.

Danen: *So, did you hit me up earlier just to criticize my jokes?*

She was shocked to see Danen's text. She waited about five minutes and responded.

Lena: *Maybe . . .*

Danen: *Okay, I was just checking.*

Lena: *I thought about you, that's all.*

And actually, she was wondering if he thought about her, too.

Danen: *You? Thought about me? Wow.*

After his response, she wanted to take back her text. She thought, *Damn, I shouldn't have sent that.* She continued to convince herself that it was harmless chatting and it was fine. She texted him back.

Lena: *Really? Stop flexing.*

Danen: *What made you think about me?*

Wow . . . What do I say to that? I dreamed about you? She decided not to respond. All of her daily conversations with friends and family felt so mundane, and she was getting a rise from texting him, but she didn't want to start anything.

Ten minutes later, her phone rang. "Yes?"

"So . . . are you going to answer the question?" Danen asked.

She blushed. Although she hadn't heard his voice in almost a year, it sounded the exact same as the last time she'd heard it, like a late-night radio host's.

"I had a dream, and you were in it. Nothing major."

"A dream sounds pretty major to me." He laughed deeply.

"Stop!" She laughed. "My mom told me she saw you the other day. How have you been?"

"I'm good. Trying to get these boys to the state championship, and still waiting on Mrs. Right. Same old, same old."

"And Mrs. Ronda?"

"Moms is good."

She smiled, remembering how sweet his mom was to her. "That's good to hear."

Danen sighed. "She asks about you."

She said, "Well, that makes us even."

"Yep. I tell her that you're still beautiful and soon to be married."

Lena's eyes widened. She paused and wondered, *Why would he say that? Does he know something that I don't?*

He continued. "Well, aren't you?"

"Stop fishing." She smiled, sensing his jealousy. "I have to go. We'll talk some other time."

Excitedly, he asked, "We will?"

Shit. I didn't mean that. She answered, "I mean . . ."

He cut her off. "You mean that you didn't mean it?"

Lena quickly ended the conversation, feeling like she was being sucked in. "It was nice catching up. Bye."

He laughed. "Bye, Lena Harris."

She hung up, set her phone on the coffee table, and walked to the bathroom. Her hair had fallen and lost its body. She plugged up her flat iron while looking at herself in the mirror. *Still beautiful.* She thought about him and smiled, then caught a glimpse of herself smiling in the mirror and said, "Get it together." Her phone rang again. Alonzo's contact picture lit up her screen.

"Yes, Lonnie?"

"Hey, I'm starving. Are you okay if I grab us something on the way?"

"That's cool."

"Okay. Italian or Mexican?"

"Breadsticks!"

"Okay, okay. Breadsticks it is. Lasagna?"

"Yep!"

He laughed. "You sound so excited."

"I am!"

"All righty then. See you when I get there."

"Okay."

That was close. She hadn't done anything, but she felt like she was being sneaky. She didn't want Alonzo to know that she'd spoken to Danen. Danen was . . . Danen was that guy. Danen had been the *one* at one point of her life, and Alonzo had his insecurities. She decided to keep her and Danen's conversation to herself. She unplugged the flat iron and pulled her hair in a short ponytail, carefully removing each black-and-auburn strand from her tawny-colored face. It was time to get her roots colored. Her eye makeup was still sort of fresh looking. She took off her earrings, set them on the counter, and then made her way back to the couch to wait for Lonnie. She closed her eyes.

Forty minutes later, Lonnie walked in, waking her from her catnap. "You smell like Eden," she said, wiping her eyes.

"I bet your breath doesn't."

"Stop teasing," she whined.

He smiled and set the food on the table. "Stop whining. Let's eat."

They almost inhaled their meal. "Hungry much?" Lonnie teased her.

"You can't talk. I didn't even get to taste your alfredo."

"And I had a chance with your lasagna?"

"Nope!"

"Exactly!"

They cleaned up and found themselves retiring to the couch, each with a glass of wine in hand. Alonzo started scrolling down the guide.

"Hey, *Golden Girls* is on."

"No."

She laughed.

"You aren't going to ask me about my talk with Mike?"

"I was getting to it." She really wasn't. She was tired and fighting sleep already. She had had a hectic day at work, too. Alonzo told her that he had accepted the offer, but with either his own additions or the promise that they would make some changes to the deal. He wanted to run the new shop in Charlotte, where he lived. Mike still lived in Concord. He told her that it only made sense for Mike stay in Concord and work with his mom-in-law. She asked him if he was fully ready to run a new shop. He looked at her with a confused face and asked why he wouldn't be.

"You doubting me, Lena?"

"No . . . I'm only saying that it's easier to run something that is organized and established. It's a different ball game building a business up from scratch."

"It won't be from scratch. Mike will still be involved with new shop. Ya know? I thought you'd be more enthusiastic. I'd be working closer and wouldn't have to commute no more than twenty minutes. If my commute isn't as long, then I wouldn't be getting up as early and be so tired from driving home. That means more time for us."

"I'm not trying to sound like I'm not enthusiastic. I know it's a great opportunity. I was just letting you know that there's a difference. I don't doubt that you can do it."

"Okay," Alonzo said dryly. "How was your day?"

She shrugged. "Fine. Mr. Edwards is giving another one of his family members a hookup with a job. He also told me that we're getting ready to hire big, but my department isn't where it needs to be. A lot of stuff is on me, but no one seems really concerned." Lena felt in over her head. She was a manager with no one to manage. She was doing way more legwork than she felt she was supposed to be doing. *My new hires can't come soon enough!*

"You don't have any interviews coming up?"

"Yeah. I have a guy coming in on Thursday. His résumé was pretty nice. He used to work for the HR department at a college. I'm hoping he interviews well so I can go ahead and hire him."

Sleep crept in on them. Both of their wineglasses were empty and sitting on the end table closest to Alonzo. She snuggled up under his arm, wanting to be closer to him. His head was lying back on the top of the couch, and his legs were propped up on the coffee table over hers. She looked up at his face. His five-o'-clock shadow was turning into a full beard. She thought it complimented his maple syrup–colored skin. He looked so sweet, and she wanted to press her lips on him. She leaned in to kiss his neck when her phone rang.

"What in the world?" she said aloud. It was two in the morning, and no one should be calling her that late. Alonzo, in his deep sleep, didn't even budge.

"Hello?"

"Lena. It's Doug. I just got arrested. I need you to come and get me."

Chapter 6

Lena started slapping Alonzo's leg, not knowing her strength at the moment, and nudging him to wake up. Alonzo mumbled, pushing her away, then jumped up. "What?" he nearly shouted, sounding irritated.

She muted the phone for a second and said, "Dougie's in jail. We gotta go."

His eyes widened. He stretched, yawned, then got up and walked to the bathroom. Lena watched him calmly walk away. *Wow. No questions asking why he's been detained?* After her moment of curiosity, she went back to her and Dougie's phone call.

"Hello? Lena." Dougie made sure she was still on the line.

"What happened? Are you all right?"

"Yeah, man. My bail is two thousand five hundred dollars. Are you coming?"

"Wait. What? What happened?"

"Man, it's not my fault, but I got a DUI. Are you coming? Please don't call Mom and Dad. Please."

"Okay, me and Lonnie are on the way. Are we going to be able to get you out or will you have to stay overnight?"

"I don't know."

"Okay, we're coming."

"Yeah."

She got up and walked to the bedroom, rummaging in her closet for the matching jacket to her velour pants. She couldn't believe it! Alonzo asked if it was a DUI. She told him yes and asked how he knew. He waited until she was done in the closet, tired from yelling and irritated from being woken from his sleep.

When she came out of her closet, Alonzo was sitting on her bed. "He lives in a college town. That boy is in school. You know he's going to party. They're always getting those kids for DUIs. You went to college. You should know."

She blew out a loud breath and sat next to him, putting on her socks. She knew her brother would party, but she wasn't expecting this.

"Let's go get him. I'll drive."

"Okay." She sighed.

"Calm down, Lena. He'll be okay. He's just in a holding cell or something."

"Should I call my mom?"

"I'm sure he probably wouldn't want you to, and I mean, if you do, you should wait until the morning."

"He asked me not to."

"Well, that's on you."

She packed an overnight bag, then they headed to the car. They climbed into Alonzo's black Ford F150. Alonzo quickly moved the clutter from the front seat, tossing it to the back. He turned the volume down of Wale's voice blaring from the speakers while Lena was buckling up her seat belt.

As he pulled out of Lena's apartment, he tried his best to reassure her. "It's going to be okay, Lena. We'll get him out. He'll pay a fine, take a class, and be on probation at the most. Was there a wreck or something?"

She said, "He didn't say."

"Just calm down."

"Okay. Stop me by the bank."

"We'll stop when we get to Greensboro."

She was quiet. They were an hour in. All she could think about is why he would put himself in that position. Then, she felt bad for judging him. *We've all been tipsy and driven home,* she thought. *I hope he's okay.*

They had forty minutes to go. Alonzo looked over to her. She was gazing out of the window. Her worry showed on her face. Lena and Dougie were sheltered. Not only did they grow up with both of their parents, Doug Harris Sr. and Vivian Harris had great jobs. She owned a salon and he was a finance professor. They had never seen much trouble growing up, so this was a big deal to Lena. Alonzo placed his right hand on her knee. She grabbed it and held it tightly.

Alonzo grimaced as they pulled up to the jail. Lena asked him what was wrong. He told her that he hated going there and explained that when he was growing up, so many of his friends had been in and out of the place. He said he was blessed to never have been caught up with them when they were out breaking the law. He parked.

When they got out of the car, he put his hand on Lena's back. Alonzo told Lena that they would probably want him to stay overnight as they walked to the building, but Lena wanted to try anyway. Several minutes later, they indeed walked back to the car without Dougie. Lena was devastated. Alonzo called his mom as they were pulling off. They listened to the dial tone through his truck speakers as they waited for her to answer.

"Hello?" They could hear the sleep in his mom's voice. It was already past four in the morning.

Alonzo quickly responded, "Hey, Ma. Sorry to call so late or early. Everything's okay, but me and Lena need to stay there tonight."

"Okay. Sure, come on."

He had a key to his mom's house, but both his mom and Sherman, her boyfriend, owned guns. It was best that Alonzo call ahead instead of having a gun pointed at him while he and Lena were tiptoeing in the house. They saw that the kitchen light was on when they arrived. Alonzo told Lena that he knew that she'd be up. His mom was a light sleeper.

She opened the door for them with a sleepy smile on her face. "Good morning, Lena. Baby." She kissed them both on the cheek as they entered the house.

Lena smiled as her nostrils were filled with the scent of cocoa butter. Lonnie's mom, Ms. Ray, had a welcoming spirit. She was old school, yet still upbeat. She kept up with all of the newest trends, which she reminded everyone weren't new, anyway. Her smile, like her name, was bright like the sun. She always boasted about her name.

"I'm Ray, a sunray, because God gave me a hippie for a mother and a father that wanted a boy."

She closed the door behind them and sat in the recliner next to it. "I know you guys weren't up hanging with the college kids. What's up?" She had on her robe and some slippers. Her curly hair was pulled into a ponytail and wrapped in a brown, satin scarf. She blew her hot tea while she waited for their response.

"My brother was arrested. We came to get him, but we have to wait until the morning." Lena answered, sounding ashamed. Alonzo silently mouthed to his mom, "DUI."

She nodded. "Oh well, everyone makes mistakes. He'll be fine." She sipped her tea. "You guys should go lay down and rest a little before you go back out there."

"Yes ma'am." Alonzo grabbed their things and walked back to his old room, which was now a guest room. He walked in, cut the light on, and looked around. He told Lena, "I remember when there was a Li'l Kim poster on that wall." She shook her head, thinking about how a lot of guys had that infamous photo in their room. Alonzo grabbed a navy-blue Nike sweatshirt off of the bed. "I've been looking all over for this thing."

His mom had peeked her head in the room. "You left it here the last time you came down. I'm going back to bed. I'll have some breakfast for y'all in the morning."

"Thanks, Ms. Ray."

She walked in and kissed Lena on the cheek. "No problem."

Lena took her shoes and jacket off and lay on top of the covers. Alonzo lay next to her with his hands behind his head. She turned on her side to face him. He looked at her, still sensing her worry. He reached under her, wrapping his arm around her back, and pulled her closer. "It's going to be fine." He kissed her on the forehead.

"I know."

He kissed her again on the cheek.

Lying there, she remembered how she had felt before she got her brother's phone call. She kissed him on the lips. He let out a breath, and she kissed him again, engaging him this time. His hand slowly moved lower down her back. She thought, *I should be worrying about my brother, not making out . . . Well, it's not like I'm going back to sleep, anyway.* She went in to kiss his neck. He moved back a little so she couldn't reach it.

Alonzo turned away from her. "Come on, Lena. Stop trying to get me in my mom's house."

She laughed and reached for him. "You started it."

"I was trying to comfort you."

"I'm comforted, now come back."

She reached his neck and pressed her face into it. She scooted up for better access, then kissed all over his neck. He squeezed her side, trying to keep his composure.

"Look." He pushed her away.

She fought through his resistance. "Stop running, Lonnie."

"I'm not running, but it's been a minute, and we can't do what I want and *need* to do here, in this room, at my ma's house."

"Says who?"

"Says your moans. You aren't the quietest."

She giggled. "Okay!"

"You can do this and more when we get back to Ballan-tyne. As soon as we get back." He sucked his teeth. "Man." He patted his loins to put them back at ease.

"Don't sound so frustrated." She laughed. "This is your choice." She laid her head on his shoulder and closed her eyes. He followed suit.

About two hours later, her phone was going off. She turned off the alarm and walked to the bathroom that was in their room. She washed her face, then patted her strays down and readjusted her ponytail. She pulled her toothbrush from her bag and brushed her teeth. When she walked out of the bathroom, she saw Alonzo sitting on the side of the bed, rubbing his face.

Chapter 7

It was a gloomy Saturday morning. The sky was gray, cloudy, and looked like it wanted to sleep longer, too. To top it off, it was misting outside. Lena was anxious to get on the road to pick up Dougie. Alonzo was moving much slower. Her irritation showed as she asked him for the third time if he was ready to go.

Alonzo checked the time on his phone. "I am ready, but we need to go to the bank first. They aren't open this early."

Lena had forgotten about the money.

They sat around his mom's house for another hour before they left. He explained to her that she would only be paying a percentage of the amount Dougie told her. She wondered how he knew that information. They stopped by the bank before heading to the county jail. Alonzo yawned the whole ride there. He pulled up in the parking lot and turned off his truck. "I'll go get him. You wait in the truck." Alonzo began unfastening his seat belt.

"No, I think I should. He's my brother."

Alonzo patted her hand. "Just let me handle this." He held out his hand, and Lena handed him the cash. He opened the door, got out, closed it a little harder than normal, and walked to the building. Lena turned in her seat and watched him walk to the building. His hands were tucked away in the pockets of his dark-blue jeans. His head was down to try to avoid the mist droplets hitting his face. The brim of his Charlotte Hornets fitted cap covered his neck.

Twenty minutes later, he was walking out of the building with Dougie.

He asked Dougie, "You all right, man?" as they walked out of the building.

"Yeah. Thanks for coming to get me."

"It's no issue. You know your big sis has your back. Look, man, she's pretty worried. I don't know what she's going to say. I told her to keep a cool head."

Dougie asked, "Did she call my mom?"

Alonzo shrugged. "I'm not sure. I don't think so."

Dougie let out a deep breath. "Man, I'm glad to be out of there."

"I bet."

They both climbed in the truck. Lena turned around to look at Dougie as soon as he sat down. "Dougie, what—"

Dougie stopped her midsentence. "Please Lena, don't start."

Alonzo turned around to look at him, also, and gave him a look. "Dougie. Chill."

Dougie flopped back and sucked his teeth.

Lena raised her voice. "Dougie, who are you talking to? We drove here in the middle of the night to come and get you. I just spent my money, and you're getting an attitude with me?" Lena was fuming.

"I'll give you your money back!"

"Both of y'all calm down!" Alonzo looked in the rear-view mirror at Dougie with his best I-will-jack-you-up face. He rubbed Lena's leg. "He's upset."

"And I'm not?" she snapped back.

Dougie was quiet.

Alonzo pulled out of the parking lot and started heading back to Alonzo's mom's house.

"Man, where are we going? My apartment is back that way," Dougie blurted.

Lena looked out of the window. "We're going to Alonzo's mom's house."

Rudely, he said, "Man, I'm trying to go home."

"His mom cooked breakfast for us."

"I'm not hungry."

Alonzo chuckled. "You know you're hungry." He took a breath. "Look, I'll stop you by your apartment so you can change clothes and stuff, then you're coming with us."

"I don't see why I have to."

Alonzo stopped at a red light. He turned around to face Dougie. "Because you don't have a choice." Irked, he turned back around and watched the road. He made a route by taking a few side streets and went through a neighborhood to get to Dougie's apartment. Dougie was the first one out of the car when they arrived.

Lena shook her head at the thought of her brother. "I've never been so happy to see his raggedy Altima." His silver 2011 Altima, fully equipped with Carolina Panthers decals on the back, was parked outside. "I thought it may have been impounded."

"Come on," Alonzo said as he was getting out.

Lena, not turning from the window to face him, said, "No, I'm staying in the car."

"Lena."

"You made me stay in the car at the jail. What's so different now?" Lena had a full-blown bad attitude.

He shook his head. "Okay." He took his keys out of the ignition and walked to Dougie's apartment. He walked up the stairs. When he walked in the apartment, he heard the shower running. Dougie's apartment had clutter everywhere, ashtrays on the coffee table with cigarillo guts inside, a flat-screen, and a gaming system. Dougie was cutting loose and having a good time in college away from Vivian and Doug Sr. He sat on the couch. It was best that Lena had decided not to go to Dougie's apartment. Alonzo laid his head back, hoping for a few minutes of peace.

Fifteen minutes later, Dougie was walking in the living room. "I'm ready."

"All right." Alonzo stood up. He was almost towering over Lena's little brother, who stood at about five foot seven. "Look. I told you she was worried. Why would you go and jump on her like that? You seriously need to apologize. I mean, are you trying to make her tell your parents?"

Dougie still had his attitude. "I thought she was about to start with me and ask me a million questions. I didn't feel like hearing it."

"Even if she did, you owe her. You're a man now. Act like one." He stopped walking and placed his hands on Dougie's chest, causing him to stop just before they got to the stairs. "You're pissing her off, and you aren't the only one that has to deal with it, if you catch my drift." They walked down the steps, walked to the truck, and got in.

Dougie tapped Lena on the shoulder. "I'm sorry, Lena. Thanks for coming to get me." He sighed. "I mean it."

Lena didn't say anything, but wondered what it was that Lonnie said or did for Dougie to apologize. Dougie could be really stubborn. A smile crept on her face.

Alonzo let out a breath of relief, then started to his mom's house.

When they arrived, Sherman was outside smoking a cigarette on the porch and talking with Mr. Roland, the neighbor. They spoke as they walked toward the house.

"Alonzo. Look at you, man!"

"What's up, Mr. Roland?" He went and shook his hand. "I'm going to walk them in. I'll be back out."

"Okay."

He gave Sherman a hug and went inside with them. Ms. Ray's kitchen was small, but she'd call it cozy. Lena imagined that Ms. Ray had shared many meals at the small, round, brown table that was more suitable for a nook. The pale-yellow walls needed to be repainted—especially the stove's backdrop, which had food- and grease-splatter stains on it. Lena could tell that Ms. Ray had not changed much in the kitchen. Her refrigerator still had a million magnets on it. She remembered from a previous visit that Lonnie told her those same decorative dishes had hung on the wall when he was in middle school. Ms. Ray's house looked and smelled like a home.

Ms. Ray welcomed them. "Come on in and eat. All of the food is on the counter. Help yourself. I have orange juice and coffee."

They washed their hands, then started filling up their plates.

"Coffee, please," Lena said desperately.

Doug said, "Orange juice for me. Please."

"Coming up." Ray was excited. She didn't have guests often.

Alonzo fixed his plate and started walking toward the door when his mom stopped him. "Where are you going? Eat at the table."

Dougie laughed, and Alonzo gave him a look. "I'm going to talk to Mr. Roland, Ma. I haven't seen him in a long time."

"Okay." She smiled. "Tell him that I said good morning."

Dougie and Lena sat at the table and enjoyed their home-cooked breakfast. Alonzo made a beeline to the front door. He stepped out of the house and onto the porch. The mist had subsided some, but it was still a dreary day. There was even a hint of coolness to the air as the seasons neared their change.

"Alonzo, how's Concord treating you? You still working with Mike?"

"Yes sir. I'm still working with him. Concord is cool. You know, I only work in Concord now. I moved to Charlotte about six months ago. I'm in north Charlotte, the Derita–Statesville area."

"That's good, man. So, when are you going to do right by that woman in there?"

Sherman laughed, cleared his throat, and looked at Alonzo. "Yeah. When?"

"Uhhhh. I'm going to get back with y'all on that."

They all laughed. Sherman let out a hearty laugh louder than everyone else's, which turned into a cough. A deep smoker's cough, at that.

"I keep telling Sherman that he needs to give up those cancer sticks."

"You don't smoke anymore, Mr. Roland?"

Sherman laughed again. "They weren't cancer sticks when he was smoking half a pack a day, but they are now."

Mr. Roland scratched his head. "I gave it up, Alonzo. I don't know what happened. I woke up one morning and didn't have a taste for them anymore."

Sherman watched with a yeah-right expression. "Yeah. It was the same morning that his wife left."

"He's right!" Mr. Roland laughed.

They all laughed again. Sherman waited a second, then said, "Your mom wants grandkids."

Alonzo looked over his mom's yard. "She'll get them one day."

Mr. Roland leaned in and placed his hand on his knee. "Well, what you waiting for, man? You 'bout twenty-nine, right? You got a good job. She's nice . . . and she looks like candy."

Sherman laughed. Mr. Roland laughed and stroked his black-and-mostly-gray chin strap. Alonzo eyed him. Mr. Roland held his hands in the air and laughed. "I'm just saying, man. It seems like you have a good thing."

"I do." Alonzo stuffed the rest of his scrambled eggs in his mouth and said with a half-full mouth, "I'm working on helping Mike open a new shop in Charlotte. I need to handle this transaction first. I don't think she likes her job much. I've been saving since I was twenty-three, but I need to know that I can fully take care of her and a child just in case, and I'm thirty now."

Mr. Roland smiled and nodded. "I hear ya, man. A man with a plan. I'm proud of you. We all are."

"Thanks. I'll keep y'all updated." He needed to be getting his update on Dougie.

"Do that," Sherman mumbled.

Alonzo walked back in the house. As he entered the kitchen, Dougie was explaining the events that led to his arrest last night.

"They were all yelling and pushing each other. So, the bouncer made us leave."

Lena and his mom were listening intently. Alonzo leaned in the doorframe and joined the listening party.

"We got in the car to go. My friend Trey was driving, I was in the front seat, and AJ was in the back. I was fussing at them, you know, like what the hell?" He paused, then looked up at Alonzo's mom and said, "Excuse my language."

"It's okay, Doug. Go ahead."

He continued. "But I was really mad, they were in the club fighting over some girl that neither of them really wanted. She was dancing on Trey, and her boyfriend saw and got mad. Trey should've just left her alone, and that's what I was yelling about in the car. I told him he should've just walked away, but he pushed up on the guy. His friends jumped in, then AJ was in the mix, too. I was trying to break it up. So, AJ started getting on Trey's case, too. He was really drunk and talking shi—I mean, mess. They started getting into it. Next thing I know, AJ reached up from the back seat trying to push Trey. I yelled, 'Stop the car.'"

He drank some of his orange juice. "We pulled over about fifteen minutes away from my apartment. Trey and AJ were now outside of the car trying to fight, and I broke it up. I was like, 'Come on, let's go. Y'all know the cops are out. Stop BS'n.' Trey was mad and was yelling, 'I ain't going nowhere, especially with this punk in my car.' AJ tried to swing at him again. I took Trey's keys and said, 'Come on. I'm going home.' I was tipsy. I had maybe two drinks and didn't get to finish my beer, but I was good, and all of that mess had sobered me up. We all got back in the car. I started back driving. I was driving for maybe five minutes, and the car was quiet. Then, AJ said something under his breath, and Trey started yelling again, they started swinging at each other in the car, and one of them hit me, and I swerved. Then there were lights flashing behind me, and I pulled over. Y'all know the rest."

Lena dropped her head and shook it. Alonzo sighed. They felt bad for Dougie. They knew Dougie actually was a good guy. "Did they get arrested?"

"Yeah. They were still acting crazy when the cops got there."

Ms. Ray shook her head. "Foolish."

"I think they got arrested for disorderly conduct or something. I don't care. They have nothing to say to me."

Lena looked up. "What happens next?"

"I guess I have to go to court. I'll have probation and a fine."

"What about your car?"

Alonzo jumped in. "He can keep his car—he can still drive to work and school—but we know some people down here. We might have someone that can help him with his case." His mom nodded her head and agreed.

"Thank God." Lena looked at Dougie. "That's who you need to be thanking."

It was after noon, and everyone looked exhausted. Lena knew Alonzo was especially tired from everything. There was work, riding to her apartment, driving to Greensboro, dealing with attitudes, and riding around Greensboro. He walked over to his mom and put his arm around her shoulders. She wrapped her arm around his back. "Ma." He bent over and kissed her on the forehead.

She squeezed him. "You getting ready to head out?"

"Yeah. I'm going to drop him off and head back."

"Okay. Y'all be safe." She kissed him and patted him on the back. "Call me when you get there, and get some rest, Alonzo."

"Yes ma'am."

Dougie and Lena had already gone to the guest room to get her and Alonzo's things. Alonzo grabbed the bag from Lena. "Thank you for everything, Ms. Ray." Lena hugged her.

"Yeah. Thanks. Your food was really good," Dougie added.

She laughed. "I'm glad I got to see y'all, maybe not on these terms, but it will all work out. I will pray for you, Doug. For all of you."

She walked them out. Sherman had gone.

"Tell Sherman that I'll talk to him later," Alonzo yelled from the truck.

"What y'all got to talk about?" she yelled back.

"Stop being nosy!" She eyed him. He laughed and blew her a kiss. "I'll call you when we make it back."

She waved from the doorway as they were pulling off.

Chapter 8

They were on the way back to Dougie's apartment when Lena's phone rang. She answered, "Hey, Mom."

Dougie sat up from his slouched position and listened in. Alonzo could see the nervousness on his face as he looked at him in the rearview mirror.

"We're, uhh," Lena continued, "we're leaving Lonnie's mom's house in Greensboro." She paused to listen. "Yeah, we saw him. We stopped by his place, but he had to go to work or something." She mustered up a laugh. "No, tell Dad that there were no girls over there."

Dougie released a sigh of relief as Lena ended the call.

She looked back at Dougie. "Dad asked if there were girls over there, and then sounded upset when I said no, but if that was me and I had guys over, he'd be raising sand."

"You're a girl!" Alonzo and Dougie almost said in unison and laughed.

She shook her head and looked at Alonzo. "My mom said hey."

He smiled. Dougie smiled, too, but Lena wasn't smiling. She was upset that she had lied and felt guilty for not telling her mom about the whole night and what happened. She did not want to be burdened with this secret.

They made it to Dougie's apartment. Alonzo gave him some dap while he was getting out of the car. Alonzo rubbed his eyes. She got out of the car and looked at Dougie. He hugged her.

Dougie stepped on the sidewalk. "Thanks for not saying anything."

Lena followed him. "Are you going to tell them?"

Dougie looked away and shrugged. "I don't know."

"Yes, you do." She shook her head, thinking about how he looked in their eyes and the secrets he kept from them. There were probably more.

"I mean, I don't think they need to know."

"What about your insurance? Who pays for that?"

"I do."

She put her hand on top of his head. "Dougie, you need to think long and hard on this. They will be devastated if they find out any other way. Okay? Just think. I'll call and check on you later."

"Ten-four," he said in acknowledgment.

She got in the truck and they watched him climb the steps to his apartment. Once he was in, Alonzo started pulling off. "Wait, Lonnie."

"Did he forget something?" Alonzo asked, looking in the back seat.

"No, I'll drive."

"Drive my truck?" He laughed.

"You're tired. Let me. I won't fall asleep. I've done it before."

He hesitated, then put the truck in park. He got out and walked to the other side and climbed in. He directed her to the interstate. He tried to fight his sleep, but once they were thirty minutes out of Greensboro, he was out. The drive didn't seem that long to Lena this time.

She thought about the whole night and how it had turned to shit. *My little brother was arrested.* She really didn't have too much experience with the jail process and stuff. The only person close to her, besides a few cousins, that ever got arrested was Danen. It was back when he was in college. He and some of the football players had been in a bar when a brawl broke out. The police came in and arrested almost every guy in the bar, and then later let them go. The people who had caused damage to the bar and who actually had beaten some guy up were the only ones who remained in custody. She wasn't even as worried as she was with Dougie because Danen hadn't told her until the next day.

Instantly, she was triggered.

She was back in Danen's apartment, and he was lying on his bed with an ice pack on his left side and eye.

"Wow. You definitely lost the fight."

"You should see the other guy," he joked.

She sat on the bed next to him. "My baby." She lifted the ice pack and saw a reddish-purple bruise on his abdomen. "Oh, I'm mad now. It looks like you gotta six pack of grape soda."

"That was lame." He laughed, then grimaced. She felt even more concerned when she saw that it hurt him to laugh. He had tried explaining what had happened earlier over the phone, but she had rushed over as soon as she heard that something was wrong. Now, he explained to her what happened in detail while Lena doted on him.

"You recover quickly. You'll be good. Are you going to practice Monday?"

He said, "Yeah. I'm so glad this happened on a bye week. This could've been a lot worse, but you're here."

"I sure am."

"You're going to nurse me back to health, right?"

"Yep." She took the ice pack off of his side and kissed his bruise. She looked up at him. He looked back and smiled. Her kisses trailed farther down.

Lena smiled to herself. Then, she heard Alonzo snore. She snapped out of her daydream. She switched from his CD to the radio. She found an R&B station and put the truck on cruise control. She liked driving it. She really liked being in Lonnie's spot. In his space. She thought, *Damn. It will be almost three when we get back. The day is almost over. I may take Monday off.*

"So, callers, if you are just tuning in, we've been discussing 'Maybe I Deserve.' Y'all know the Tank song. A lot of women have been chiming in. We want to hear from a man."

Lena laughed. *They deserve to taste their own medicine.* She liked that song.

"Caller, caller, where are you from?"

"North Carolina," the male caller stated. Lena turned it up and glanced at Alonzo. She didn't want to wake him.

"So, what do you think?" the DJ asked.

"I think Tank is right, but no man will honestly say that. We couldn't stand to have that happen to us."

"So, has this happened to you? What do guys do?" The DJ laughed.

"We miss out! I've done a girl wrong, and when she did it back, I left her."

She shook her head and said, "Damn right y'all miss out," like the guy could hear her. "Or you should," she added.

"Dang, brother. You're cold!"

"You're right, but I've regretted that decision. I have to live with it. I have to live with seeing her happy with someone else. She was a good woman. That's my punishment." She thought of Danen. She wondered if he had regrets.

She turned the station. Why was he popping up in her thoughts? After everything that had just happened . . . he lingered. She found herself becoming confused and turned the radio off. She looked toward the billboards. Every other sign was a well-lit fast-food advertisement. *I need to get us something to eat.* She tried to think of everything else. Anything to keep Danen Wimbush out of her thoughts. Alonzo repositioned himself in his seat. She looked at him. *I should be thinking about him and the things we need to catch up on. I need some lovin'. I need some sleep. Damn it. I need both.* Once they were in Charlotte, she stopped at a BBQ restaurant and bought two different sampler platters. She figured they could share both plates. He was up when she got back in the truck.

"You read my mind." Alonzo smiled.

She was glad that he couldn't read hers. "I gotcha, baby." Lena was stressed, and her mind was seeking refuge elsewhere.

She was trying to stop it, but it was getting the best of her.

Chapter

The apartment was quiet. Lena was quiet. It was too quiet. Their long trip from Greensboro drained them of whatever energy they had left from their work week.

"Hey. What are you thinking about?" Alonzo asked as he was tearing the meat of a rib off of its bone. He was leaning up against the kitchen counter standing over his plate. "These ribs are tender!" He smacked and licked the BBQ sauce off of his lip.

Lena was sitting at the bar, facing him. She chewed her pulled pork, and then took a big gulp of water. She shook her head. "You know I used to get in trouble for daydreaming when I was little?"

He laughed. "Why? Did you wander off and stuff?"

"No, it was later. I can't remember when I started, but I can recall my teacher sending notes home starting in maybe the . . . sixth grade."

"Wow. I always wonder where you are."

"I can be anywhere, or still where I am, just focused on one thing in particular." She shrugged.

Alonzo put his bones in the trash and washed his hands in the sink, rinsing all of the barbeque sauce and food particles away. He grabbed her dish towel and walked back toward the bar as he dried his hands. "You fantasize?"

Lena said, "Use a paper towel. I dry my dishes with that towel!"

He looked at her and waved her off. "My question?"

"Sometimes."

He leaned his back on the counter. "Do you fantasize about me?"

"Yeah. I'm just thinking, deeply. I think about a lot of things." She paused. "And people."

Alonzo's face was now quizzical. "Oh."

"Think of it as a gun."

"A gun?"

"Yeah. You can say one thing that triggers a thought, and when you pull that trigger, I blast off into dreamland. I go backward. I go forward. I stay in the present." She laughed.

He chuckled. "I get it. I don't remember you being in"—he air-quoted—"'dreamland' as often when I met you. What has changed?"

"I don't know." That was a good question.

Her phone buzzed on the countertop. She reached for it, smearing a little barbeque sauce on its sides. Lena nearly dropped her phone when she read Danen's text.

Danen: *Have you daydreamed about me yet?*

Lena: *wtf?!?!*

She responded back so fast that she did drop her phone. Alonzo turned around to check out why she was causing such a commotion. He was still standing at the kitchen counter, now eating a second helping of food. She wiped her hand on a napkin and mumbled between chews, "This barbeque sauce. It's slippery."

"You better hope you didn't crack your screen talking about some barbeque sauce."

"It's carpet, Lonnie." She stepped down off of the stool and picked the phone up to see Danen's response.

Danen: *I'm sorry. Do you want me to stop texting you?*

Danen: *It's just, I've been thinking about you too.*

Danen: *Even before you text me.*

Lena was so confused. *How did he know?* She turned her phone off. They cleaned off their plates and started putting up all of the leftovers. She grabbed a drinking glass and poured the rest of the wine that they opened the night before into the glass.

Alonzo watched her. "Whoa. You trying to get wasted?"

"Yep."

"Me, too, then." He laughed. He grabbed the cognac bottle out of the cabinet and poured some in a glass over ice.

"You ready?" Lena raised her glass.

He mimicked her. "Yep!"

She laughed. "Let's toast to you doing what you need to do to me." She winked at him. They tapped glasses.

He grabbed her and sat her on the counter. He stood in between her legs. "You don't know how much I've been missing you." He leaned in close to her so she could feel him.

She grabbed him at his waist and pulled him closer. "Yes, I do." Their touching turned into kissing. She gulped when he sunk his teeth in her neck. Lena had always liked biting. He pulled her shirt over her head and kissed her breast while he removed her pants and panties. She leaned back, allowing her head to rest on the medicine cabinet. His kisses trailed lower and lower until his head was resting on her inner thighs. She held his head in both of her hands, rubbing his soft hair. Alonzo was due for a haircut, but that was the last thing on her mind. She let her mind and body float to a place of some well-needed relaxation. Alonzo stopped and lifted her off of the counter. He gave her a soft push to start her walking toward the bedroom and walked behind her all the way there, leaving kisses all over her neck. They caught up on lost time, and he did everything that he needed to do.

They fell into a deep sleep, having missed out on rest the night before. Lena was lying in Alonzo's arms when she felt her bladder throbbing. *Too much wine.* He had his arm laying over her and cupped under her beasts. She shuffled slowly, feeling heavy, and managed to release herself from the suction of his body curled around hers. It didn't help that they were sticky with sweat from the previous hours' activities. She moved his arm, placing it on his side, and rolled out of bed. She looked over at the clock to see it was about one a.m. *Wow, we were really knocked out.* She stood up, and her legs buckled a bit. She felt heavy. Her whole body felt heavy. It had been a while, and she could tell that Alonzo had really missed her. She was standing at the bathroom door when she stopped, turned left, and exited her bedroom.

She walked to the kitchen, grabbed her phone off of the counter, and powered it on. She walked back in her room, bypassing the bathroom in the hallway, and went into her master bath. Alonzo rolled over when he noticed Lena wasn't in the bed. He briefly opened his eyes and watched her leave the room. She came back in with her phone. Its bright screen illuminated the whole room, and she didn't notice that Alonzo was awake. Lena used the bathroom and washed her hands. She stood there for a second, looking at her phone on the bathroom counter. Then she picked it up and sat back down. Lena reread Danen's text, *I've been thinking about you too,* while she sat on the toilet. She stared at it until her screen went black, then she went and got in the bed.

Sunday was filled with long showers, naps on the couch, leftovers, and beer. Lena had already decided that she was calling in. She was going to need an additional day to process her weekend. Alonzo, however, didn't have that option. His weekend was gone and he would have to recuperate on the weekend coming up. "What are you going to do tomorrow?"

"Sleeping in."

"You're going to sleep all day?"

"No, I'll probably get some work done from here too." Lena was changing the channels from the news to a movie on one of the premium channels.

Alonzo checked the time. "I think I'm going to head to bed. Are you coming?"

"No. I'm going to watch TV for a while. I'll be back there later."

"All right." He watched to see if she was going to grab her phone off of the end table as he walked to the bedroom. She didn't move or even notice him watching.

Lena thought about Danen. She didn't know what to say back. She didn't know if she was happy or mad that he texted her that he was thinking about her. She was torn. *What was he thinking? Does he think I would leave Lonnie for him? What is he trying to do?* She asked herself a million questions with no answers. *I may have to ask him.* She really wasn't watching TV.

She just needed time to think. In fact, that's what she planned on doing on her day off. She turned the thermostat up. The temperature was dropping in little increments. She pretended to watch TV for a little while longer, then turned it off and went to bed. She left her phone in the living room.

Chapter 10

Alonzo's alarm went off around five forty-five a.m. He got up and ran through the shower quickly, hoping it would wake him up even more. He'd be glad when he could leave from Lena's place for work and not have an hour-long drive. It was really starting to weigh on him. He wondered if Lena was really excited about him working in Charlotte. She didn't sound as eager as she did before when he told her that he may be running the shop in Concord. They did have something like a long-distance relationship. She lived in south Charlotte and he was in the north. They were about thirty minutes away from each other. Maybe she enjoyed her space more than he originally thought. But how could he marry someone who needed space between them? He'd never heard of people wanting to be in a long-distance marriage.

He grabbed his things and started walking out of the bathroom. He saw her phone in the living room as he headed to the front door. He unlocked the door, then stopped and set his things on the floor. He walked back in the bedroom and kissed Lena on the cheek. She mumbled and rolled over. He smiled at her and left.

On his way to work he thought about how he was letting her phone make him paranoid. She could've taken her phone in there with her for anything. It really wasn't a big deal. He thought about Dougie and decided that he would give his mom a call on his lunch break to ask her about her lawyer friend. *I have other things I need to take care of. I need to figure out how to convince Mike to let me work in Charlotte.*

He made it to the shop at seven thirty. The parking lot was empty, and all of the lights were off in the shop. He had beat Mike there. *Good,* he thought. *I need a few seconds.* He opened up the garage and made a pot of coffee. He sat at the front desk and went over the customers that were scheduled to come in. Then, he estimated how many walk-ins they would have. He didn't think they would have many. It was pretty cool and rainy. He looked outside, watching the rain run down the shop's windows. He looked through the windows at his truck and wished that he had stayed up while they were on the road on Saturday. *I bet she looked funny driving my truck.* He smiled. He really loved her. He thought about her a lot. He thought about all the things he wanted to do for her. He thought about all the ways he could repay her for being there. Then, he thought about her and her phone. *What was she up to?* He was going in circles. The door opened, and in walked the owner.

Mike's blonde hair was cut down into a buzz cut. He wore a light-denim and short-sleeve brown button-down in which his baby beer belly protruded. He was built like a shorter J. J. Watts. He was actually told that he looked like him from time to time. "Good morning, black brother."

"Good morning, white brother." Alonzo laughed and they pounded their fists. Alonzo had always looked at Mike as a big brother, and Mike's feeling was mutual. They always joked that they were black-and-white brothers. Mike's mom also considered Alonzo a part of the family. He had been around for years. She invited him to almost all of their family gatherings. Josh never liked it.

"Hey, man, I want to talk to you." Alonzo sipped his coffee.

"Dang, bro. Let me get in the door." Mike laughed. "I've been thinking about your counteroffer."

"I do want to talk about the shop, but I was talking about something else . . . something personal."

Mike blurted out, "Lena's pregnant?"

"Hell no." Alonzo gave Mike a look and they laughed.

Mike's mother-in-law, Ms. Susan, walked in. "What are you boys laughing about?"

Mike sighed. "Nothing, Susan." He signaled Alonzo to follow him. "Come in my office. I was thinking about opening thirty minutes late today since we don't have anyone scheduled at eight. Want to run through a drive-through really quick?"

Alonzo nodded. "Sounds cool."

They headed out the door. "Hey, Susan, we're headed to grab some breakfast, and I'll probably get the guys some doughnuts. What do you want?"

She asked, "Where are you going?"

He politely repeated his question: "What do you want?" Mike whispered to Alonzo, "She's so difficult." Alonzo laughed.

With a half smile, she said, "A sausage biscuit."

"Okay!" They walked out of the door and started walking toward Mike's Navigator. "See how simple that could've been?" Alonzo laughed hard. Mike pointed out some things in his passenger seat. "You're going to have to move some toys from the front seat. I've been meaning to clean my car."

"No prob." Alonzo started moving the toys to the back seat. "Let me ask you something. How long does Ms. Susan plan to work?"

Mike burst out laughing. "I don't know, but I told Trisha that I may get her mom to retire. She's fudging up my books."

"Oh." Alonzo laughed, too. "Yeah, she is."

"So, what'd you want to talk to me about?"

"Lena."

"I knew it had something to do with her." He laughed. "How?"

"'Cause you were sounding like a sad puppy." He laughed again.

"Stop." He chuckled. "Naw. I don't know. She seems distant."

"Did you tell her about maybe working in Charlotte?"

"Oh, so that means I'm working in Charlotte?"

Mike looked over to Alonzo. "I said maybe."

Alonzo laughed. "Just checking. But yeah, I did. She didn't sound totally excited. She questioned if I was ready."

"That's reasonable."

"Why do you say that?"

"If it's one thing I've learned about women"—he paused—"well, smart women, is that they are logical thinkers. Your friends will congratulate you and not give the work much thought. A smart woman will give the work thought, then congratulate you later. You know what I mean?"

"Yeah."

"She's just looking out for you." He pulled up to the drive-through and ordered their food.

"I'll get it." Alonzo handed Mike a twenty.

"Aww shucks. Thanks," Mike joked.

Mike grabbed the bag and headed to the doughnut shop, which was five minutes away. "I really don't think you should be worried. I know you may be paranoid, and you have your reasons, but don't let your imagination get you in trouble."

"Yeah. You're right."

Mike started talking about one of their customers who always came in with her cleavage out. Alonzo cut him off.

"Mike, she took her phone in the bathroom with her."

Mike looked over at him. "First of all, I'm trying to tell you about these big tits that come bouncing in here every three months, and you cut me off because she takes her phone in the bathroom with her? Do you know I've been looking at the same breasts for six years now?"

Alonzo burst out laughing again. "My bad."

"Get a grip, bro. I take my phone in the bathroom with me all the time. I play games, I text, and if it's my wife, I talk on it. What's the problem?"

"No problem. There is no problem. I'm tripping."

"Yeah, you are! Tighten up."

They picked up a dozen assorted doughnuts and headed back to the shop.

Chapter 11

Lena woke up refreshed at ten a.m. *What a marvelous Monday it is,* Lena thought as she lay in her bed. The white walls of her room were illuminated by the sun. She pulled her comforter over her head and rolled over. She couldn't remember what she had dreamed about. That made her happy. That meant she hadn't dreamed of Danen. She thought maybe the lack of rest had caused her to do all of that extra daydreaming and thinking of Danen. It was because she was stressed. The stress made her have those thoughts to get away. *Danen shouldn't be my getaway, though.* She shrugged and fell back asleep.

She ran a bath, then remembered her lavender-bath-wash gift set that her mom had given her for Christmas last year. This was the perfect time to use it. It may have been noon, but it was the beginning of her day. She lit the one candle she had in her possession and soaked in lavender-scented bubbles. Her mom would be proud for the special time she had dedicated to herself. Relaxation, finally. Her Internet radio was streaming smooth R&B. She listened to Brian McKnight's "Anytime." She hummed the lyrics as he sang. He sounded like a man in longing. He begged to know if he ever crossed her mind. He needed to know if she dreamed of touching him. The sound of the song was perfect for her mood, but the message wasn't. It made her think of her old flame even more. She wanted to know those same things.

Danen. Why was she so intrigued? Did she ever cross his mind, she wondered? By his last contact with her, the answer was yes. She thought of all of the time they had spent together. They really had a lot of good times. The grass seemed so much greener there. *This is fucked up.* Her thoughts interrupted her thoughts. She got out of the tub feeling guilty. It felt like she had no control over her thoughts at all. She rinsed off, wrapped her towel around her wet body, and lay on her bed, hoping that her mom was not busy as she dialed her cell.

"Hey, baby. On break?"

She smiled hearing her mom's voice. It was just what she needed. "No, I took off."

"Really? Why?"

"I just needed a little time."

"Oh, I understand, baby girl. So, what are you up to?"

"Just used your Christmas gift."

"Oooohhh. I know that was good. Lavender smells so good."

Lena knew her mom enjoyed feeling useful to her children. They were both grown now and fully on their own. "It was."

"Have you talked to Dougie?"

Lena's face tightened. She needed the focus to be on her this time. She didn't want to think about Dougie's situation with the frame of mind she was in, and it upset her that he was avoiding their parents. "No. Not since I left. Why?"

"I've been calling him. I guess he's working."

"He probably is."

"I'll try him later. Is everything okay with you and Alonzo?"

She sighed. *Yes, bring it back to me.* "We're okay."

"Just okay?" She could tell that her mom was concerned. "Well, he has been questioning me about my daydreams lately. He said that he's noticed that I daydream more. I've noticed it, too. I feel like I can't control it."

Her mom simply said, "Oh," and then, "Hmmm . . ."

"Well, what do you think? What did you do to help me stop? I remember you doing things."

"Selena. Have you not realized what's happening when you daydream?"

"I mean . . . Yeah. I drift away." Lena turned on her side and looked toward the light shining through her half-closed blinds.

"Yeah, you drift away, but where do you go?"

"Anywhere, Mom. You know that."

"Lena, you drift away to a happier place."

Lena didn't say anything. She waited for her mom to explain further.

"Are you there?"

"Yes ma'am."

"Lena, when your teachers started sending notes home, I always thought you zoned out because you finished your work early and were bored. So, we found more activities for you to help you focus, but the issue still remained. I don't think you even realized what we were doing. It was a Tuesday when I sat you down and asked you why you were daydreaming so much. Don't you remember what you told me?"

"No." Lena searched through her memories, seeking the answer. "I don't. I can't remember."

"You were eleven, and you told me that you were happier there. So, I asked you what you did in your daydreams, then made it happen in real life. Your dad was also in the hospital around that time, and I spent a lot of time tending to him while I left you and Dougie with your Aunt Elise or Grandma Ethel. When you stress, you daydream more. When you're not being fulfilled, you go to a place where you are. That place is in your head. It's one of your traits, baby. I can't recollect a period when you've had no daydreams. They definitely subside when you are in a good place."

"You don't think I'm happy with Alonzo?"

"Baby, I didn't say anything about Alonzo, but there is an aspect, or some aspects, of your life that you aren't content with. Are you happy, baby?"

"I don't know. I think so."

"It looks like you need to do some thinking. Some life searching. Some regrouping. You can't run away to your fantasy worlds because you don't like your reality. Nothing is permanent. You can change whatever you like in your life except me." She laughed. "And the rest of your family, too."

Lena chuckled. "Is that a fact?"

"It sure is." She could hear her mom's smile.

"I'll figure it out, Mom. Thank you. I needed it."

"My pleasure, baby girl, and I know you will figure it out, but you need to hurry. You'll be thirty next year, and I'm ready for some grands."

"I'll get Dougie on it."

"Child! How many times do I have to tell you not to play with me?"

Lena laughed again. "Love you, Mom."

"Love you too, bad girl."

They hung up the phone. Lena had a plan now. She would find some clarity. She pulled out her laptop and checked her e-mails for work. *I guess I will attempt to get some work done.* Then, she sat her laptop on the coffee table, picked up her phone, and dialed Dougie. He picked up on the third ring.

She could hear music and guys talking in the background when he answered. "Hello?"

"What are you doing?"

He coughed. "Chillin'."

"You don't have class today?"

"I've already went. I have one more at four. What do you need?"

"For you to call your momma."

"Man, Lena. I'm doing something right now. What do you want for real?"

She almost cursed. *This lil boy!* She shook her head. If he were there, she would've punched him in the arm like she had when they were younger. "DOUG! If you don't stop playing that game or whatever you're doing and listen to me, I swear I will call Mom right now and tell her everything!"

"Man, hold on." She heard him talking to one of the guys in the background. "Aye, man, play for me real quick, and don't lose!" Dougie walked to his room and closed the door. "Yeah."

Lena calmed herself down. "Why aren't you answering their phone calls? Do you want them to come out there?"

"No."

"So . . . why?" She was becoming irritated again.

"I don't know."

"Yes, you do! It's because you feel guilty and you know that you are her little baby, and she'll be able to sniff out something wrong. I'm telling you right now. If I talk to her one more time and she asks me whether I've spoken to you, then I'm telling her. So, you better get to calling her now!" Lena hung up the phone. Dougie called her right back. She watched his picture on her phone screen flash as her phone rang. She declined and composed a text.

Lena: *I need to see you tonight.*

They responded: *Our same spot?*

Lena: *Yep.*

Lena went into the kitchen, fixed a cup of hot green tea, popped two aspirin, and went back to her work e-mails. Her phone buzzed.

Her mom texted her. *Dougie just called me.*

Lena: *I told you he was probably working.*

Chapter 12

Lena was tired from a day of playing catch-up on work and had hardly parked in her parking spot at her apartment when her phone rang. Grabbing her things in one hand and hitting the answer button on her Bluetooth headset with the other, she answered the call and briskly made her way to her apartment door. The night air was still warm, but her attitude was cold.

Dryly, Lena said, "Hey."

"What's up, baby? Everything okay?"

"Yep. Just getting home."

"Why so late?"

Because I damn wanted to get home late! She opened the door, dropped her purse on the table, and sat down. "I went out to eat."

"What'd you eat?" Alonzo asked while chewing his food on the other end of the phone. The sound of his chewing was bothering her today.

"I met with Sheree." Saying that reminded Lena to let Sheree know that she was home. She got her phone out of her purse and texted her.

Alonzo continued to question her. "Y'all go to Glaze?"

"You know it. I'm surprised that you still have to ask."

Sheree lived thirty to forty minutes away from Lena, going toward Gastonia, so they'd picked an area halfway between both of them to meet up to socialize during the weekdays. Glaze was one of a few restaurants in the area that they had tried out and really liked. They had found a small BBQ spot that was good, but they enjoyed the ambiance much better at Glaze. It always quiet, dimly lit, and served great dishes like balsamic-glazed chicken breast or bourbon-glazed pork chops with heaping, homemade sides. Because they were considered regulars at this point, they'd almost always had a chance to try some new concoction by Larry, the bartender, and would often receive appetizers that were compensated by the manager, who had a crush on Sheree. Most of the servers knew them and were super friendly, so they always left big tips.

"Hold on for a minute." Alonzo answered his other line.

"Alonzooo!"

"'Sup, Mike?"

"You busy?"

"Not really. I have Lena on the other line."

Mike chuckled. "That means you're busy."

"No. She sounds like she has a really bad attitude. So, hold on." Alonzo clicked over back to Lena. "Hey, baby. This is Mike. Let me call you right back."

Lena was okay with him ending their call. In fact, she rushed him off of the phone. Her day wasn't as soothing as she had planned it to be. She had so many emotions swirling inside of her. She thought about her dinner with Sheree. It was supposed to have been a meeting to help her clear her mind and vent, but it concluded with her evoking old, hurt feelings and with Sheree feeling out of the loop. She replayed it in her head. They were sitting there enjoying their loaded potato skins and drinks. Sheree was discussing the new money man for their boutique.

"He is so cute. I might give him my number the next time he comes and picks up the money. Would that look too forward?"

"Maybe." Lena laughed wryly. She was barely paying attention to Sheree's rant about the money man. All she could think about was Danen and how her thinking of him worried her.

"What's up with you, Lena? You seem off today."

Lena sighed. "Don't judge me, but I've been thinking about Danen lately."

Sheree blankly stared at her. "First of all, never start your statement with 'don't judge me,' because then judging you is the first thing I'm doing!" The server came back with their orders. Sheree wiped the blank stare off of her face and turned and greeted the waitress. "Oh yes! I am ready for my steak!"

The waitress laughed. "It looks really good, too. I'm a little jealous."

"Be jealous, girl. Be very jealous." Sheree laughed as she moved the appetizer plate over, making room for her steak and macaroni and cheese.

Lena smiled as she was given her bowl of seafood gumbo. "Thanks."

They both prayed over their food. Sheree looked up at Lena as she was cutting her New York strip.

"Ugh, Danen. I never liked him for you like that. Y'all were *too* perfect. It was so cookie cutter."

Lena looked shocked. She put her spoon down and looked at Sheree. "I never knew that."

"What do you mean you've been thinking about him, anyway? In what way?" Sheree was pouring steak sauce over her sliced pieces of steak.

Lena calmed herself. She felt herself becoming moved by Sheree's comments. She didn't know why Sheree was on her case about him. She took a minute to gather her thoughts. "I've just been thinking about him . . . you know, like how he's doing." She swirled her gumbo with her spoon. "And old times."

"Old times? Poor Alonzo."

Poor Alonzo? "Sheree, you won't even hear me out. I talked to my mom today and I've been thinking about some of the things she said."

Sheree cut in. "He took your virginity."

Lena raised her eyebrow. She was appalled. "Yeah. So what? It has nothing to do with that."

"I'm sure it has everything to do with that. In fact, for the both of you." She placed a heaping spoonful of macaroni and cheese into her mouth. She chewed it up, took a sip of her drink, and continued. "He doesn't want anyone else eating his cookie, and you have that longing to be with your very first. I've solved it."

Lena's volume rose a bit. "You haven't solved anything!" Sheree tilted her head and looked concerned that Lena was becoming heated. Lena continued. "Why have I not known about your feelings about mine and Danen's relationship?"

"That was so long ago, and back then I had nothing to compare your relationship to, but if I use the present as an example, which I have been, then I just can't see you two together now. That was a different time for y'all. You and Danen didn't have worries. Life worries, careers, kids, money, etc. Who's to say that y'all would even work out now? What I'm saying is you and Lonnie have friction. That friction makes a fire. It's a beautiful blaze. Enjoy its warmth, girl."

Lena, who was becoming more heated by the minute, reached for her water. "Sheree."

She cut her off. "Don't 'Sheree' me. Why would you risk this? You guys are awesome together!" Sheree scooted her plate away as if she'd lost her appetite.

Lena hadn't even tried her food yet. She was taking a sip of her water when she heard Sheree's comment, and she slammed her glass on the table. "Sheree, he cheated on me!" Sheree's eyes widened. Lena felt her face flush. Her emotions were taking over. She got up from the booth and went to the restaurant's restroom. Sheree got their waitress's attention and looked around to see if anyone had heard the commotion. No one seemed affected.

The waitress quickly returned to their table. "Yes ma'am? Are you two ready for dessert?"

Sheree managed to make a half smile. "No, just two boxes and a check."

Still chipper the waitress asked, "Will it be separate or together?"

"Together."

The waitress cleared the table of its empty appetizer plates and swiftly walked away to retrieve the to-go boxes and check. She returned before Lena was back. She bagged the food as Sheree dug in her wallet for her card. Sheree signed for the food, grabbed their things, and went to the restroom to check on Lena, who had been in there for about ten minutes now. When she walked in, Lena was patting her face with a wet paper towel, carefully trying not to smear her makeup. Her eyes were puffy and dark pink.

She held up the bags containing their meals. "I've already paid for the food. Are you okay?"

"Yeah. I'm ready to go." She grabbed her purse from Sheree. They greeted the servers as they walked through the restaurant, and then made their way to their cars. Once they were in the parking lot, Sheree followed Lena to her car and sat in her passenger seat. She looked at Lena. Lena was looking out of the window at all of the cars that were pulling up to park. They had just missed a rush. Lena looked heartbroken.

Sheree decided to break the silence in Lena's car. "When? Lena, why didn't you tell me?" She was holding back tears. Lena didn't answer or look Sheree's way. "Lena, I'm sorry. I didn't know."

Lena sighed. Still not facing Sheree, she turned and looked out of the windshield. "I know."

"What happened?"

"The only person that knew was my mom."

Sheree waited for Lena to tell her, but Lena started to cry again. She set her forehead on the steering wheel and whimpered. Tears streamed from her eyes down the steering wheel, over the Acura emblem in the center, and onto her lap. Sheree rubbed her back and tried to console her without crying herself. Lena's head was still down. "It was in April."

"Lena, I'm so sorry for scolding you like that in there. I didn't know. I'm so sorry. I feel so horrible." She patted Lena on the back. "I can't believe Alonzo!"

Lena looked up at Sheree, whose eyes were glistening with her own tears. "It's okay. I was embarrassed. I didn't want to say anything."

"Don't ever be embarrassed. Don't ever feel like you can't tell me anything. You know we're better than that. I'm the friend who got drunk and peed herself when you came to visit me in college. Never forget that!"

Lena burst out laughing. Sheree joined her. Lena knew that they would be friends until they grew old. How were they able to find a smile in that moment of heartache? It was because Sheree loved her and would do anything to see Lena smile.

"I know, but that was the first time that I had gone through that. I didn't know what to do. I just called my mom, girl. I was devastated. This year is giving me a run for its money. Dougie got arrested Friday, and my mom doesn't even know. It's too much going on, I feel like I can't take it."

They sat in the car talking, crying, and not caring about the onlookers that saw. They sat there until the sun went down. Sheree even went back in the restaurant for to-go waters. Larry politely obliged. Lena cried and told Sheree everything.

"It was the second weekend in April, I think. Lonnie came over after work on that Friday night. Everything was cool, like normal. I was going to church with my mom that weekend. Originally, the plan was for me to leave on Friday, but I stayed to hang out with him. Lonnie brought a list of client invoices with him. That was the week that Ms. Susan was sick, so he and Mike took work home. We had a great night. We went out to eat and to a bar. There was a girl there that kept looking toward our table. Every time I caught her, she turned away. I knew something was up and asked if he knew her. He said no.

"We went home and enjoyed each other, for at least two hours. He did everything to me. Girl, it was a *perfect* night. He made breakfast the next morning while I packed for my mom's. We were both a little hungover. He left around noon. When I was leaving, I saw that he left his folder and laptop bag on the floor by the sofa. I called him and he didn't answer. I figured he was asleep. So, I went to drop it off before I went to my mom's. I texted him when I was about fifteen minutes away to tell him that I was coming to drop it off. He didn't respond.

"His truck was parked outside when I got there. I walked to his door, and I heard music playing as I stood outside of it. I knew he wasn't asleep then, but I guess he had missed my phone call and text because of the loud music. So, I figured that he may have been cleaning up. I unlocked the door and walked in to an empty living room and kitchen. I set his stuff on the couch. His phone was on the kitchen counter next to an empty beer bottle. I walked toward the music, which was coming from his room. The door was open. As I stood in the doorway, I saw him and a girl sitting on the edge of the bed. They were facing the window with their backs to me. She had her head on his shoulder and her arms wrapped around him. He sat straight with his arm around her back and rubbing it. I must've stood there silently for at least three minutes before I took off my wedges and threw them at her."

Sheree cut her off. "You threw your shoes at her?" She laughed hard. "Which ones, girl?"

Lena shook her head and chuckled. "I did. I didn't know what had come over me. I didn't want to throw my purse, but I needed to throw something. I had on my black, six-inch BCBG strappy wedges."

"Those shoes are nice, sturdy, and heavy! Good choice!"

"Girl, one flew right past her and toward his window. It just missed the window and left a long, black scuff on his wall. The other one clocked her right in the back of her head! Lonnie turned around quick as if he was going to assault their attacker, but when he saw me standing there, he froze. The girl was bent over, rubbing the back of her head. She sat up, turned around to look at me, and then stood up. Alonzo grabbed her arm. She snatched it away and tried to walk toward me. He almost jumped across the bed, he was moving so fast, and he stiff-armed her, preventing her from getting to me. She was crying and fuming trying to get to me. She was yelling to him to let her go and was calling me a bitch and everything. He told her, 'Look, you need to leave.'"

"What were you saying, Lena? You didn't say anything back to her?"

"No. I didn't have anything to say. She was the same girl from the bar the night before. I was dumbfounded. Lonnie had looked me square in my eyes and lied to me."

"Wow," Sheree said. "A lie doesn't care who tells it!"

"He walked her to his room's doorway. I was standing right there in it. He blocked her from touching me. Her arms were flailing while she tried to reach me. I hurried and retrieved my shoes, then followed them into the living room. She was still eyeing me as he put her out. He sat his back on the door and looked to the floor. Then, he took a deep breath and looked up to me."

Suddenly, Lena was triggered.

"Are you all right?" Lena remembered his every word. She saw herself standing in Alonzo's living room. She hated that it couldn't be a bad daydream; this scene was real. This had happened. He was looking at her, waiting for her answer.

Lena yelled, "What the hell is going on?" The woman was still outside his door, banging on it. Lena walked toward the door, and Alonzo tried to restrain her. "If you don't let go of me—" Alonzo didn't give her a chance to finish her sentence. He held his hands up and stepped away from the door. Lena opened the door wide enough for the woman to see her only. "You need to go home, or wherever. Don't make me take my shoe off again." (Sheree giggled in the background.) The woman continued to beat on the door for about three more minutes, then left. She knew Alonzo wasn't coming to her rescue. "Alonzo, talk. NOW!"

Alonzo sat on the back of his couch, looking down and rubbing the back of his neck. Lena was now standing with her back on the door. "Lena, that was Tiffany."

"Tiffany, huh? The damn chick you didn't know in the club last night? The Tiffany that you dated before me? And what the fuck was Tiffany doing here, in your room, on your bed, with your damn arms around her?"

"I made a mistake, Lena."

"CLEARLY!"

He held his head down. "I made a terrible mistake, and I'm sorry."

Lena went and stood directly in front of him. She stood there with her arms crossed. "What did you do?"

Alonzo told her the story of how he ran into Tiffany at the store two weeks earlier. They had chatted and she'd recommended that they catch up. He'd told her he wasn't sure about that, but she had been persistent and suggested that they meet at a coffee shop. He had felt a coffee shop was harmless and had met her two days after the store run-in on a Thursday. They had talked at the coffee shop until its closing time. She'd decided that they should finish their conversation at a bar that was close by. He had hesitated, but indulged. They'd had a few drinks and talked. She'd asked him to dance. He thought they shouldn't and had said he was leaving and would walk her to her car. When they got to her car, she had kissed him, and he'd kissed her back.

Lena stared Alonzo down as he told the story. She was growing more irate by the minute, but he continued. "Next thing I know, she was opening her car door and was pushing me in the back." He looked away.

"And?" Lena knew what was next. She knew, but she wanted him to own up to what he did.

He sighed. "We did it."

"You did what? Had sex with your ex Tiffany in a car outside of a bar?" Lena slapped him. "I bet you didn't even use a condom!" She stepped back. "No class!"

He looked at her with red eyes. "I did, Lena. I had one in my wallet . . . and she wasn't my ex. We just messed around." She slapped him again, harder, and walked off toward the kitchen counter. She leaned over it, using her arms to hold herself up. He stood up, rubbing his stinging cheek. He did not walk toward her. "It was a horrible and dumb mistake, Lena. I wanted to tell you, but . . ."

Lena held up her finger, signaling him to stop talking. She was still leaning over the counter and not looking at him. "When did this happen?"

"I told you. It was two weeks ago."

"Well, I forgot like you forgot to tell me that you cheated, dumbass." Lena stood up. "Okay." She started walking toward the door.

Alonzo's apartment disappeared, and she was back in the car with Sheree. "Girl, I left. He was calling after me and followed me to my car. I asked for my keys back and burned rubber on his ass."

"Then what happened?"

"I didn't talk to him for all of May, I think."

"How'd he get you to take him back?"

"Sheree, I don't know. I just took him back." Lena shook her head.

Sheree looked confused. "Lena, he must've done something to get you back after all of that?"

"I just took him back. I did. I mean, he said things and called, texted, e-mailed, and left gifts at my place. He begged . . . and to tell the truth, I was tired of going home with no one to talk to. I missed him, and I hated being alone. We were making life plans before he did that. And after it happened, he was doing everything possible to let me know that he made a mistake. I didn't think anyone else would love me like he did." Lena paused. "He's tried his hardest to please me since, but something just doesn't feel right. I've been denying my feelings, Sheree. I've been trying to go along with it, but I'm not happy. My mom even told me that."

Sheree sat up. She was leaning her cheek on her hand, which was propped up on the to-go boxes in her lap. "What did your mom say about everything?"

"When it happened, she laughed at the shoes stuff."

They both laughed, but Sheree laughed harder. "Ms. Vivian is a trip!"

"She is. She helped me. She talked me through it and told me that I had to make a choice. She said she'd never personally dealt with it, but a lot of her clients had, and ultimately I have to decide if I could forgive him and move on." Lena laid her head back on the seat. "When I talked to her today about my daydreaming, she told me that I do it most when I'm not happy with life, and I go inside of my imagination for a happier place, and you know what? It made perfect sense, Sheree. I don't know if Danen is my happy place or not, but I'm going to figure it out."

Sheree held her hand. "I definitely wouldn't want you to be in a relationship that you aren't happy in, but I don't think hopping over to Danen will make it any better. You need some time to think everything over."

"Maybe." Lena leaned over the divider and laid her head on Sheree's shoulder. Sheree caressed her best friend's hair. "We need to be getting home. It's seven, and we both have to go to work tomorrow."

Sheree agreed. "You are right." She started to gather her things. She looked over to Lena and placed her hand on her lap. "Take some time, Lena. Just think about every-thing. Don't make any hasty decisions." She got out and walked over the driver-side window. She leaned in and kissed Lena on the forehead. "Call me when you get home. Okay?"

"Yes ma'am." Lena watched Sheree put her things in the car. Sheree closed her passenger-side door and walked back to Lena's window. Lena rolled it down.

"I still cannot believe Lonnie's stupid ass." She shook her head and walked to her car.

Lena laughed. Sheree pulled off first, and Lena fol-lowed. She drove home in silence. In the car alone with her thoughts, Lena wondered if she was making the right deci-sion by staying with Alonzo. She consciously blocked out his cheating, but her heart had not forgotten. Old thoughts surfaced. Could she trust him? Was he actually working late on those nights when he claimed to be so tired? *Maybe I should give him a surprise visit.* Lena wasn't up for games, though. She knew it, and she didn't think her heart could take another infidelity surprise. She caught a glimpse of Danen's face in her mind's eye. She saw them at her parent's house, watching movies on the couch. She snapped out of it and realized what her mom had been saying. She could see that she was avoiding her thoughts and problems with Alonzo by daydreaming and fantasizing, but this was a fantasy that she surely wanted to come true.

Chapter 13

Alonzo's alarm was sounding off. He snoozed it twice and slowly rose from his bed twenty minutes later. He checked his phone for text messages. He had called Lena back the night before, but she hadn't answered. He didn't see her falling asleep so early when she'd had the day off. He made his way to the shower and hopped in. He stood under the stream of water. His thoughts were with Lena as each drop and splash of water magnified the dark-brown hue of his skin. He wanted her. He wanted to feel her, entangle his fingers in her hair, and tug it while she went down on him. He wanted to grab her and kiss her mouth until she was out of breath. He felt like he owned her when his fingers seized her waist. He felt himself elevating. *Not now.* He had no time to handle it, but gave himself an extra five minutes to "get the man down," as Lena would say. He got out of the shower and dried off, being careful not to give any special attention to the now-sensitive area. It wasn't long before he was heading out of the door to his truck. He drove a little faster than he normally would because of the extra time he had spent getting ready. Mike had called him the night before to inform him of a meeting today, and he could not be late.

Everyone beat him today except the new kid, and that was because Mike had put Joe on breakfast duty since he ran late so often. There was one additional car there that he didn't recognize. It was a silver BMW 3 series GT. It looked brand new. He walked in and was greeted by Mike, who was leaning over the front counter, talking with Susan.

"Late start?" Mike sipped his coffee.

"Yeah. Sorry I'm running late." Alonzo hurried in.

Mike chuckled and looked at his watch. "We still have five more minutes before the shop opens. You're the only guy I know whose late is still on time."

Susan interjected, "That's a good thing, Alonzo. Don't let Mikey pick on you."

"Thanks, Ms. Susan." Alonzo grabbed a magazine addressed to him out of the mail and headed to his closet-sized office.

Mike followed him with an extra cup of coffee and sat it on Alonzo's desk. "Are you ready for the meeting?"

"I sure am. I see you have on khakis. It must be big." Alonzo laughed hard.

Mike mimicked a woman batting her lashes and said, "Oh, you noticed?" in a girly voice. They both laughed. "Yeah. I miss my Levi's, bro."

Alonzo sipped his coffee. He was actually starting to feel a little nervous. "Whose car is that outside?"

Mike smiled. "You'll see." He stood up and walked toward the doorway. "Come on to my office after you get settled in. We'll go ahead and start a little early. I've already told one of the guys to cover your morning tune-up."

"Okay." Alonzo gulped the last of his black coffee.

He went to the restroom and checked himself. *I look good*, he thought. There were no crumbs on his face from the toast he had eaten on the way to work. He looked at himself in the dingy mirror, but found himself distracted by the flickering lightbulb in the fixture. He looked up at it, then back to himself in the mirror, and said aloud, "I got this. I work hard. I deserve this."

As he walked to Mike's office, he stopped and told Ms. Susan to get one of the guys to tend to the lightbulb in the men's restroom. When he finally got to his boss's office, the door was cracked and he heard Mike and a woman talking. It was a familiar voice. He immediately felt less anxious. He lightly knocked on the door. He heard Mike sarcastically ask his mom, "Did he just knock?" Alonzo smiled.

"Get in here, man!" Mike yelled from the other side of the door. Alonzo walked in and smiled.

"Good morning, Mrs. Alice." He held out a hand for a handshake. Mike's mom grinned and stood up for a hug.

"You should be ashamed, Lonnie. A handshake?" He laughed and hugged her tightly. Mrs. Alice felt so small and dainty in his arms. Her blonde hair had long, gray streaks and had a floral scent. She pulled her vest together and positioned her skirt back down over her knees as she sat back in her chair, still smiling.

Alonzo fixed his mouth to say "My bad," but he knew that this was not the time for casual banter. There was a time and place for everything, and he needed to show them that he was a professional. "Sorry about that, Mrs. Alice. You two had me nervous today."

"Had? You should still be; this meeting isn't over," Mike said jokingly.

"Oh, stop, Mikey." Mrs. Alice sat down in her chair that was in front of Mike's desk. Alonzo sat in the other chair. His office looked like any other small office. He had two chairs tilted so that they were almost facing each other in front of the desk. There were pictures of his family and friends, fundraising and sponsor certificates, and his framed college diploma littering the dark-green wall.

"As you already know, Alonzo, I've been wanting to open up a franchise in Charlotte. My mom and I have been doing some major thinking about expanding the shop. You know Automotive Works was my dad's baby." Mike chuckled. He had been twiddling his thumbs the whole time he spoke and looked down at his hands.

He looks nervous. Almost more nervous than me. Oh shit! They're going to tell me no. He looked at Mike, trying to gauge where he was coming from.

Mike continued. "Sometimes dad made the shop sound more like a sibling when he talked about it."

Mrs. Alice chuckled. "Indeed, it was another child to him, and that's why this was a very important decision for us to make. Big Mike was a stubborn man. He made sure we knew that he only wanted his shop family owned and operated."

Alonzo chimed in, "I understand." His tone wasn't as excited and anxious as it was before.

"Me and my mom . . . we've held true to his wishes. His shop, the original shop, is family owned and operated." Mrs. Alice pulled out an attaché case from the side of her chair closest to the wall. Alonzo hadn't seen it when he walked in. Mike continued. "Well, Alonzo, and so will the rest of our shops." Alonzo shifted in his chair. He didn't want them to see how uncomfortable he was. He couldn't believe it. He had worked so hard. *It would be different if I was white. They'd hand me the job if I was white.* Mrs. Alice starting pulling papers out of her case. *What are these papers for? Am I fired now?*

Mike was still talking, but his voice had faded. All Alonzo could hear was Mrs. Alice shuffling the papers. They made eye contact while he watched her, and she smiled at him and continued to shuffle the pile of papers.

Mike cleared his throat. "So, Alonzo, what do you think?"

Alonzo snapped out of it. "Think about what, exactly?"

"About all of this. About everything we've said."

Alonzo straightened up in his chair. "I totally get what you're saying. You're honoring your father's wishes and keeping your business in the family. I think he'd be proud. You know I consider you my big brother, and I think you're making the right decision."

Mike cheesed. "That's right! I knew you'd understand. That's why I call you my black brother."

The smile left Mrs. Alice's face. "You do not call him that, do you?"

"Yeah, Mom. I do."

"That must stop." She eyed both Mike and Alonzo down.

"Mom." Mike chuckled.

"I'm serious. I better not hear that ever. It sounds weird. I think 'brother' by itself will do." Alonzo laughed and she gave him the "mom eye."

"Sorry." Alonzo smiled and looked away.

Mike's mom patted the neatly stacked papers in her lap. "If you two will get back to business, we can finish this. I have a spa appointment in an hour and a half."

"Yes ma'am," they both said in unison.

"Lonnie." She grabbed the papers from her lap, set them on the desk, and faced Alonzo. "This is a contract. I've had our lawyer draw it up. You're right, we are honoring my late husband's wishes. He wanted Automotive Works to stay in the family. He put his all in this and invested so much into this company. I really hate that he's not here to see how much this shop is flourishing. He wasn't about expansion and branching out. He was about the simple life. He was a country boy, but my sons," she smiled, "they are not. Mike Jr. here is very business savvy. You saw what he's done here in Concord. Let me rephrase that—what you two have done here." She placed her hand on Alonzo's. "You are family. You have worked at the shop longer than Josh has. My husband, he wasn't much of a talker, but he saw something in you. He gave you a job for a reason. He spoke of you often. No one really knew that, but he respected you for respecting him. So, I know he's in heaven smiling at us right now. He seemed serious all the time, but he had a sense of humor. I know he's laughing hard at us right now for beating around the bush and scaring you into thinking you don't have this job."

Alonzo looked away from her and turned to Mike, who was grinning. Alonzo felt a smile creeping onto his face. "Really, bro?"

Mrs. Alice laughed and wiped a tear from her eye. She stood up and Alonzo stood up and hugged her. Mike came from around his desk and hugged the both of them. Alonzo sat down and shook his head and smiled. "You two." He sighed.

"I'm sorry." He apologized out loud for his earlier thoughts. "You two really had me on edge."

Mike placed his hand on Alonzo's shoulder and patted it. He walked back to his desk chair and sat down. "All jokes aside. This was really a big decision. We interviewed some other people, Alonzo. I don't want you to think that we were looking over you, but that is just the business side of things. Maybe we did waste our time. You were always our first choice, but we had to be sure. At the end of the day, my father's wishes were the deciding factors. You're family, bro. You've been through it all with us. My dad's death, my wedding, my kids, my mom's cancer scare, I mean all of it! You've worked at both shops, and we want you to help us with the third. My mom and I have been looking at a few garages for sale in Charlotte. We have it down to three. We're waiting for some phase-one info on the sites. Our lawyer is working on that. My mom has your contract. You can take it home and read over it. This isn't a quick process. It won't be until maybe next summer or fall for us to have everything together with the property, more employees, et cetera. Alonzo, the thing is, you're a young guy. You have Lena and all, but you aren't settled. You two aren't married and don't have any kids. So, who's to say that you and her want to stay here? Y'all might decide that you want to live in another city, state, or hell, another country. I'm like my father. This company is one of my babies now. My business plan worked here in Concord, and I'm sure it will work in Charlotte, but it takes dedication. Plus, you have to prove yourself." Mike stopped talking and looked at his mom and Alonzo. "Do y'all need anything? Water? Restroom break?"

Alonzo answered, "No. I'm okay."

His mom stood up. "Actually, I do, but you guys continue." She left the office.

"Mike, no offense, but I've worked with you since I was a teenager. What more proof do you need?"

"No offense taken. I know you've been patient with this, and I thank you for your patience. Maybe proving yourself wasn't the best choice of words. I take that back. You have proved yourself to be a great assistant manager. You have worked your way up for sure, but I won't be there when something goes wrong. I'll be at the least thirty minutes away without traffic. My family is here, my kids have their friends here, and I don't want to commute. I may come to check on the shop a few times a month once it's good and running. You will be responsible, Alonzo. You will manage this shop."

"Okay. So, I'll be pretty much on my own. Tell me about this contract."

"Sort of. The contract says you will be there full time for two years. The first year there tackles establishing our shop in the community and gaining new loyal customers. The second year is where we make the real money. So, I need to know that you're willing to invest two years, Alonzo. I have a cousin who just graduated with his degree in accounting. Right now, he will manage with you and handle the books.

"You know I wear many hats, and you will have to as well. Along with managing, you will need to be over marketing and the employees. It shouldn't be a problem for you. You've helped me in those departments plenty, but this time you have a budget, and you make the decisions. I'm sure that my cousin, Ralph, will move on after this. He's a fresh graduate and will want to go off somewhere. This job will be a resume filler for him, and starting money in his pocket. That's why I haven't offered him any ownership. After two years, he'll probably be finding or training his replacement, but if you would like to stay, then you'll be manager and part owner by twenty-five percent. Of the shop in Charlotte, that is. You'll get a raise, of course, and keep your benefits. All of it is listed in the contract."

Alonzo flipped through the contract. "Well, it looks like I have some reading to do."

"You sure do." Mrs. Alice was walking back in. "We really want you to take your time. This is a big decision." She looked at her watch. "Well, boys, I have to be heading out." They both rose from their seats to walk her out.

Alonzo had an overwhelming feeling of joy. He left his cell phone in his office before the meeting, and he couldn't wait to get to it to call and tell Lena the great news. Ms. Susan signaled him to come by as he walked past the desk.

"How'd the meeting go?"

He smiled. *Nosy.* "It went well."

"I was hoping they picked you." She patted his hand and he continued to his office.

He sat behind his desk and dialed Lena. No answer. He composed a text, but erased it. This was something big. He didn't want to text it. He wanted to hear the pride in her voice and see her ecstatic face. He would take his time and read over it like they had said, but the decision seemed like an easy one to him. He had enough money saved to get a house for him and Lena, but moving in together in her apartment would be great for starters. Her place was nicer than his, and they could save money. *I have my woman, and now my career. I have enough for both of us. Lena is happy. I'm happy. My family is here and so is hers. This is perfect. Two years is nothing. I never planned on leaving, anyway. We're set.* Alonzo was so elated. Everything was working out. He called his mom to tell her the good news.

Chapter 14

Lena looked at herself in the mirror. She looked tired. She had bags under her eyes and worry wrinkles. *I'm going straight to bed tonight after a glass of wine. No phone calls. No TV. Just sleep.* She exited the women's room and made her way back to her office. She spoke to a few coworkers in the hallway. She wondered if they were happy. Like truly, family-sitcom happy, or were they too plastering on fake smiles? She got back to her office and sat in her soft, comfy desk chair. It was the best piece in her office because she had brought it from home. She sat back and turned to look out of her window. She didn't have much to look at, only pavement, cars, and a few trees. She looked past the parking lot to the expressway. *I'd love to be on my way home right now.* Lena was beyond stressed with catching up on work and with the situations outside of it. She was far too ready for the work day to be over. She had the work that she had put off on Friday to do, the work that she had missed on Monday, an interview to prep for, and she had to take on Tammy's role because she had called out. She was kind of happy that Tammy wasn't there, because she planned on backing out of their after-work bookstore date. She just wasn't up to it. Lena turned to face her desk and saw the notification light blinking on her phone. She checked to see a missed call from Alonzo. *Why does he keep calling me?* Once again, she found herself leaning back in her chair. She ran her fingers through her hair, closed her eyes, and murmured to herself, "It's because he's your boyfriend. Duh!" She didn't know why she felt so angry with him all of a sudden. She wasn't even this angry when it happened. She was mostly hurt, but now she was livid. All of the pretending that everything was okay and going along with him had made matters worse. Her hurt and rage had too much time to sit and fester inside of her, and she knew what she needed to do. It was what she had needed to do in the first place. Take some time, some real time away from Alonzo. With her epiphany, weight was lifted from her chest. The release she felt was unreal.

Lena had gotten through Friday's and Monday's work and was putting a dent in her present workload when Tammy called.

"Hey there, Tammy. You feeling better?"

"No, not really. I'm going to be out tomorrow, too. Just giving you a heads-up."

"Everything okay?"

"Yeah. See you Thursday."

"Oh, okay. Hope—"

Beep. Tammy hung up the phone before Lena could finish her sentence. *Okay . . . that wasn't weird.* She texted Tammy.

Lena: *Let me know if you need anything.*

Before she got back to work, she opened their schedule server and requested three days off in the last week of September. *It is time for a vacation,* she thought as she lunged back into her work. September in North Carolina was still warm, but the breezes made the days feel like true fall days, with the temperatures averaging in the seventies.

Two hours went by, and her stomach was making its empty state known by rumbling so loud that someone would've thought a rabid dog was hiding under her desk. She had missed breakfast and had forgotten her leftovers from dinner with Sheree, so she headed out. Lena picked up a grilled-chicken-sandwich combo from a drive-through and sat in her parked car at a nearby park. She ate half of the sandwich and all of her fries. Then she lay back in her seat. She wanted to spend the remainder of her break letting her brain rest. She thought about where she would spend her three days off. *The beach?* She could definitely see herself on the warm sand with her feet in the saltwater. *Yeah, the beach it is.* Her phone started ringing. She hesitated, thinking, *I'm on break,* but she knew she wasn't answering any phone calls once she left work. She hit "answer" on her steering wheel without even opening her eyes to see who it was.

"Hello?"

"Lena Harris."

Lena quickly sat up and read the name on her console. "Danen?"

"Uhhh . . . yeah. Did you delete my number or something?"

His voice was coming through her car speakers in surround sound, and he sounded so good to her. "No."

"Okay . . . how are you?"

Lena was hesitant. "Fine."

"What's up with the one-word answers, Lena?"

"I don't know. What do you want?"

She could hear him saying "wow" under his breath. He raised the volume of his voice. "What do I want? To know what you were doing? To chat. Hell, to hear your voice!"

Lena stared at his name on her console.

Danen added, "But I see that this was a bad decision."

Lena abruptly blurted out, "Planning my vacation!" She sighed. "That's what I'm doing."

"Oh."

"I'm thinking about the beach."

"Sounds cool. I'm sure he'd love it." Lena knew that Danen was trying so hard to sound not affected by the thought of Lena and Alonzo on the beach.

She quickly responded, "It's just me."

"Just you? What about him?"

"Why are you asking me about him, Danen? From what I remember about our last conversation, you weren't too worried about him. You confessed that you had been thinking about me."

"I have. I mean, I do. I just wanted to check on you. You never said anything back."

Lena thought about how she sat up that night reading his text. "Right, and that didn't mean anything to you?"

"No." Danen sounded unbothered.

"*No?*" Lena was frustrated. Danen could see right through her.

"It would've meant something if you didn't answer my call today, but you did."

"Danen—"

"You got scared and didn't respond to my text. I know you, Lena. I know you like no other man on this earth, and our feelings are mutual. You can't deny it."

Lena was quiet. Her mind was back racing again. She couldn't fix her mouth to respond to what he said. He awoke something within her. It was a feeling that she hadn't felt in years. It was a feeling that she hadn't felt since she had been with him.

"Lena, why isn't he going with you?"

"That's none of your business!"

He let out a loud, deep breath. "Lena, I'm sorry. I really am. I don't mean to break up anything that you two have going on, but I know you wouldn't have reached out to me if you were totally happy. You're an all-in woman, Lena. Always have been and always will be. I have been wanting to give us another chance for the longest time, but I was out of state. When I came back to North Carolina, you were with him."

"You never said anything. Why, Danen?"

"Long distance isn't our thing, Lena. I didn't know I was coming back here."

She cranked up her car and headed back to work. "Danen, I don't know if this is a good time. I need some time to myself."

"You've been on my mind so much in the past week I thought I was going crazy. I miss you, but if you don't want me to contact you, then just say the word. To be honest, part of me hoped that you didn't answer so I could bury these feelings for good, but you answered, Lena. That means something."

"I didn't check to see who was calling. I just hit 'answer.' I didn't know it was you, Danen. Not until I heard your voice."

"Damn, Selena."

She smiled. It gave her satisfaction to hear him twinge. "I'm glad I answered, Danen, but I can't tell you anything right now. I don't know what to say. I gotta go."

"Okay. We need to talk about us, Lena. Please call me back." She hung up.

Her brain was a wreck. She walked back into the building, submerged in her thoughts. She didn't want to be just satisfied. Her mom was right. Lena was never one to be complacent. She needed to get what she wanted, but she didn't know what or who that was exactly. According to Danen's last statement, they were "us." She had no idea that they even existed as "us." Everything was so real. She was bored with her job. She didn't know how to tell Alonzo that she needed a break, or if she should give Danen chance. And how could she give Danen a chance? She would have to leave Alonzo. *No wonder I daydream. The real world is demanding. Whatever decision I choose makes or breaks my chance at happiness.*

Once again, she was back at her desk trying to work and not think about everything floating around in her head. Every time she got in the groove of her paperwork, she heard an echo of Danen's voice saying, "We need to talk about us, Lena." She loved how the L sound rolled off of his tongue whenever he said her name. She opened her desk drawer to get a piece of gum. As she shuffled through highlighters, boxes of gym clips, and staples, she saw a picture of her and Alonzo. Sheree had taken it last year while they were all out to eat at a fancy restaurant in downtown Charlotte. She had it printed and gave it to them in a Christmas card. Lena plopped back in her chair and looked at the ceiling. *God, why is Danen on my mind if I'm supposed to be with Lonnie? I'm confused. Please help me.* She sat back up and worked, doing her best to ignore all of her thoughts.

It was five forty-five, and she had worked late just to catch up. She had everything on her checklist scratched off except a phone call to Kalvin, the guy she would be interviewing on Thursday. She gave him a call. He didn't answer, and she left a message. "Hi, Kalvin. This is Selena Harris from Powers Communications. I was calling to confirm your interview on Thursday at ten a.m. Please give me a call if you have any questions or need to make any changes. Have a good one." She hung up and thought, *If he shows up, then he's hired on the spot. I need help!* She grabbed her things and was on her way out. She drove home in silence.

As soon as she walked in her apartment, she poured herself a glass of wine, taking a swig from the bottle before putting it back in the fridge. She leaned on the kitchen counter, took off her shoes, and left them there.

She walked barefooted across her carpet with her glass in one hand and her phone in the other. She plopped down on the couch and lay her head on the armrest. She turned on the call rejection on her phone so that it would reject all calls except for her parents'. She finished her wine and fell asleep. She woke up a little after eight and relocated to her bed, stripping as she headed there, then climbed in her bed with only her panties on.

Chapter 15

Alonzo tried calling Lena three times after he got off. One call went unanswered and the others went straight to voicemail. *What is she doing?* He texted her.

Alonzo: *What's up, baby? I've been calling you. Wyd?*

His mom called him as he was driving home.

"Hey, Ma."

"Hey, baby. I talked with Mr. Howell. He's going to meet with Dougie Thursday. They already set it up. He's a great lawyer. I know he will handle this."

"Okay. Cool. How much is it?"

"He's going to let me know after he talks with him."

"Okay, keep me posted."

"Did you tell Lena yet? I know she'll be so proud of you!" His mom was bubbling over with excitement.

"Not yet. She's . . . busy." *Doing what, I don't know.*

"Okay, well, congrats again! I'm so pleased right now!"

"Thanks, Ma. Love you."

"Loved you first."

He tried Lena one more time and it went to voicemail. *Why is her phone dead? She keeps a charger on her.* He arrived at his apartment and sat in his car for minute. He reflected on his meeting with Mike and Mrs. Alice and couldn't believe where he was now compared to where he had started off. This was an awesome day, and Lena was nowhere to be found to share it with him. He went into his apartment and took a shower. He ate some leftover pizza, then sat on the couch and watched TV. Four hours later, he was in the chest of drawers, grabbing some clothes and heading out. He was going to Lena's house. He didn't know if she was there or not, but he would be there when she got home if she was out.

His thirty-minute drive was filled with plenty of scenarios of why she wasn't available. *She's probably with Sheree. I know she's not with another man. What am I thinking? Maybe she's asleep. I know she saw my calls earlier. I wonder why she didn't call me back. I hope she's okay. Mike's right. I need to get a grip. Lena loves me. I'm paranoid. I was the guilty one.* He pulled up outside of Lena's apartment, peeping at all of the cars. They were the same cars that were usually parked near her place. They belonged to the other residents. There was one that he didn't recognize. He put his duffel bag over his shoulder and walked to her door. He unlocked it and was opening it when the inside chain obstructed him from entering. *Why does she have on the chain on the door?* The living room was dark and empty from what he could see. He loudly knocked on the door and yelled for her. "Lena! LENA! Open the door!"

Lena woke up from her sleep hearing Alonzo's voice and banging on her door. She slowly got up, put on her silk black robe, and walked to the door to remove the chain. She stood there rubbing her eyes. "What are you doing here?" Alonzo walked in and closed the door behind him. "The better question is why are you screaming and banging on my door?"

"Is someone here? Why is the chain on the door?" he asked sternly.

"What?" She pulled her gaping robe together, preventing her bare chest from becoming exposed to her irate boyfriend. "I always chain my door, and you know that. It's not like I knew you were coming to spy on me tonight."

"I couldn't get in touch with you. I've been calling you all day!"

"So you come bang on my door and accuse me of having someone over?"

"I didn't accuse you. I just asked." He was looking around the room. His eyes stopped on her shoes on the floor in the kitchen. Lena was very tidy and kept her shoes on the rack in her huge bedroom closet.

"Well, go ahead, Alonzo. Check the other rooms!" She sat in a chair at her table. "What is your problem?"

"I was worried!"

"I was and still am tired, and you woke me up!"

He sat down at the table with her.

"Damn, Lonnie! You were outside beating down my door like a crazy man!"

"I'm sorry. I had been trying to reach you. You weren't picking up. I didn't know what was going on."

Lena was fed up. She was exhausted, and this was the last thing Lonnie needed to do. "So you come over to catch me?"

"No! I just came over to check on you."

"I'm not you, Lonnie!"

"Low blow, Lena. Was that called for?"

"It's the truth."

"Why is your phone off, or dead?"

"It's rejecting all calls except my mom's and dad's. I'm tired, Lonnie. I need some uninterrupted sleep, but I see you aren't having that."

"You don't want to talk to me? You could've called me back earlier."

"Or I could've done what I was doing, which was work! You know I have a lot on my plate."

Alonzo raised his voice. "Five minutes would've made me happy, Lena. Just five!"

Lena was looking down and tapping her fingers on the table. She sat up and let the anger rise from her heaving chest and dissolve in the air between them. She held up her head and looked Alonzo in the eyes. She removed the sting from her voice. "It would've made you happy? What about what makes me happy? Sleep would've made me happy tonight. I'm exhausted, Lonnie. I'm exhausted from working everyone's job at work. I'm tired from hiding Dougie's mess from my mom and dad, and I'm especially tired from pretending like I'm happy after you had sex with Tiffany. I'm just tired! So excuse me if I took a break from making everyone else happy."

Alonzo leaned his head back and raised his eyebrows in shock. He was blown away. He stood up, walked into the kitchen, and went to the refrigerator. He came back to the table with a beer. He opened it and drank some of it. "You don't want to be with me?"

"I didn't say that."

"You said you were tired of pretending."

"I know what I said."

"I thought we were okay. I thought we were past that."

"Past you having sex with another woman? Did you really think that?" She dropped her head. "You know what, I believe you. I thought it had passed too, but those kinds of issues don't just disappear, Lonnie. I tried to imagine that it didn't happen, but it did! And it is devastating!"

He got up and started pacing. He stood in one spot, and then knelt in front of Lena, placing his hand on her hands, which were lying in her lap. "Lena. I'm sorry for today. I was paranoid and scared and worried. I am guilty. I think about what I did to you, and I thank God all the time because you are still with me. I did think we were okay. I have been in awe at your strength to move on from it, but I see now that it has been disturbing you the entire time. I will do everything and anything in my power to make you happy, and to make it up to you. Just let me know what I need to do. I'll do anything, Lena."

"Anything?"

"Yes!" He got up from the floor and sat back in the chair, scooting it close to Lena so that he was directly in front of her. "Anything."

"I've been thinking. Not this whole time, but just recently." She held his hand. "I think I need—I need some time, Lonnie. To make sure this is what I really want."

"This? Us? Me? You need time to figure out if you want to be with me?"

"Yes."

He backed up a little bit, but still held tightly to her hand.

"What the hell, Lena?"

"You said anything!"

"Isn't there another way?" He clenched his teeth and pulled his hand out of hers and placed them behind his head. "I can't believe this."

"I can't believe you cheated."

"Stop saying it! That was months ago!"

"Whatever, Alonzo. You don't get it. I'll keep pretending. Maybe I'll just cheat, too. It will make us even, right?"

Shit. You win, Lena. You win. "Fine, Lena! I can do that. I can give you time."

"I wonder what changed your mind so quickly. The thought of me doing to you what you did to me?"

"Never mind that. I'm giving you what you want. I mean, it's a good idea that you make sure that you're sure. I have big plans for us. I know it's you that I want, Lena. I have no doubts."

"Okay."

"How long do you need? I don't know how to take a break from you. Can I still call you and come and stay with you?"

"I don't know how long I need."

Alonzo didn't think she wanted to be without him, and he didn't want to be by himself. He sighed. "Is this a breakup?"

Lena teared up. "Yes."

Alonzo let out a heavy breath. *I bet none of this would've happened if I had stayed my ass home. I pushed her. I pushed her to the edge. Shit.* He put his hand over his face and leaned back. "Damn! I wasn't expecting this today!" He stood up. "Okay. I'll go."

She grabbed his arm. "No. Don't leave me tonight. Stay here, Lonnie. I don't want you to leave."

He let his anger get the best of him. He couldn't believe it. This day was supposed to be one of the best days of his life, but it was ruined. He had thought of marrying her earlier, and now she was breaking up with him. "Whatever makes you happy, Lena."

"Lonnie, this is hard for me too. I know you don't believe me. Please stay. You should be with me tonight."

"You're right, I should. I'm not sure when I'll see you again." He placed his hand on her shoulder, and then moved to her chin to lift it up. He pulled her closer and kissed her on the lips.

They went back to her room and got in her bed. She lay right under him. They were silent. Lena looked over to her alarm clock to see that it was midnight. She forced her eyes closed. They would both be even more tired at work that day.

Alonzo could see and feel Lena's tension. She tried to keep her eyes closed and make herself sleep, but she couldn't keep her eyes off of him even though she could barely see his face. She looked toward him in the dark. "Lonnie, I love you."

He kissed her on the forehead. "I know you do." He knew it.

Lena taking him back with such ease was too good to be true. He had made his bed, and now he had to lie in it. "I can't stand the thought of me being blind to the fact that you've been unhappy this whole time. I've enjoyed you being with me, and I love you. More than you know." He turned on his side and placed his hand around her waist. "But I want this if it can help us. I want to marry you, Lena. I want you to mother my children. I want to take care of you. I want to make you happy."

They both closed their eyes, but neither of them went to sleep. Six hours later, he was heading out for Concord.

Chapter 16

Lena looked over her almost-bare, deep-mahogany walls. *I should put some paintings up in here. Maybe if I decorate more, it'll feel like my space. I need to do something to make this place feel like my "work home." My bills aren't going anywhere . . . so I have to be here. No, what I need to do is hit the lotto!* Lena was a week in and not feeling much better about the decision she had made about Alonzo. She remembered their last night together and how she had felt like she was failing him. The decisions that she thought about earlier not only made or broke her chance at happiness. They also did the same for Alonzo's happiness, but she had to stand up for herself this time. *Be strong, Selena. You have to do what's right for you. You've been there for him. Allow him to be there for you.*

Work was flowing much better. She had hired two more people in her department, Kalvin and the newer recruit, Rachel. They had stepped up to the plate, eager to gain more experience. However, when she had gone to dial Alonzo to tell him the good news, she had realized that wasn't her best idea. They had not spoken since that night and she had a feeling that he now hated her. She couldn't run to him for everything anymore. It came with the territory. Tammy knocked on her door. Lena told her to come in. *Come on in, girl, and tell me what's up, 'cause you've been antisocial.*

Tammy asked her about the location of their benefits files. Lena directed her to ask the new hire, Rachel, who was working on deleting all of their old files, replacing them with the new ones from their insurance provider, and organizing them on the server. Tammy, who didn't look satisfied with Lena's answer, started walking toward the door.

Lena stopped her. "Tammy."

Tammy stopped and turned to face Lena. "Yes ma'am?"

"Is everything all right? Did you sprain your ankle or something?" Tammy walked with a slight limp. It was barely noticeable, but she saw it when Tammy turned to walk out of her office.

"I twisted it yesterday. Lisa and I were washing the dog and he got away. The bugger ran off and I tripped over the water hose trying to catch him." Tammy smiled a little. Lena smirked as she left her office.

As soon as Tammy cleared the room, Lena pulled out her cell phone and called Sheree. She pondered what type of paintings she would buy. *Floral, scenic, pop?* The phone rang four times before it was answered.

A deep, male voice answered. Lena was confused at first and thought she had the wrong number. The guy chuckled and asked her to tell him her name. He insisted that she had the right number. She pulled her phone from her ear and checked to see if she dialed the right number. Surely enough, Sheree's name was being displayed. The guy mumbled something else, but she could not make it out because the phone sounded like it was being pulled away from him. Sheree hopped on the line. Relieved, yet still confused, Lena questioned Sheree about the guy who answered her phone. Sheree giggled and played it off without giving Lena a name, but after a few more minutes of questioning told Lena that is was Tony. Sheree also immediately tried to change the subject after making her confession by asking Lena to dinner at Glaze. Lena was not thrown off by the gesture. "Tony? I thought y'all stopped talking months ago?"

"Well, we started back two weeks ago. Is Glaze a yes or a no?"

"Glaze tonight is a no, but I would like to step out this weekend."

"That's even better! I know just the place. It's new!"

Lena's office phone started ringing. She rushed Sheree off the phone to answer it. "Hello. This is Selena Harris speaking."

"Hi, Ms. Harris. This is Sam Howell. I've been speaking with Alonzo and Ms. Ray about your brother, Doug. Alonzo gave me your work number. Is this a good time for you?"

Oh Lord. I forgot all about Dougie. What's next? "Hi. Thanks so much for contacting me. I'm actually busy right now. May I call you after four thirty?"

Mr. Howell was very formal. "That would be fine." After hanging up, she texted Alonzo.

Lena: *Hey. Just spoke with Mr. Howell.*

Lena: *Thanks for doing this. Tell Ms. Ray too.*

She thought about sending *I love you*, but decided that he may not have wanted to see that. *He's still looking out for me.* Lena worked through lunch. She had a staff meeting with Mr. Edwards at two thirty and didn't want to be behind the next day. She glanced at her desktop calendar. It was August 26. *I officially have five weeks until my vacation. Lord knows I need it.*

Lena called Mr. Howell after work and talked with him as she drove home. They discussed Dougie's case. He mentioned that he could try to get his charge knocked down to reckless driving. He would do it as a favor to Ms. Ray, whom he had a long history with, but his assistance wouldn't be free of charge. She walked into her apartment, downtrodden. She was somewhat mildly relieved with the new information because it meant Dougie wouldn't be charged with a DUI. She called Sheree.

Lena told her about the conversation with the lawyer. Besides him mentioning that Alonzo's mom had called Lena her future daughter-in-law, he said it would cost $1,400. She knew Dougie didn't have the money to pay for it. Sheree assured her that everything would work out, but Lena wondered when things would work out for her. Lena grew more frustrated as they talked. Her mind was on the $1,400 that she was now out of on account of her brother.

"How the hell can I go on vacation now?" Lena slammed her wineglass down on the counter. The base shattered and the stem broke in half. The bowl of the glass rolled along the counter, leaving a trail of its red contents. "Shit!"

"What was that? Lena are you okay?"

"I have to call you back."

"Lena!"

Lena hung up the phone. She went to the sink and pulled a small shard of glass out of her finger and washed the blood away. She cleaned up the broken wineglass and wiped the red wine from her counter and off of her floor. *No vacation for me.* She got a Band-Aid from the cabinet by the sink and sat at her kitchen table, drifting back to her and Alonzo's last night together. She felt herself about to cry. *I can't be here. I gotta go. I have to leave.* She snatched her purse off of the table and left her apartment. She rode around town for about forty-five minutes, just listening to music in her car and settling down. She found herself pulling up to a bar called MVPs. She had never heard of it. She wanted to be someone else, at the bar, alone. MVPs seemed like a good place to be that person. She normally didn't recommend emotionally induced drinking, but she was down for anything that would take her mind off of everything. She walked in the sports bar and was met by the stench of stale smoke. There was a nice after-work crowd there that was mostly guys and a few scattered women hanging on their arms. Pennant flags and other memorabilia from each professional football, basketball, and baseball team lined the walls. She walked in and was startled by an uproar of laughter. Her eyes followed the sound to a group of guys by the pool table. She scanned the scene and watched them as she walked to the bar. Her stare was met by a woman trailing behind one of the men. *What are you looking at?* Lena cocked her head to the side and woman looked away. *Thought so.*

The bar almost spanned the length of the building. She could tell that the place was very busy on weekends just by the size and atmosphere of the place. The guys at the bar watched her as she walked past. She ignored their eyes and didn't even offer a smile. One half of the bar wasn't lit. She sat closest to it so that there were four barstools between her and the next patron. Lena looked down the bar for the bartender. He was chatting up a customer when she saw another customer signal she needed his service. The guy pointed toward Lena, and she nodded and smiled, expressing her gratitude for his assistance. The bartender looked like a scruffy out-doorsman type. He was tall and slender with his brown hair pulled back in a ponytail. He had on denim with a red-and-brown, flannel-looking shirt. He smiled as he walked toward Lena.

"You expecting someone, sweetheart?"

"Nope. Just me."

"Shame."

She gave him a smirk. *Why yes. Yes it is.*

"What can I get you? Do you need a menu?"

"That would be awesome . . ." She paused, gesturing to indicate he should introduce himself.

"My apologies. I'm Winston." He handed her a menu and leaned on the counter as if he were admiring her. She looked up from the menu, peeped at his gray eyes, and giggled at him. "Are you going to stay down here?"

"Why wouldn't I?"

Lena leaned her head toward everyone to her left sitting at the bar. "What about your other customers?"

"They'll be all right. I'm here for you right now."

"Charming."

He laughed. She noticed his small gap. It was fitting. "I try."

She smiled and handed him the menu. She ordered a top-shelf Long Island and nachos.

He walked to the computer that was about two barstools away from her and put in her order. She watched him mix her drink and check on the others at the bar. She was enjoying herself, just living in the moment and pretending that her world wasn't crumbling all around her. He came back to her and placed a napkin on the bar. Following the napkin was her drink. It was huge.

"What's your name?" he asked as he poured a whiskey shot and placed it next to her glass.

"It's Lena, and I didn't order that."

"I know." He smiled. "But it's yours if you want it."

Lena tried her best not to blush, but a smile snuck onto her face. "Thanks, Winston."

He returned her smile before he left to check on his other customers. Lena had never had a such an attentive bartender. *I bet he's like this with all of the ladies . . . he is fine, though.* She sucked a big gulp of the Long Island through her straw. *I better hold off on this shot until I put some food in my stomach.* That was a good idea because she was already feeling a slight buzz. *This thing is strong! Oh, he makes good drinks.* The music playing in the background grew louder, and she nodded and bounced with it in her chair. Ten minutes later, Winston was back with her nachos.

He wiped down the bar as she ate. His arms were well defined. He was definitely a gym rat. He threw the damp bar towel over his shoulder and walked back to the other side of the bar and then to the kitchen. She watched his every move.

After some fifteen minutes, she pushed her nachos away. She had eaten all of them except for the soggy chips. It wasn't a large serving. Winston came back to take her plate.

"So, why'd you give me this?" she asked after taking her shot.

"Because . . . you seem tense."

"You can sense it?"

"Yeah. People come in here to relax, and you looked like you needed it."

"I did. I think I want another."

"I can make that happen. Whatever you want, Lena."

Someone yelled from the other end of the bar. "Hey, Winston!"

He threw his head up, held up a finger, and yelled back, "Be there in a sec." He poured Lena another shot of whiskey, smiled, and walked off.

She took the rest of her Long Island to the head as she watched Winston talk with the guys at the other end of the bar, and she immediately felt a swimming sensation. *Bad idea.* She snickered to herself, then took her second shot. She shook the burn off. *Yes. This is it. This is the feeling I've been looking for.* She felt whimsical. She also felt like kissing, but as the minutes went by she mostly felt like she couldn't drive. She put her elbows on the bar and propped up her head, then bobbed her head to the beat of the music. *I'm done. I can't drive.*

"Are you okay over here?"

Winston snuck up on Lena and startled her. "Yeah, may I have my check, please?"

"Of course." He came back with her printed check. "So, is there a Mr. Lena?"

She flashed him a flirtatious smile. "Wouldn't you like to know?"

He dropped his head and laughed. "I would. Badly."

"No. There's only Lena." She slid her card and check across the bar to him.

He placed his hand on top of hers as he grabbed her payment. "Well, does this lowly bartender have a chance at receiving your number?"

The warmness of his hand on hers brought to her attention that he was the first guy to touch her since Alonzo. *Alonzo would be so angry, but I'm single now. Sort of. I don't know. He's really cute! Bump it!* "He most certainly does."

He smiled and walked off. He brought her card back and handed her his phone. Lena took it and started dialing her number. He watched her squint at his phone screen as she saved her contact information. "Are you going to be okay to drive?"

"Nope."

He laughed loudly. She handed him his phone back. "Would you like me to call you a taxi?"

"No. I'm going to call someone."

"Okay, Lena . . . anything else?"

"Water." She pulled her phone out of her purse and dialed Alonzo.

Chapter 17

"Hello?" Alonzo's voice sounded raspy. It was a sign that he was tired, sleeping, or both.

"Hey. I need a favor."

He sucked his teeth. "What, Lena?"

"I'm at this bar, and I've had too much to drink."

He cut her off before she could say she couldn't drive. "Where are you?" She could hear him getting up and stretching.

"A sports bar on Dawn Street. MVPs."

"I'm on my way. I'll go get Tony. He can drive your car home."

"Okay. Thanks, Alonzo."

"Yeah."

She sighed. *He's pissed.* She waited and sipped her water.

Winston stopped by and checked on her a few more times. Twenty-five minutes later, Alonzo was walking in. Lena saw him and grabbed her purse. She carefully stepped down from her stool and walked over to him as steadily as possible. She walked past the remainder of the guys at the bar. They still watched her and she still ignored them. As she got to the end of the bar, Winston yelled, "Bye, Lena." She smiled at him and waved. Alonzo looked him up and down and opened the door for Lena.

"So what, you're a regular here? The bartender knows your name and shit?"

She bumped into him as they walked out of the bar. "Nope. Just met him tonight." Tony was standing outside by the door. She waved at him as she pulled her sweater together to block the chill in the night air.

Alonzo stopped walking. "Where are your keys and who were you here with?"

"No one, Alonzo." She handed him her keys.

Alonzo sucked his teeth, then passed the keys to Tony. "Let's head out."

The car was silent. She hated it. She wanted to say something, but didn't know what to say. *Sorry about this? It won't happen again? I miss you. Kiss me! Can you stay the night?* She felt him looking at her. She looked up at him and he was indeed looking at her. His eyes went from her to the road. She looked out of the window to avoid meeting his eyes. Alonzo let out a long yawn and mumbled something under his breath. She ignored it. She didn't think it deemed a response, but she did look at him while he drove. He looked like he had jumped right out of bed. Sweat pants and a hoodie. *Look at my Lonnie. My ex now.* Alonzo was in his thoughts and she could tell that he was becoming more bothered by the minute.

"What is this, Lena?" He couldn't hold his silence any longer.

"What?"

"Why are you drunk? It's a weekday, Tuesday! You have to go to work tomorrow."

"I was stressed. I wanted a drink. It won't happen again."

"This is stupid."

"I said it won't happen again."

"I'm talking about us."

"Lonnie." She started over. "Alonzo, we already talked about this."

"And I thought it was stupid then."

"Well, there's no going back."

"Says who? Why not? I miss you, Lena."

She looked out the window at the few cars that they shared the road with. *I should've ridden with Tony.* Her eyes went back to Alonzo. "I miss you, too. I do. So much, but—"

Alonzo was upset, and when he reached that level, there was no listening. "So why aren't we together? That's why this shit is stupid. You need to stop playing, Lena." He looked at her hard.

"Keep your eyes on the road."

"I got this. I'm not the one who's drunk!"

Lena shook her head and looked out of the window.

"Lena, for real. I just can't see you not wanting to be with me or being okay with this. There was a time when we inseparable."

Before she knew it, "That was probably before you fucked Tiffany, though" slipped from her alcohol-induced loose lips.

Alonzo banged his fist on the steering wheel and yelled, "Lena, stop with that shit!"

"You started it."

"All right."

They drove the rest of the trip in total silence. Lena was okay with it this time. She no longer hated it, because Alonzo was talking nonsense. His truck drove smoothly, and you couldn't hear any outside sounds from within the cabin. She laid her seat back and closed her eyes. Alonzo turned on the radio. Slow jams filled the atmosphere, and Lena floated to sleep.

Alonzo tapped her on the shoulder when they arrived at her apartment. Lena woke up and put her seat back in its normal, upright position. His truck's clock read a little after ten o' clock. Tony was parking her car beside them. Alonzo and Lena both got out of the truck. Lena thanked Tony while Alonzo got her keys from him. Tony got in the truck, and Alonzo walked Lena to her apartment and unlocked her door, then handed her the keys. He stood in her doorway for a second, then turned to walk away. She caught his hand, then pulled him toward her by his arm. He stood there, coldly looking down at her. She hugged him. He didn't hug her back, and she didn't let go. Eventually, he gave in and hugged her back.

He held her tighter. "You don't understand how this affects me, Lena. I don't think you get it."

"You have to give this time."

"No, I don't. You don't, either."

"Yes. I do!" She backed away.

"You're not telling me something, Lena. I can tell."

"No. You're paranoid." *Way to fudge up this moment.*

"Who is it, Lena? I know there's someone else."

Lena slapped her hands over her forehead and slid them down her face. "Thanks for picking me up, Alonzo. You have no idea how much I appreciate it. I'm going to bed. Text me when you get home. Good night."

"This is the last favor." He walked to his truck.

I know. She closed the door, locked it, and went to bed.

Chapter 18

Alonzo drove to work still troubled from dealing with Lena the night before. He questioned whether they were having a break or if it was indeed the end. Besides that, he was still in the process of making his new career decision. Mike told him to take some time and think about the proposition and where he'd want to be a few years. With the changes he was faced with in a week's span, he finally understood what Mike was explaining. That dream of running the shop with Lena on his arm was fading, but Alonzo refused to give it up. *Maybe she's going through some stuff that I don't know about. We're not over. I love her too much.*

The first half of his day was pretty easygoing. It was occupied with bunch of routine-maintenance appointments that he oversaw or performed himself. Mike was out of the office for the day, meaning that Alonzo was acting manager. Alonzo was thankful for the break when lunch rolled around. He was still sleepy from riding around Charlotte the night before. He closed his office door and stopped by the front desk. Ms. Susan stopped him before he left for lunch. Alonzo thought she was being nosy again. She asked him where he was going to lunch as if she wanted to order something, but eventually told him that she had brought lunch.

Alonzo walked out of the shop and was met by Mike. Mike stopped him in the parking lot. "Bro! I'm not in today and you're sneaking out?"

"Yeah, man. Playing hooky!" Alonzo held out his hand for a fist bump.

"Where you headed?"

Alonzo yawned. "I don't know, man, I need to put something in my stomach."

"Late night drinking with Lena, huh? That explains why you look like shit!" Mike laughed hard. Alonzo didn't. "What?"

Alonzo rubbed his hand across the back of his hair. He needed a haircut. Bad! "Late night with Lena, all right. Drunk-and-can't-drive Lena."

Mike twisted his lips up. "Oh . . . Still sounds fun, unless she's an angry drunk or something?"

"Man, I don't even want to talk about it. I only want to talk about food right now."

Mike volunteered to drive them to lunch. They got into Mike's SUV. He drove to the parking-lot exit and stopped before pulling out into the oncoming traffic. "Where to, bro?"

Alonzo shrugged as he looked out of the passenger-side window and said, "Doesn't matter."

"All right, sounds like we're eating subs to me."

A few minutes later, they were at the sub shop. "I'm feeling a Philly cheesesteak." Alonzo rubbed his stomach as they walked through the door. The smell of the freshly baked bread was inebriating. The place had an old-fashioned, seventies-diner look. The walls were green with white-and-green-checkered tiles along the top of the walls. Alonzo always thought it was tacky in there, but the sandwiches were amazing. The meats were great cuts and piled high. It was really a bang for your buck.

"No, man. I'll Hulk smash a turkey melt!" They ordered their meals, got their drinks, and paid.

Mike approached Alonzo while he was grabbing napkins and condiments. "So, what's up with you and Lena?"

"Bruh."

"Alonzo, eat a Snickers. Why? 'Cause you're a Catholic priest when you're hungry."

"Mannn!" Alonzo laughed hard as he sat down at their table.

They talked while they waited for their subs to come out. Mike told him more about the updates on the shop location in Charlotte. Alonzo needed to retrain his thoughts and focus on work and not his Lena problems, but he knew it was a temporary transition because Mike was itching to know. The food arrived, and they ate. Alonzo was halfway through his Philly when Mike couldn't resist hearing what had Alonzo so dreary.

"Okay, man. You've eaten. Spill it!"

Alonzo took one last bite. "You're acting like a woman, Mike."

"Call it what you want! Spill it."

"Lena broke up with me a week ago . . . We're supposedly taking a break." *I hope.*

Mike shifted in his seat. Alonzo had no trace of happiness in his voice. There was only dread. Mike tried to lighten the mood. "Oh, a break is nothing." He chuckled. "Next time, lead with that!"

Alonzo sighed. "It doesn't feel like a break. Why end the relationship if it's only a break?"

There was no lightening Alonzo's mood, but Mike continued to prod. "Where did the idea come from? Did something happen?"

Alonzo stared out of the restaurant's cloudy windows. They needed to be washed, but even through the windows' film, he could see that it was a really pretty day. He felt he couldn't enjoy it. All he could think about was Lena and how she had dismissed him. *I drive to pick you up from a bar because you're drunk, and you give me a sorry thank-you, oh, you really appreciate it . . . bullshit.* He sighed. "You already know what happened."

"What?"

"The fucking Tiffany incident finally caught up with me."

Mike looked confused. "I thought you told her."

"She knew about it. She saw us together. I guess she never really got over it, and now she wants to make sure that she's making the right decision by being with me."

"Oh."

"Right . . . part of me believes it. Another part of me thinks she has someone."

Mike shook his head in disbelief. "You think she would try to get back at you?"

"I don't know anymore."

"You know what? Lena is almost thirty. Women get crazier when they creep up on thirty. Especially if they aren't married with kids. It's the biological-clock thingy. She's going through that confused-ass-woman stage where she's questioning everything. Y'all will be fine. Just give her some time. I'm sure there's no one else."

"There better not be."

Alonzo's underlying hostility made Mike uneasy. "Bro. Don't talk like that. Even if there is someone else. There's nothing you can do."

"There's plenty I can do."

Mike looked at his watch. He signaled to Alonzo that it was time to head back, then he went and refilled his drink and picked up a couple of to-go boxes.

Mike told Alonzo to take the rest of the day off as they returned to the shop. Alonzo initially disputed the order, but his fight subsided. He knew that he needed some rest and a mental break. He went back home and slept until about a little after five. When he woke, he checked his phone. There were missed calls from Tony and his mom. His listened to his mom's voicemail. Her voicemails always started off with phone-fumbling sounds and her talking in the background as if she didn't know the phone was already recording. "Hey, sugar. Call me back. I want to cook dinner for you this weekend. You and Lena should come down. Call me back now . . . I mean it!"

He dropped his phone and rolled over. It was time he broke the news to his mom. He knew she'd be devastated. She loved Lena. Every time Lena came around, she'd pull him to the side and whisper, "I'm so proud of you. You did good, son." What killed him was the question why. "We broke up" is always followed by "Why?" *Why? Because I slipped up. I made a damn mistake. Why can't she see it that way? I'll never do it again. I need one more chance.* His mom always taught him to fight for what he wanted. He could see them on the porch talking, her in her sundress in the rocking chair and him getting ready to meet his friends at the basketball courts. Saturday-afternoon talks was what he came to call those meetings.

"Where you going, son?"

"To play basketball."

"Did you get your homework done?"

"Some of it. I have the whole weekend, Ma."

As soon as those words slipped from his mouth, a look of disappointment would make its way onto her face. She'd ask him, "What are you waiting for?" and tell him, "You could've done it already." He always wondered why she was tripping. All he wanted to do was go and play basketball with his friends, but he'd never question his mom. She was all he had. She would lecture him and tell him that he was lazy and needed to prioritize. He needed to make sure that he knew what were the most important things in his life. He could clearly remember her saying, "You'll find out that nothing worth having comes easy in this world."

He'd go meet his friends at the courts. It would appear that he was blowing his mom off when she tried to talk to him about life, but he listened, and those lessons had saved him many times. Alonzo didn't know if Lena had someone or not, but it didn't matter anymore. The new guy was no competition to him. She was who he wanted to marry, and he was going to marry her. She didn't know it yet, but he did. After calling his mom and telling her everything, he texted Lena.

Alonzo: *I apologize for the way I spoke to you last night. I'm here if you need anything. Always.*

His accusations had to stop. It was now time to plan how he would get her back.

Chapter 19

Lena crashed on her sofa. She had had the longest day. Waking up with a ringing head and queasy stomach, she had a hard time getting out of bed, let alone finding something to wear that wasn't sweats. She settled for a quarter-length-sleeve dress that went past her knees, and flats. She couldn't handle wearing anything that was too constricting. She arrived to work late, slept in her car for lunch, and overall regretted her night of drinking. All except for Winston. He seemed pretty cool. She felt like she could enjoy a conversation or two with him. Sheree had called her a few times, but she wasn't up for bragging about her drunken night. So, she texted her instead.

Lena: *I'm about to take a nap. I'll call you later.*

She was sure Sheree already knew about the night before. Tony couldn't keep a secret. Sheree didn't respond. She was probably upset.

Just as Lena was deep into her sleep, her phone rang. *Ugh . . . I forgot to turn the ringer off.* She checked her phone and saw a number that wasn't saved. Curious, she answered.

"Hi. This is Marie from the law office of Sam Howell. Am I speaking to Selena Harris?"

Shit. I shouldn't have answered. "Yes. This is Selena."

Marie was calling to notify her that a payment was needed. Dougie's court date was scheduled within the next month or so. They needed a payment before they would proceed with his paperwork. Lena was confused. She told Marie that she had spoken with Mr. Howell previously and he hadn't mentioned a court date. Marie explained to her that they had recently received new information from Doug, and that he had listed her as the responsible party.

Something has got to give. Lena closed her eyes and listened as Marie went through the details of the agreement and invoice that she was preparing to send. They wanted half of the total fees up front and the other half after the case was over. Lena asked when the first payment was due.

Marie let out a breath as she answered. "All of the information is on the invoice. I don't know the exact date. I didn't generate this particular invoice. I'm only sending it to you, but I can tell you that if his court date is within a month or month and a half that your payments are needed ASAP to start his case preparation."

Lena thanked her, although she didn't find her answer helpful, and ended the call.

Lena laid her head back and said a little prayer to herself. She opened her eyes and composed a text to Dougie.

Lena: *Maybe you should tell your responsible party about your case updates too. Grow the fuck up, Dougie.*

Between Dougie and Alonzo, Lena was done with men. She even found herself mad at Winston for being too flirty. She amused herself. *Winston hasn't done anything wrong . . . yet.* She thought about going back to the bar, but she still felt drained and dehydrated from the night before. With that thought, she made her way to the kitchen for a glass of water. With her bare feet pressing into her lush carpet, she walked around her living room, pacing and moving from one room to the next. *I should go walking . . . No, I'm still tired.* She walked over to her stereo and turned it on. She danced in the middle of her floor, prancing around and rocking her hips to the slow beat of a soft drum tap. Alonzo had left his jazz CD in the player months ago, and the saxophone player took Lena to another place—a small, dank club with blue lights. She imagined herself sitting at a small table in the corner with an unrecognizable man, and he whispered sweet nothings to her and made her smile. She danced, swayed, and sat on her floor. With her legs stretched, she lay down. She grabbed a pillow from the sofa and propped it under her head.

Dougie called her. Alonzo texted her. But Lena didn't answer or text back. She just lay there with her eyes closed, dreaming about the vacation she would no longer have.

Chapter

It was Friday, August 28. Lena was getting in her car again to leave work. *Finally Friday!* It was pretty yucky outside. The sky was dark gray. It had been raining all day. She was thankful that it had subsided as she and her coworkers walked to their cars. She had contemplated calling out as she lay in her bed, but eventually forced herself to leave her apartment that morning as it stormed. It really made her appreciate her college days when she could skip class on the rainy days.

The day was a drag and she worked slowly. Tammy looked just as exhausted as she did, and the new kids were so upbeat that it was nauseating. Every day felt like it was blending together. Her exhaustion was taking a toll on her overall well-being, and she felt like she had no energy. She didn't look forward to the weekends by herself. She contemplated going to see her parents, but couldn't bear to be around them knowing that they didn't know what was going on with Dougie.

She thought about how much she missed Alonzo as she drove home. The roads were packed and it was pouring down rain. She wanted to be home right then, but she was stuck in traffic. The local radio stations reported two wrecks that had everyone backed up. She sat there in the car watching the raindrops slide down her side window. She thought about how good her bed would feel once she got out of the shower. *A bed in oceanfront hotel room would be even better.* She was pretty disappointed about cancelling her vacation. Although she couldn't go anywhere, she decided to take the days off anyway and just chill at home. *I'm going to eat myself into a coma, have some drinks, and throw in some missed seasons of my favorite shows.* She loved crime series.

Lena was singing along with Mary J. Blige when she was suddenly cut off. Her music stopped playing and a phone call came through. Danen.

He greeted her with his normal "Hey, Lena Harris." She smiled, but decided to cut the small talk.

"What do you want?"

He laughed. "You. But you already know that."

And all of a sudden, Lena remembered where she and Danen left off. He had told her that he wanted to talk about them, as if there were a *them.* Then, Alonzo crossed her mind. He was temporarily out of the picture. She indulged. *Why not give him something to talk about? He's always accusing me, anyway.* She decided to return the flirtatious banter. "Well, what are you going to do about it?"

Danen was stumped. "Umm . . . I would say take you from your man, but I don't want to cross any lines."

"You wouldn't have to take me." Lena inched up in the traffic.

"Quit playing."

"I don't play."

He asked her what she was doing. She told him that she was stuck in traffic. It was bumper to bumper. She wasn't going to be home anytime soon. Danen told her that he was on his way home from the high school, but quickly changed the subject back to her previous comment.

"Now what's this nonsense about me not having to take you?"

"Take a wild guess," she teased.

"Lena, are you single?"

"I am."

Danen was quiet. She could hear his music in the background, so she knew the call hadn't dropped. "Danen?"

No response.

"Danen? You there?"

"Yeah."

"What the heck were you doing? You didn't hear me talking to you?"

"Yeah, I did. I was saying a prayer. I had to thank God for what you just told me. No slight to your guy. Well, ex-guy. But the Lord knows my heart."

Lena laughed. "Man! You do not have it all."

"Yes, I do, and I'm about to have you."

"Whatever!"

"I'm not worried. You'll see. I let you slip away one time. It won't happen again."

Lena reddened. She may have not spent time with Danen recently, but she knew when he was resolute, and he was not joking around. He spoke with evocation, causing her to recall his facial expressions. Danen was an eyesome fellow. Danen was fly, and Danen had the power to blow her mind, or whatever was left of it. His words held so much power, but she refused to display any signs of the mini explosion in her body. She wouldn't give up her propensity to fall for him so easily. "If you say so."

He chuckled. His laugh rumbled through her speakers. "So, what's been going on with you, Lena Harris?"

"Too much, Danen. Too much." She sighed.

"Well, you're stuck in traffic. You might as well talk. I'm listening."

She told him about her ending it with Alonzo and how she felt like she needed to be sure about him. She didn't mention his infidelity. She didn't want him to be judged. She was still protecting him. She talked about her job, and even about going to the sports bar and exchanging numbers with Winston.

"I don't know about this Winston guy. He's in line after me, and technically, he shouldn't be in line at all, because the buck stops here!"

"No, technically, you've had your chance already. So, it may or may not be his turn."

"Not if I have a talk with him."

"Shut up, Danen!" Lena was finally close to her apartment complex, but because of the traffic had another fifteen to twenty minutes until she got there. "I'm so hungry."

"Do you want me to bring you something to eat?"

She laughed. "No."

"How's Dougie, man? I haven't seen him in forever. Your mom told me he was in school at A and T."

"Wow, I can't believe I didn't tell you! I've been trying my best not to think about it."

"What?"

"Dougie was arrested. And don't tell my folks!"

"I won't say anything. What happened?"

Lena told him what happened and the updates with the lawyer and his court date. "He's so ungrateful. He barely says anything to me. I can't stand him right now, and I'm afraid that if I talk to him that I'll say some stuff that I'll regret. So, I'm giving us a break, too."

"Well, you're just breaking it off with everyone, aren't you?"

She laughed and smiled at him, finding some humor in all of her mess. "You're next."

He proclaimed that she'd never break it off with him, because she loved him. "You'll always love me, Selena." She laughed at him and acted as if she was going to hang up. He begged her not to, then told her that he loved her, too. Danen told her that he had never stopped loving her. Lena wouldn't say it back. Instead, she tried to change the subject by adding more details about how she paid Dougie's lawyer and cancelled her vacation.

"When were you going?"

"The end of next month."

"Where?"

"I hadn't decided on a place yet, but I was thinking Virginia Beach."

"I'll take you."

"No, Danen."

"Why not?"

"I don't know. Just no. I can't let you do that."

"Let me? Who says you have a choice? You deserve a break. You deserve to be happy right now. I'm going to be the one to give you something to look forward to."

"Why would you do that? We haven't seen each other in a year, I think."

"I already told you why. I love you. None of that other stuff matters. I'm making us reservations tonight. One room with a king bed. I'll send you the info tonight."

She burst out laughing. "Two rooms!"

"So, you are coming? I knew you would. I'll talk to you later, Lena Harris. I can't wait for our getaway."

"Bye, Danen." Lena smiled all the way home.

Chapter 21

Danen is so silly . . . but it would probably be so much fun hanging out and catching up with him, especially on the beach. Lena was back home and reflecting on her and Danen's conversation. She sat at her big dining-room table with her Chinese takeout that she picked up while on the way home. After a bite or two, she was putting the rest of the takeout in the fridge. The long ride home was enough to decrease her appetite in and of itself, and the rain made her sleepy. She would rather lie down than sit at the table and eat. It was a perfect night for resting. She couldn't distract herself with the TV. The storm took care of that by knocking out her satellite reception. Carrying her heels, she slowly walked to her master bath. Her feet ached from her pointed-toe pumps. She didn't wear those black pumps often, but when she did, she felt sharp. They looked great with her black, pinstriped pantsuit. She smiled, thinking about all the stares she had gotten as she walked through the office. With Alonzo in

151

mind, she barely noticed all of the guys that watched her, but in his absence, she did.

Lena turned on the shower and let the steam fill her bathroom as she undressed. She pulled her hair back and put on her shower cap. As she stood in front of the counter looking in the mirror, she felt a slight vibration near her foot. It startled her, but then she remembered that her phone was in her pocket. She dug into her pants pocket and retrieved her phone. There was a text message from Danen.

He wrote, *What days did you take off?*

Oh my God. He's serious! Lena stood there in her bathroom, naked. *I can't let him do this. I can't.* She stared at her phone and smiled. The gesture was flattering, and she enjoyed the butterflies that she felt just from thinking about seeing him. It had been such a long time, but he still haunted her thoughts. She looked up from her phone and into the mirror, and what she saw there made her decision easy. She saw herself naked, holding her phone, but the one thing that she saw that made all the difference was her smile. A true, genuine smile. She hadn't felt this way in quite a while. *I'm doing it.* She texted Danen back.

Lena: *Sep. 30–Oct. 2.*

Lena: *I was aiming for Wed. or Thurs. through Sunday.*

He responded a few seconds later.

Danen: *I thought you were going to back out and not give me the dates. You never cease to amaze me, Selena* ☺ *. I'll get something to you by the end of the night. Send me your e-mail addy.*

She blushed and sent him her e-mail address. Soon after she was in the shower, washing away her cares. She stepped out of the shower after a long thirty minutes, wrapped her extra-large and soft towel around her wet body, and walked into her room. She hung up her suit and placed her dirty clothes inside of the hamper in her closet. Her towel slid off of her as she was plugging her charger into her phone on her nightstand. She caught a glimpse of her naked body in the mirror on her wall. *What will Danen think about my body? I'm not as slim as I was back then. Oh gosh, I need to work out. Wait . . . why is he seeing me naked? Get your head out of the gutter, Lena! I don't have to be naked. I could be in my bathing suit.* Lena shook her head at herself and laughed. Clean and relaxed, she got into her bed, only to have her phone vibrate ten minutes later. Excited, she grabbed her phone, assuming it was Danen with room information, but it was her mom.

Immediately, her excitement went away and she became edgy. Lena was paranoid every time her mom called, out of fear that they had found out about Dougie. She wasn't in the mood to talk to her, but answered anyway. After their greetings, her mom moved on to what was really on her mind.

"Well, I was just calling to check on you. I haven't heard from you in a while. Or Dougie, for that matter. I have two grown kids that don't call their mom. Y'all know I still want my progress reports."

Lena apologized and told her how busy she had been. Soon after, her mom began to question her about Alonzo.

Lena reiterated that they were "taking a break." Her mom wasn't accepting that answer.

"I know what you told me, but I don't get this break stuff. You are either with him or not with him."

"Okay. We aren't together right now."

"Mmhm. We'll see how long this lasts. You better not let Danen find out."

"Huh?"

"If you can 'huh,' you can hear. You heard me, Selena."

Lena laughed. "Why are you always bringing him up?"

"'Cause every time I see him, he asks about you. Every single time. You know he coaches your little cousin now. He's in high school."

"Who?"

"Monty!"

"Oh yeah! I forgot."

"You should come see him sometime."

"Who, Danen?"

"No, child! Monty! You ought to come see him play some time. He's really good. Plus, you'll be able to see Danen too, since you're asking."

"I'm not asking!"

"Mmhm, girly. Well, I'm going to let you go. You sound tired."

Lena was glad she had answered. Talking to her mom was soothing, although fearing that she had found out about Dougie's arrest was nerve racking. She was even more thrilled from learning of Danen's inquiries about her. She was really in his thoughts as much as he was in hers. She closed her eyes and saw his face. She grabbed a memory from way back when. This wasn't a daydream. It was her reliving a moment that she shared with Danen. He was in her bed, in her room, in her apartment near campus. She had loved that apartment. It was a two-bedroom townhome. Her roommate, Chasity, was okay, but the place was spacious, well decorated, and had an amazing balcony porch.

She remembered trying to keep quiet so her roommate wouldn't hear her moan and giggle as her and Danen's playful wrestling in her bed turned into kissing and then rolling around on the floor. Lena climbed on top of him and rocked back and forth with their clothes on, going down to kiss on his neck and lips at every chance she got. Danen almost ripped her clothes off, literally, in a heated passion. He bit and sucked all over her inner thighs so hard that he left hickeys all over them. And when he finally made it up to her wet center, he ate as if he had never tasted anything that sweet. He licked and shook his head in it. He sucked on her lips and kissed between her legs as if it could kiss back. Her legs shook with each stroke of his tongue against her body, and he'd use her juices to help guide his fingers inside and out as he kept her body warm in his mouth.

Lena shuddered in her bed at the thought of the way Danen made her feel. She even felt her insides tighten as if she were back in that moment. *I have to control myself, but it's over if he kisses me. He can't kiss me. I can't let him.* Sheree said to take things slow. She was weak for him. Lena could try to use all the self-help tools in the world to not give in to her cravings for Danen, but the only thing that could really stop her was a relationship. Lena did not believe in cheating whatsoever. She kept her promises. However, she was not in a relationship, and her body was craving an old feeling. Lena was looking forward to this vacation for more than a few reasons. The next morning, she woke up to an e-mail with the subject titled, "Reunited and it feels so good . . . It's official, Lena Harris." He had forwarded her the confirmation e-mail for their room reservations.

Chapter

Another Friday down! *September is finally here.* Lena crossed out September 4 on her desktop calendar. The sun's rays seemed less intense, and the afternoon breezes were present and refreshing. She looked forward to afternoon lunches on the terrace and sipping wine during sunsets on her porch. She had had a stress-free week. Work was going smoothly. She and her team really had the ball rolling. It felt great having the load taken off of her, and she finally had a chance to direct others. She even enjoyed eating lunch and talking with the newbies. Normally, Lena would eat by herself if she wasn't heading out or in the office eating with Tammy. She did miss her lunch dates with Tammy. Tammy looked as if she had been under the weather all week. Today, she had called in sick again.

Everything else was good, too. She was back on good terms with Sheree. She explained what happened the night she hung up. Sheree, being Lena's oldest friend, knew how Lena could react when under a lot of pressure, so she didn't stress it. Plus, Tony had already told her what happened, as Lena figured he would. Lena was sure not tell her about her vacation with Danen. In fact, she told no one. As far as she was concerned, everyone thought she was going by herself, and she'd like to keep it that way. Sheree especially couldn't know, because she was afraid that she'd tell Tony, and then it would definitely get back to Alonzo.

She questioned whether it was a good idea to go through with the trip with Danen, just for Alonzo's sake, but every time she thought about whose sake she was basing the decision on, she'd make up her mind to go. *I'm doing something for me* was what she'd tell herself. She spoke with Danen almost every day, and every day he was more convincing without trying. He was so ready for the trip and had even planned stuff for them to do while down there. Lena ate it all up.

Things with Dougie and her family were getting better. He was giving her the updates she needed. She finally felt that he was appreciative. Her paranoia with her family subsided as Danen told her not to worry. Everything was finally working itself out.

It was getting close to lunchtime, and Lena was deciding whether she'd eat her leftover chicken and rice or go out and get something. She was attempting to go on a diet to be beach ready, but something fast and greasy was calling her name.

"Hey, Selena." Kalvin knocked on her open door and leaned into her office.

"What's up, Kalvin?"

"We're all going to the pizza place. Would you like to come?"

"No, I have leftovers." Lena frowned.

"Oh, right, vacation diet. I forgot. Enjoy your boring food." He laughed.

She gave him a side eye and he left with the rest of the coworkers. She gathered her things. She wasn't eating with the group, but she also wasn't eating her boring food. She picked up her phone to call her mom. She and her mom talked during her lunch breaks on some days, but she noticed she had three missed calls and a voicemail from Tammy. She checked the voicemail first.

"Selena. Please call me. I had no one else to call. I . . . I need your help. Please call me back." Lena sat back down at her desk. Her response was imminent. Tammy's voice was cracking and frail, and Lena feared the worst. She dialed Tammy's number, and Tammy picked up fast.

"Selena."

"Yes, Tammy. Are you okay?"

"Can you meet me? Please."

"Meet you where? You need to tell me what happened."

"At the Days Inn on Sugar Creek Road. I had to get away."

"I'm not sure where that is, and get away from who?"

Tammy let out a wail before she murmured, "Jason."

Jason? Her husband, Jason? "Okay. I'm coming. I'll GPS it."

"Thank you, Selena."

Disturbed by Tammy's request, Selena sat there for a second. Tammy's standoffish behavior made sense now. Everything made sense: the missing days, the limp, and the change in her hairstyle. Tammy always wore her hair back in a bun. Lena could recall many a conversation about trendy hairstyles where Tammy reiterated her dislike for hair in her face. *I hope she's okay.* Lena searched the hotel's address on her computer. *That's across town. Makes sense if she doesn't want her husband to find her.* The hotel was in the same area as Alonzo's place. *I'm looking at a thirty-minute drive. I might as well take the rest of the day off.* She packed all of her things since she wasn't returning and composed an e-mail to Kalvin.

> *Kalvin,*
>
> *I have a family emergency to tend to and will be out for the rest of the day. Please forward all calls to my voicemail. The new-employee packets are not complete. Please complete them by the end of the day. We will have five new employees completing orientation on Monday. Be sure to add the new full-time-benefits forms. Also, Mr. Edwards was out today, but have him reach me on my cell if he calls and asks for me. Have a great weekend.*
>
>
>
> *Thanks,*
> *Selena Harris*
> *HR Manager*
> *Powers Communications*
>
>

That should keep him busy for the rest of the day. Lena left the office and drove the thirty minutes to the hotel where Tammy was hiding. The whole ride there, she pondered what that fear felt like. *How could he do that? I wonder if Lisa saw it. Oh God, I hope she didn't. That poor little baby.* Lena had had a peaceful childhood, and situations like this reminded her of how grateful she should be. *I've been over here worried about my grown little brother and Alonzo while Tammy has endured physical abuse at the hands of the man that's supposed to love and protect her. Oh God, please help her. My life could always be worse.* She saw Tammy's car as she approached the hotel from the street. She called Tammy.

"Are you here?"

"Yes. I am pulling in to the parking lot now. What room are you in?"

"Is it just you?"

"Yeah."

"I'm in room twenty-one."

"Okay."

There weren't many cars in the hotel parking lot. Lena could imagine why. The hotel looked outdated from the outside. The beige-and-blue paint was plain and atrocious. She thought the whole place needed remodeling. Lena parked next to Tammy's car. As she got out, she saw baskets of clothes, shoes, and toys in the back of her coworker's car. Everything was disheveled. Tammy must've been rushing and thrown the things back there. *She's running away while he's at work. He'll be furious when he finds out. We need to call the police.* Lena walked to Tammy's room and didn't get a full two knocks in before Tammy opened the door. Lena hesitated to walk in. She momentarily checked out the outdated room first and saw that Tammy was the only person occupying it. "Are you okay?"

Tammy was standing by the door holding it open with her head down, her hair falling in the same direction as her head. "No. I don't know what's wrong with him." She looked up and exposed her blackened right eye. She had dark-red bruises around her neck.

Lena stood there in shock at the sight. She covered her mouth to hold her cry in.

"Selena, I can't close the door with you standing there."

"I'm sorry! I'm so sorry." She stepped out of the doorway toward Tammy. "We need to call the police!"

"No!" Tammy walked to the bed. "I can't."

"Why?" Lena followed her. "Look at what he did to you!"

"I know, but he's been locked up before . . . for other things. If the police find out, he will go to jail for a long time."

"He needs to be there!"

Tammy sat at the foot of the hard, queen-sized bed. The blanket on the bed was beige, just like the walls, but with a dark-brown, floral pattern on it. "I can't take care of Lisa on my own!"

"And you can't if you're dead! Did he choke you?"

"Yes." Tammy started crying.

Lena sat next to her and wrapped an arm around her and rubbed her back. "Where's Lisa?"

"A friend came and got her. I didn't want her in school. I thought that he might go and take her. You know, to get me to come back. She's staying with my friend tonight. She will take her to school tomorrow with her daughter."

"You sure you don't want to call the police?"

"I'm sure."

Chapter

"Yeah, man. I'm most definitely down tonight!" Alonzo laughed as he turned out of his doctor's parking lot. "I'm off for the rest of the day! I'm ready to pregame right now!"

"Man, whatever. Some people have to work," Tony joked. "Hey, let me hit you back."

"All right." Alonzo hung up. He turned up the music as he cruised down the street. He was on his way to the pharmacy to pick up a few over-the-counter things his doctor told him to get. The traffic was clear for the most part. His windows were rolled down. The September air felt calming as it flowed through his car and brushed his face. He liked the combination of the sound of the air passing his ear and his music. He felt like living.

Alonzo hadn't been off since the day Mike had sent him home; that was the night he had picked Lena up from the bar. He pulled into the pharmacy's parking lot. There were only a few cars parked around the bright-red building. He pulled into a spot right in front of the store, next to a green Ford Explorer. He was really fond of Explorers. He had always said that he would get Lena one once they had kids. He sat in his truck looking at the green SUV. The car beeped and the lights came on. A tall, slender woman with long, black, curly hair walked out of the store. Alonzo watched her as she walked to the driver's door. She caught him staring and smiled. Embarrassed that he was caught watching her, he grinned back.

She giggled and said, "You like what you see?" as she opened her door to get in her SUV.

Alonzo lifted his eyebrows in disbelief. He leaned over his divider so that he was a little closer to his open passenger-side window. "Most definitely. You're the highlight of my day."

She sat there with her door open and smiled. "Really? That's sweet."

"Yep."

"Okay . . . Well, have a good day."

"You too, beautiful." She gave him one more inquisitive look, then closed her door and drove off. Alonzo told himself to stop her the whole time she was pulling off, but when he decided to say something, she was already backing out of the spot. He couldn't make himself reach out yet. He still had *most* of his faith in Lena. He pulled his keys out of the ignition and returned to his errand.

Alonzo hummed as he walked up and down the aisles of the pharmacy. There was so much excitement to look forward to for the rest of his Friday. He strolled down the aisle, grabbing items from the multicolored-package-filled shelves. *Vitamins, fiber, beer . . . I gotta get some beer, water.*

Oh, those chips look good. Spicy nacho. Getting 'em. Might as well get some soap while I'm here too. Yeah . . . soap. Oh! Trash bags! He tossed the items in his buggy and went to go check out. "Hey ma'am, how are you doing?" His phone rang as he reached the cashier.

"Fine." She barely looked up at him.

He fumbled in his pocket for his phone before reaching it, placing it to his ear, and holding it there with his shoulder. "Yo." Then, he fumbled in his other pocket for his wallet. Very excited about the night's festivities, he asked Tony more about their plans. "So, who all's coming out tonight?"

The cashier raised her voice over his phone banter. "Your total is thirty-four dollars and twenty-five cents."

He surveyed all of the candy that sat underneath the register and grabbed a pack of Now and Laters. "Oh. Add these, too."

She looked frustrated as he handed her two twenties.

Tony told him that their friend Rob was thinking about coming. Rob hadn't been out with them in a while. Hence, Tony's comment that he stayed "caking," or continuously spending all of his time with or talking to his girlfriend and/or current female companion.

"Thank you, ma'am." Alonzo grabbed his change and bags from her, then walked out of the store.

He was fully back into their conversation once he exited. "You can't talk, Tony."

"Ahh, here you go. You didn't hear me say anything when you spent *every* weekend with Lena."

"Yeah, yeah," Alonzo dismissed him.

"'Yeah, yeah' nothing. I'm right. Speaking of Lena, have you heard from her?"

Alonzo put his bags in the back. "Nope. I saw Dougie last weekend when I went to see my mom. He said that she was still snapping on him about the DUI." He chuckled. "I figured I'd give her the time she asked for."

"Oh, okay. Where are you, anyway? I haven't been to lunch yet."

"Man, I'm over here on Sugar Creek. I'm leaving the pharmacy and about to head to GNC. I gotta start back hitting the gym, man. She said I need to watch my cholesterol."

Tony laughed. "You're getting old, man."

"Tell me about it. I almost freaked out this morning. I thought I saw a gray hair on my balls!"

Tony laughed out loud. "On that note, I gotta go. I'm hungry as hell and don't want to hear about your balls!"

Alonzo laughed. "Peace!"

Next stop, GNC. He purchased almost $120 worth of products ranging from protein powder for shakes, fat burners, and protein bars. He packed his car up and was finally headed to the house to pregame before his boys got off. *We're partying tonight. Just like the old times!* He turned up his radio as he rode down Sugar Creek Road. J. Cole's "Forbidden Fruit" was blasting through his custom speakers. He hummed along. He was jamming, enjoying the ride, and checking out the scene. People were out. It was a beautiful day. The transport-like van in front of him completely stopped in his lane before merging into the left-turn lane to turn into a hotel. *Man! Gotta know how to drive with all those damn kids in your van.* His eyes followed the van as he pulled off to continue going straight, then he did a double take at a car parked at the hotel. *Damn, that looks like Lena's car.* He kept riding. *That really looked like Lena's car . . . Stop tripping, Alonzo.* He rode for a few more minutes, then he turned around in the parking lot of a fast-food burger joint. He rode back down Sugar Creek and pulled into the hotel parking lot. Alonzo pulled up behind the car he suspected to be Lena's. It was her car. *What the fuck. No! She is not creeping with someone in my neck of the woods. At Days Inn? SHE IS NOT!* He parked next to her car and called her. No answer. He called her again. No answer. *Damn, I don't know what room she's in. I should go bang on every damn door!* He called her one more time. His heart was beating a mile a minute. Every dial tone seemed to be held longer and longer, every second going by slower. She didn't answer, and he sat there in his truck, silent, but the song continued to play. *Well, you're right, J. Cole. Love comes and it goes.*

Chapter 24

Lena sat with Tammy and listened to her tell the story of Jason. He had been drinking more. She didn't know why. He had been attacking her for weeks now. "He's just angry." He'd hit her so hard that she fell out of her chair and twisted her ankle. Lena grew more furious with every word. She really wanted to call the police, but felt she had to respect Tammy's wishes. Jason's parents were up in age, and his mom had gone through the same issues with his dad. After hearing that tidbit, Lena assumed that Jason's abuse toward Tammy was a learned trait. Tammy said that he never hit Lisa, but he was becoming reckless and she was afraid that he would. "I've got to leave him. At least I could get child support."

"Yeah, but what you need now is protection. That's why you need to report it."

"I think I'm going to go to my mom's house. I don't know what to do. I don't want to lose my job."

"You're missing so many days, Tammy. It's inevitable if you miss any more. You need to have a meeting with Mr. Edwards. Maybe if you explain the situation, we can come up with something."

"You're right." Tammy walked to the bathroom.

Lena walked over to the table where she'd set her purse. She'd been hearing it vibrate, but wanted Tammy to have her undivided attention.

Tammy walked out of the bathroom and saw Lena at the table with her purse. "Are you leaving?"

"No. I have some missed calls. I told Kalvin to tell Mr. Edwards to call my cell if he needed me, and someone has been calling me." Lena shifted the stuff around in her purse, looking for her phone. *I need to clean this thing out.* She finally pulled it out from under a pile of old receipts and wadded-up tissue.

"Was it Mr. Edwards?"

Lena looked surprised. "No. It was Alonzo." She walked toward the door. "Give me a second, this may be about Dougie."

"Okay."

Lena placed the latch in the doorway so it would be open and stepped into the hallway of the hotel and called Alonzo. "Hey. What's going on?"

Sternly, he said, "Selena, come outside."

"Huh? What do you mean?"

"I'm outside the hotel. Come outside."

Lena walked down the hall and passed the front desk, where she smiled at the receptionist. "What are you doing off?"

"What are you doing at a hotel when you're supposed to be at work?"

She walked through the dingy double doors of the hotel and stepped into a cloud of cigarette smoke. She started sneezing and waving the smoke away from her face. She looked toward the origin of the smoke and saw a tall, skinny guy with a long, gray beard taking another drag. He unapologetically looked back at her and flicked his ashes on the ground. She cleared her throat and continued to the parking lot. Alonzo was standing beside his truck. She hung up the phone and went to him. "Are you spying on me?"

He met her halfway and pointed to her car. "I saw your gold," he mimicked her voice, "I mean, your *champagne* Acura outside." He walked over to her car and looked in it. "I was passing by this hotel and thought, 'Hey, that looked like Lena's car.' Once I noticed the UNC tag, I knew it was you. Who are you in there with?"

"Calm down. It's not what it looks like."

He yelled, "Who's in there?"

"So I look like I'd meet someone at a Days Inn?"

"Stop playing, Lena! Answer me!"

She laughed. "Number one, you need to lower your voice."

He walked to the hotel. Lena didn't stop him. She was pissed that he'd accuse her of being with someone else again. She walked in behind him.

"What room number?"

"Twenty-one."

He walked down the hall with fast and wide strides. He was finally going to find out what man was stealing her away. He opened the door and saw Tammy sitting on the bed with a bruised eye. Tammy was startled and jumped.

Stunned at the sight, he blurted out, "I'm sorry." Alonzo stepped out of the doorway and back into the hall. He looked at Lena, wide eyed, and mouthed, "What the fuck?"

Lena apologized to Tammy. "I'm sorry, girl. He came to check on me and wanted to see for himself . . . that we were safe. I'll be back."

Tammy, clutching her chest, softly said, "Okay."

She hated that she had allowed him to scare Tammy like that, especially with what she was going through, but Alonzo needed a rude awakening. She wanted him to feel like the fool he was being. Lena closed the door, then walked back outside without saying anything to him.

"Lena." He walked beside her. "Lena! What's going on in there?"

She didn't say anything to him until they had reached their cars. "Alonzo, you don't trust me?"

"You've just been different lately. I don't know. I thought maybe there was someone else."

"Alonzo, I'm fed up with your accusations. I can't live with your guilt! What if there was someone else? Would you not want to get back with me? Would we be over? Would you not give me another chance? Like how I did for you?"

"Who is it, Lena? I know there's someone. Who is it?"

"You can't even answer my questions! All you ask is who, who, who? Don't you get it? That's not the point! I gave you so many chances, and you probably wouldn't give me one if I did to you what you did to me! This is bullshit!"

"It does matter, but I *need* to know. Who?"

Lena looked at him with a face that showed her thoughts. *You're so lost, how can you not see?* She turned toward the hotel, walked off, and whispered "Danen" under her breath. He walked to her and grabbed her shoulder. "WHO?"

She turned around and screamed, "DA-NEN! Damn, did you get it that time?"

He stood there with an open mouth, his hand still on her shoulder.

She knocked his hand off of her. "You feel better now?"

"What the fuck, Lena? When? What happened?"

"I don't owe you any explanations!"

"What? Did you cheat on me?"

"No! Nothing, Alonzo! Nothing!"

"What do you mean, nothing?"

"Nothing happened! We've been talking. I think about him. He doesn't stress me like you!"

"So you haven't had sex with him?" He folded his arms across his chest in disbelief.

"No."

"Have you seen him?"

"No." *But I'm going to.*

"Do you want to?"

Lena didn't answer.

"I don't know what's worse—sex with him or him in your head."

Lena shrugged. "To be honest, I don't give a rat's ass what's worse to you." She walked off.

He followed her. "Lena, but . . ."

She turned around and held up her hand. "Stop. Don't come any closer."

He stopped. "You need to listen to me!"

"I'm not your girl! I don't need to listen to shit! I don't want to hear any more. I have a coworker that's going through a traumatizing situation right now! I need to help her find a resolution. I don't need your paranoid ass up here being foolish! You've changed, Alonzo. You keep saying all this crap about 'someone taking' me, but you've been pushing me away. So fuck it! I took myself out of the picture. There was a time where I wanted us to work out, but I think that time is over." She walked toward the hotel.

Alonzo stood there and watched her walk away. "Lena!" he yelled for her.

She yelled back, "Kick rocks!" She left Alonzo standing there and went back in the room with Tammy. A feeling of relief engulfed her body.

Chapter 25

Lena let the passenger-side seat back and sang along to the songs on the radio as Sheree drove. The leather seats felt soft. She could tell it was genuine. Sheree sang along with Lena as she drove her white Jeep Cherokee around downtown Charlotte. "So, where are we going?"

"How about you just enjoy your ride and find out when we get there?"

"Whatever, Sheree."

Sheree had managed to get away from Tony for a weekend and was taking Lena out. Having an insider, Tony, she always knew about Alonzo and Lena's situation before she and Lena talked about it. She sometimes felt awkward talking with Tony about them because he always took Alonzo's side, and of course she took Lena's. She wanted some time with her best friend and to see how she was holding up.

"Why are you over there smiling so hard? Who are you texting? Danen?"

"No." Lena looked over to Sheree and smirked. "Winston."

"The white man?" Sheree looked over at Lena with a raised eyebrow.

"Yes." Lena laughed.

"Girl, I just don't know what to say about you." Sheree glared at Lena while they waited at a red light.

"What? I can't talk to white men?"

"No. It's not that. You went from Alonzo to two options! Fast! Is there anyone else that I should know about?"

Lena rolled her eyes. "No. I'm not out here being promiscuous, Sheree. I'm socializing and entertaining. I'm single."

"I know you aren't. I didn't know you had it in you . . . to be so single."

In a cocky voice, Lena patted Sheree on the shoulder and said, "Never underestimate me!" Lena was feeling herself, and it was about time. She had Danen schmoozing her up daily and Winston vying for her attention on the regular. Between them, Dougie's case, Tammy, and work, she had enough people and responsibilities to keep her busy and her mind off of her and Alonzo's situation. She had not spoken to him since the day outside of the hotel. Immediately following the incident, he had called her repeatedly and left her numerous messages and voicemails. He stopped trying after three days. Initially, she had regretted some of the things she said, but in the days following, Alonzo in his anger said some things to try to hurt her, and that caused Lena to stand behind her words and recognize that those were undeniable statements that he needed to hear.

"Trust me. We are not underestimating you." Sheree turned the corner and pulled up in front of a huge club with a not-so-short line of partygoers in the front.

"Who is 'we'?"

"Umm." Sheree was circling the club parking lot looking for a closer spot.

"Umm? So . . . what? You and Tony talk about me? And when did y'all become we?"

Lena was coming up with more questions when Sheree mumbled, "A few weeks ago."

"What? You two are official?"

Sheree parked the car and sighed. "Yes, Lena. Stop making a big deal out of it!"

"Stop? It is a big deal!"

Sheree shook her head and grabbed her clutch.

She began to check her face in the mirror. "Why didn't you tell me? That is vital information. In fact, this is worth a demotion from BFF to BF if you ask me." She chuckled then stepped out of the car and closed the door. *I wonder how much the VIP is. I'm not waiting in that line.*

"Whatever, Lena. You already had a lot of things going on with Alonzo and Dougie, and I decided not to say anything. We were seeing each other on and off for a year. It didn't seem like much news to tell." *Beep.* Sheree hit the lock button on her key, and they walked toward the club's entrance.

Lena walked with her head down, staring at her phone. "You still should've told me. How'd it happen? And what's the name of this place?" She almost bumped into a parked car but caught herself.

"It's called 'Look Up When You Walk'! Maybe if you weren't on your phone the whole ride here, you would've seen that big sign that says Blaze."

Lena laughed. "Shut up."

They approached the front of the line. "This line is long, Sheree."

"Yeah, but my friend is going to let us in."

"What's up, ladies?" The bouncer shot them a smile.

"Hey. How are you tonight?" Sheree smiled.

"I'm good. VIP line is thirty dollars tonight."

"Please. Eric would not accept a dime from me."

"Oh, are you Eric's friend, Sheree?"

"That's right."

"My bad. I didn't know. Come on through."

"Thank you." He lifted the velvet rope, let them in, and latched it back to its stand behind them. Security checked their IDs and purses, then they were in.

"It's nice in here. How does this Eric look?" Lena asked as they walked to the bar.

"Don't you have enough guys?"

"Hater." Lena checked out the bar's décor. The bar's base was covered with glass, and it was topped with a frosted-glass bar. The colors from the strobe lights around the club danced in their reflection on the glass.

Sheree ordered two margaritas, both with sugar around the rim instead of salt. They watched as the mixologist prepared their drinks. He stacked three martini glasses on the bar. Next, he grabbed the tequila bottle and flipped it in the air without spilling a single drop before he began pouring it and all of the other ingredients into the shaker. After dancing and shaking, he poured their drink into the top glass. They watched in amazement as the margarita cascaded into the bottom glasses. He topped off all three drinks with a splash of tequila and lime juice. Sheree nudged Lena. "Look at all of that tequila he's putting in there."

"I know! I was thinking the same thing. Tonight is going to be epic!"

"I'm only going to be able to drink one of those."

"Sucks to be you tonight."

Sheree rolled her eyes and laughed.

"Two margaritas for the beautiful ladies!"

"Thanks." Sheree handed him thirty dollars.

"No ma'am." He waved his finger at her.

"Huh?"

He pointed to their wristbands. "Your drinks are on the house all night. You two must be special." He flashed them a flirty smirk.

A long smile crept across Lena's face. Sheree cocked her head to the side as she put her cash back in her clutch. She pulled out a few loose dollars and handed them to him. "Okay. Well, thank you!"

"This is what I'm talking about!" Lena shoved Sheree's shoulder. "We should do this more often!"

Some upbeat techno song was filling the club. Sheree held Lena's hand, and they made their way through the hopping crowd on the dance floor to an open lounge-like area with brown leather couches. They found a couch in a corner and sat, drank, and talked.

"So, I still can't believe that you didn't tell me you and Tony were an item."

Sheree rearranged herself and crossed her legs. "Me not telling you makes us even. You didn't tell me about Alonzo and Tiffany, and that was actually news."

"Touché."

They laughed. Two guys walked by them and looked at them, smiling. Sheree chimed, "We still got it!" They laughed again. "What is Tammy going to do?"

Lena finished her text, sipped her drink, and then answered Sheree. "She went to her mom's last weekend after I left her hotel. We had a meeting with Mr. Edwards on Wednesday, and he's going to give her time to handle it. Not until the divorce is final, but until she heals and finds somewhere for them to live."

"Wow, that's so unfortunate. Do you think she'll go back?"

Lena sighed. "I don't think so." *I hope not.*

The DJ mixed in some rap with the techno. The dance floor was even more packed. Sheree and Lena watched everyone grind and sweat. It was probably safe to assume that everyone was buzzed with the amount of alcohol that was being mixed into the drinks. They sat, feeling buzzed themselves, and enjoyed the light and fun atmosphere. Another guy walked by, and Sheree's eyes followed him as he passed them. "Girl, that man was too sexy. This place is going to get me in trouble." She laughed. "So, what's going on with you and Danen?"

Lena laughed at her ogling the guy. *Glad I'm single.* "You know I told Danen about the hotel incident. He wants to fight Alonzo."

Sheree sipped her drink. "Well, that'll make it a mutual feeling . . . For Alonzo, that is."

"Oh. Has Tony said something?"

"Yeah. Alonzo has been ranting about Danen. He thinks you never stopped talking to him. Tony asked me if I knew about you and Danen on Monday."

"Alonzo knows I wasn't talking to anyone else! I was all about him! Anyway, what'd you say?"

"I told him that you and Alonzo's relationship is not our problem to solve and that I wasn't discussing y'all anymore for the sake of our peace."

Lena laughed. "Good save."

They both laughed.

"You getting all ready for your vacation?" Sheree's laughing face became a bit more serious.

"Yep." Lena sipped her drink.

"I wish I could go so you wouldn't have to be alone. I'm surprised Danen hasn't tried to go with you."

"Wouldn't that be nice?" *And it is nice. Go with me? More like I'm going with him. We're going to have so much fun.* She laughed on the inside.

"Has he tried?"

Lena looked up from her drink. Sheree was looking at her. *Girl, don't make me lie to you. Shit! Promise you won't be mad later!* "No, he hasn't."

Sheree took a huge gulp from her straw. "You would tell me if he did, right?"

"Yeah." Lena loved Sheree dearly, but with her dating Tony, she didn't feel safe telling her everything anymore. It was unbelievable. Even with everything going on with Danen and Winston, there was still part of Lena that held on to the idea of her and Alonzo. It was a very small part of her, but its existence affected her decisions.

"Okay." Sheree looked around. "There is no telling where Eric is in here. This place is huge."

Lena was so relieved that Sheree changed the subject. "I know, right? Let's find Mr. Eric. I can't wait to meet him!"

Sheree rolled her eyes at Lena, then stood up. "Come on, girl. Let's check this place out."

Lena laughed and stood up. She tugged her short, red dress down, although it would ride back up with every twitch of her hips. "Yes, let's go! I need another drink!" She downed the rest of her margarita.

Sheree shook her head. "It's going to be a long night."

Chapter

Sheree led Lena through the crowd. They walked around checking out the scene. The crowd generally had a young vibe, but here and there they saw a group of people near their age, late twenties to thirties. After circling the massive dance floor, they wound up back at the bar. Lena ordered another margarita and Sheree ordered two shots of tequila and a Sprite.

Lena raised her brow. "Tequila?"

"Yes! Shots for our Saturday together! Ladies' night!"

"Hell yeah!"

"Don't get too excited." Sheree taunted her. "This is my last drink for tonight." They took their shots.

After Lena unpuckered her lips from the strong taste of the shot, she checked her phone for the time. "It's early, Sheree. It's only twelve. I think you can handle one more."

"You sure?"

"Yes! We haven't had a ladies' night in forever! C'mon!"

"Okay, let's go! Bartender, two more shots!"

Bobbing to the beat, he poured them two more shots. A couple of women waiting for their drinks at the bar cheered them on. "Turn up, ladies!"

Sheree and Lena looked at each other, tapped shot glasses, and threw them back. The two women at the bar high-fived them. They danced and bobbed to the music. "Let's go, Sheree. I'm ready to dance!" She grabbed Sheree's hand.

"Wait for us!" one of the women from the bar yelled. "You two look like you know how to have a good time."

Sheree looked at Lena and scrunched up her mouth. Lena shrugged. "C'mon, then." Lena led all four of them to the center of the dance floor. The DJ started spinning Ne-Yo's "She Knows." The colored spotlights on the ceiling swirled around the crowd and flashed. Lena was in the groove. Everywhere she looked around, people were smiling and moving. She didn't know if it was her drinks, the lights, or both, but it looked like the room was blinking in and out. The beat took her away. She felt like she was floating. With a smile plastered to her face, she rocked, bounced, and totally got loose. A group of guys moved in on them and they all danced together. She looked over to Sheree. She was grinning from ear to ear and dancing in sync with her partner. *That's right, girl. Enjoy yourself!* Lena's partner moved his hands from her waist to her hips. She turned around and looked at him. He smiled. *Hmph. Why not?* She danced harder. He held her tighter. They rocked and swayed. She felt him tap her on the shoulder. She turned around to give him a smile, but saw Winston standing there instead.

"So, can I cut in?"

Lena's dance partner raised his eyebrow. Lena giggled. "Yes!" The guy she was dancing with let go of her and bumped into Winston as he walked off. Lena walked over and hugged him. Sheree's dance partner left with Lena's. Sheree walked over to her.

Winston bit his lip. "Lena, Lena, Lena. This dress."

She blushed. "When did you get here?"

Sheree interrupted, "Hi! I'm Sheree!"

Winston held out his hand for a handshake and laughed. "Hi. I'm Winston."

"Sheree, you are so rude." Eric stepped from behind Winston, struggling not to bump into the people around them. "Dang, you can barely move out here. I'm doing numbers tonight."

"Eric!" Sheree hugged him. "How do y'all know each other?"

Eric put his arm around her shoulders. "Club owners usually know each other." Sheree looked down at Lena and mouthed, "Club owner?"

"Yeah. Well, I own a bar," Winston added.

"So, why aren't you at your bar? It's Saturday," Sheree asked sarcastically.

"Like I said—rude. That man knows it's Saturday." Eric laughed. Sheree nudged him.

"I'm here because the beautiful Lena invited me, and I couldn't pass up an opportunity to find myself next to her on a dance floor. So . . ." He held out his hand to Lena. Lena took Winston's hand. He stood behind her, blocking Sheree from questioning them any further.

Eric followed suit and snatched up Sheree. "Stop cock-blocking and dance with me, girl!" Sheree giggled like a schoolgirl. She danced with Eric. "What are you doing later?" Eric asked.

"Later? Taking Lena home and going home."

"You should chill with me. It's been a while." Eric smiled. Eric was in his late thirties, but didn't look it. He always put Sheree in mind of a young Morris Chestnut.

Sheree shuddered as he placed a hand on her shoulder. It almost covered her whole left shoulder. "Uhh . . . I can't. I have a boyfriend."

He let go of her and stepped away. "Oh really? Why are you in my club drinking my free liquor, then?"

"Excuse me?" she squinted up her face and yelled.

Eric burst out laughing. Sheree stood there, still looking upset. He snatched her up again and held her in his arms. He whispered in her ear, "Calm down, sweetie." Sheree still stood there, tense. He turned her so that she was halfway turned toward him. Mimicking the Joker, he asked, "Why so serious?" She couldn't hold her pouting face any longer and laughed with him. "You're always welcome, Sheree, even if you don't want me no more," he teased.

Next to them, Lena grinded on Winston. *Let's see if the white boy can keep up.* He met her grind. *Oh shit.* He grabbed her hands and held them over her head, then turned her so that she was facing him. She was taken aback by the move. "How did you find me?"

"I can spot you out of a million women."

"Quit! I'm serious."

He pointed to the DJ booth that was on the second level of the club, then placed his face close to her ear. "I was up there with Eric and saw this red dress on the dance floor. I knew immediately that it was you. You look like candy."

"Oh, really? You have a sweet tooth?"

Winston moved in closer. "Don't ask me about it if you aren't willing to find out."

Chapter

Alonzo was perturbed. Lena was his world. And now Lena was gone.

Lena had been thinking about her ex. He was angry. He was hurt. He was damn near drunk with two and a half drinks under his belt at the bar with Tony. "You know she's probably somewhere sleeping with him."

Tony sighed. "Lena's at the club with Sheree, man. Chill out."

Alonzo asked if he knew where they were, but Tony denied knowing. Alonzo was sure that he knew, but wouldn't tell him. "Ask Sheree."

Tony shook his head. "Hell no."

Alonzo stopped smiling. "That's fucked up about you, man."

"You blowing my buzz, man, and that's fucked up about you." Tony laughed.

Alonzo chuckled and took a sip of his drink. "Let's go get on this pool table."

Alonzo and Tony were at "the hole in the wall." It was a small bar named Kickbacks. It was pretty early, so not too many people where there yet. It was smoky in the building. Alonzo's eyes even burned, a little irritated from the smoke, but it was where he wanted to go. It matched his mood—old. He didn't feel new and fresh. He felt used and walked over. He felt betrayed. He walked past the round tables near the bar and got two dollars worth of quarters from the change machine. Tony was already waiting at the empty pool table. "Bring your ass, man. Come on and take this loss."

"You have never beaten me in pool, man."

"I forget you get drunk and can't remember shit." Tony chalked his stick.

Alonzo laughed. He was loosening up. "Put a dub on it."

Tony pulled a twenty-dollar bill from his wallet. "I'll put a dub and shot on it."

Alonzo held his head up. "Let's go." He put his change into the side of the worn, green pool table and pushed it in hard. The pool table rumbled and released the balls. Alonzo racked them up. "Break."

Tony lined up his cue ball and shot. The cue ball hit the racked balls and they scattered. Two striped balls fell into two separate pockets. "Highs. Uh . . . nine-ball corner pocket." He shot and missed.

"I told you, you suck, bro. If you've ever beaten me, it's because I gave it to you. I probably scratched on the eight ball or something."

"A win is a win!" Tony laughed.

"One, side pocket." Alonzo shot and it went in. "Five, right corner." It went in. "Watch and learn now." Alonzo checked out the table. "Three-seven combo, side pocket." Alonzo measured the shots, set it up, and shot as Rob walked up.

"Yooooooo!"

Alonzo scratched the ball as he was interrupted by Rob. "Damn, dude! You messed up my shot."

"Aww, you suck anyway! I'm glad y'all are getting your practice in! The champ is here!"

Tony laughed. Alonzo was still salty from missing his shot. "Man, don't come in here talking all that shit. I have money on the table."

"Stop bitching. I'm taking both of y'all's money anyway!"

They all laughed, talked, and played pool. Tony went to the bar and came back with platter of wings and fries. Rob called a waitress over and ordered a bucket of beers. The place had nearly filled up now. Men and women were coming in in waves. Alonzo hadn't been there in so long. He forgot that people were still wearing gold teeth. A few women walked in that looked like they were his mom's age. He stopped looking around after realizing that he would not see anyone that he wanted. He was hazy, but finished a beer anyway and got back to his game. The person he wanted wasn't going to come through that door. *The person I want doesn't want me anymore.* He shot the ball hard, and it jumped off of the table and onto the floor.

"Damn, man!" Rob yelled.

They played about three more games before they moved back to the bar. Luckily, there were three empty seats. Alonzo sat in the middle of the two. Rob leaned over the bar so that he could look around Alonzo to Tony. "I enjoyed taking your money, Tony." He held up Tony's two twenties.

"Whatever, man. I gave it to you."

Rob elbowed Alonzo. "This man never wants to admit to losing. Alonzo, tell him."

"Man, Tony knows he can't play pool!" They all laughed.

Tony snapped back, "Come see me on the basketball court, though!"

Rob waved for the bartender to come to them. He looked at Alonzo while they waited to place their drink orders. "Lonzo! So, what's this I hear about you and Lena?"

"*Please* don't bring that shit up!" Tony blurted out.

Rob laughed hard. "It's like that?" The bartender came over.

Rob ordered them another bucket of beers with his winnings.

"It's pretty bad." Alonzo looked off into space.

Rob patted Alonzo on the back. "Well, you'll get over it, man. Keep your head up."

Alonzo tapped his finger on the bar. "I'm good." He really wasn't. Every second without her hurt.

They spent the next hour talking about their jobs, families, and sports. Rob added news about his baby boy. "He's gonna be a little player, man. I know it! I can't stand his mom, though. I'm telling y'all. DO NOT have a baby with someone you can't see yourself marrying." Tony and Alonzo laughed.

"We told you not to mess with that girl! She's crazy." Tony laughed.

"My girlfriend and her don't get along at all, man." Rob shook his head.

"At least we didn't have a baby," Alonzo said. "She couldn't have my son around another dude. Especially not Danen. What kind of name is Danen, anyway? Fuck him." Alonzo sipped his beer. The club's music bass bumped, and a rapper sang in the background. Alonzo was fading. Then he was tugged back to reality by a familiar voice.

"Hey, fellas."

They all turned around. Alonzo's eyes widened.

Rob blurted out, "Tiffany. What are you doing here?" He was a very obvious person and expressed whatever he felt.

Alonzo sat their quietly, processing how the situation became more complex. He had not seen Tiffany in a long time, and the only time he thought of her was when Lena brought her up. She was more like a figment from a bad dream, but now she was standing in front of him in person. He faded back into their conversation.

She was still standing in front of Rob. "Dang, Rob. I can't come out?"

"I mean, yeah, but . . ."

She held up her hand to his face as if she was telling him to talk to the hand. She walked over to Alonzo. "What's up, Tony, Alonzo?" She smiled.

Alonzo looked at her. He was in a haze. At first, he was angry. He saw red. Everything was her fault. It was her fault that he was in a bar with his boys instead of at home with Lena. Then, he saw blue. He felt calm when he looked at her hips—those hips that he had seen naked on countless occasions. A smile crept onto his face. "Tiffany."

Rob sat there with his mouth open. He shook his head and turned back around to face the bar. He leaned over to Alonzo, who was still turned around facing Tiffany, and whispered to him, "Don't do it, man."

"Don't be rude!" Tiffany mushed Rob's head from the back.

He snapped back fast and eyed her. "Keep your hands off me!"

Alonzo laughed. "Y'all two kids cut it out." Tony just sat there and watched it all unfold.

"So, you still look good," she said to Alonzo.

"Thanks." He sat there, still smiling at her. His elbows were propped on the bar. His legs were gaping open.

"Why are you looking like that? How many drinks have you had?"

Rob, with his back to her, yelled out loud, "None of your business!" Tony laughed.

She sucked her teeth. "I wasn't talking to you, Rob."

Alonzo grabbed her hands and pulled her in between his legs. He held her hands up and checked them. "Still no ring, I see." She smiled.

Rob sat there with his mouth open, looking at Alonzo go down a path that he knew he would regret. He looked around Alonzo to Tony and mouthed, "What the fuck?" Tony shrugged.

She stood there between his legs. "I hear you are single now, too."

Alonzo looked surprised. "Hmmm. What little birdy told you that?" Rob dropped his head and shook it in disapproval.

She nodded her head toward Tony. "Tony did."

"Oh really?" Alonzo and Rob both turned and stared at Tony at the same time. Tony was purposely looking in the opposite direction.

"Tony, this is supposed to be your boy! How could you set him up like that?" Rob hollered.

"What's that supposed to mean?" She shoved Rob.

Jokingly, Rob stated, "You have approximately one more time to put your hands on me before some shit pop off, Tiffany." However, Rob wasn't joking.

"Man, cut it out! For real!" Alonzo was getting irritated. "That's it. I'm out. I can't witness this shit."

Rob got up. "It's shit, Alonzo." He laughed, gave them dap, and left. Tiffany rolled her eyes.

She leaned into Alonzo's face and said, "I'll be back." She walked off to a table with two other girls.

"Sooo . . ." Alonzo said under his breath to Tony. A woman bumped into him as she sat in Rob's now-vacant barstool.

"Sorry."

"It's cool." He smiled at her and she smiled back.

Tony interjected, "I told you I saw her the other day, man."

"I know, but you failed to mention that you told her me and Lena broke up."

"It slipped, bruh. I didn't know we'd see her. My bad."

Alonzo looked over to Tiffany and her friends. "It's okay. Maybe this is a good thing." *Lena's back with her ex. I might as well be with mine.*

Chapter

"So now that it's quiet . . . what happened with you and her?" Tiffany was sitting on Alonzo's couch. Tony and Alonzo had spent the rest of their night sitting at the bar. Tiffany had gone back to the bar and chatted with him as she said, but spent the remainder of her night with her friends. Pretending to let Tony talk him out of talking to her, Alonzo had texted the last number he remembered her having. He had to reach back far into his mental Rolodex. He had deleted her number from his phone after everything that went down earlier that year. He had sat there and chatted Tony up. When he'd felt his phone vibrate, he had known who it was. She had the same number. He'd told her that he wanted to see her later, and she had simply responded with "Okay." He'd called her after Tony dropped him off, and she had been knocking on his door twenty minutes later.

He was in the kitchen fixing her something to drink. "I don't want to talk about her." He walked into the living room with her glass of juice.

"Okay . . . so what do you want to talk about?" He sat down next to her.

"You."

"What about me?"

Alonzo was fully engulfed in the alcohol. "What about you on top of me?"

She snickered. Then, the smile disappeared from her face. "So, I'm a booty call?"

Alonzo sighed. He lay his head back onto the top of his sofa.

He chuckled and thought, *Yes!* "No, of course not. I just saw you. You look so good, Tiffany. My bad."

"No! Don't apologize. I just wanted to make sure that that wasn't it."

"No. You know we go back." He rested his hand on her thigh. She had on a short, black skirt with a coral, low-cut tank top. Her stilettos were black with peep toes, and her hair was full of extensions flowing down her back—the really good weave, the kind that looked exactly like her hair.

"I know." She smiled.

He rubbed her thigh. She leaned up and sat her glass on the coffee table. "Do you remember the last time I was here?"

Why do you keep talking? Then, he really pondered her question. The last time she was there, Lena hit her with a shoe. Before he knew it, a laugh escaped him.

She scooted away from him and looked at him.

He kept laughing. He couldn't stop.

"What are you laughing at?"

He tried to gain his composure, but between the alcohol and the sound of her head getting clocked with Lena's wedge replaying in his head, he couldn't stop. "No . . . not . . . nothing." He couldn't catch his breath.

"I'm leaving! Alonzo, you're drunk." She got up and walked toward his door.

He stood up and caught her arm. "Man, calm down. I just thought about something Rob said."

"I still think I should go." She pulled her arm away and walked to the door.

He walked up behind her and pinned her to the door. He laid his forehead on her shoulder. "Stop, Tiffany. Stay."

"Alonzo."

He moved her hair to the side and kissed the back of her neck. She turned around to face him, leaned her back on the door, and looked up at him. He looked into her eyes and saw Lena. He wanted to kiss Lena so bad. He palmed her face with his hands. Her breaths shortened. He kissed her lips. He sucked her bottom lip, and then her top. She gave in and kissed him back. He pushed up against her, and she moaned. He pulled her shirt over her head and dropped it on the floor. He pulled her off the door, then pushed her to the sofa. She tripped over her shoes and fell onto it. He lay on top of her. He grinded into her, hiking up her legs with each push. He kissed and licked all over her chest. He went back to work on her neck as he pulled her skirt up. Tiffany squirmed under him and moaned at his every touch. He found himself back at her mouth and inserted his tongue. As he went to unbuckle his belt and jeans, she mumbled something. She struggled to get her mouth away from his. Alonzo could kiss hard, and even harder when alcohol was involved.

She managed to get her lips away for long enough to whisper, "Alonzo. I need to tell you something."

He found her mouth again and kissed it. She moved away and repeated herself. "Alonzo. I need to tell you something. Wait . . ." she moaned.

He stopped and looked at her. "What is it?"

She sighed. She placed a hand on his face and smiled. "I still love you."

He smiled back. "I love you too, Lena."

Once again, her smile disappeared. Her eyes went from soft to irate. "WHAT?" She pushed him away and started swinging at him. "What did you call me?"

He fought away her arms. "What the hell? Stop!"

"Get off of me!"

He sat up and moved away from her. She started crying. Still not realizing what he had said and done, he told her to calm down.

"Don't tell me to calm down." She sat up and started picking up her clothes off of the floor.

"What happened? Tiffany!"

"Oh, now you know my name?" She pulled her skirt down and put on her shoes.

Her comment took him aback. He found himself experiencing the very same catapult that Lena tried to explain to him. His trigger was Tiffany's statement, specifically the word "name."

His mind hit the rewind button. Everything went in reverse. Her getting up. Her hitting him and pushing him away. His belt unbuckling. Her skirt coming up. Her breasts. Them falling on the couch. He didn't have to go back far, just minutes earlier when they were standing in his door. Right before the kiss. *I want to kiss Lena so bad. Lena. Lena. Lena . . .* "Tiffany. My bad. Too much to drink, that's all."

She was already putting her bra and shirt back on. "Leave me alone, Alonzo!"

"I'm sorry. I really am." He reached for her.

"No! You just called me *Lena*!"

"I know. Slip of the tongue! That's all."

She stood there as if she was contemplating whether she believed him. He walked to her and moved her hair from her face. "I'm really sorry. I am. You gotta believe me. You know we just broke up. I'm just used to saying her name. I promise that's all it is." *What the fuck? Why am I begging her?*

"You promise?"

He hesitated.

"No, this is a bad idea, Alonzo. I'm going." She walked to the door and he followed her. She opened the door and stepped out, but he grabbed her arm and pulled her back in. He backed her into the wall next to the doorway. She just looked at him. "What, Alonzo? What do you possibly have to say?"

He tried to think of something to get her to stay. He drew a blank. He dropped his head. "I don't know."

She started crying again. He wiped her tears away. They kept falling. "I'm sorry, Tiffany. You're right. You should go."

She pushed him off of her, walked out, and slammed his door. He sat on the floor by his door with his head in hands. "Shit, Lena!" He slammed his hand on the floor. Alonzo wanted relief. He wanted immediate relief from his heartache, and he had looked for it through the physical, but it wasn't his body that yearned so deeply. It was his heart. That was the main detail that he couldn't wrap his head around. He went back and forth in his mind, cursing and longing for Lena, but his heart had one directive the entire time. As he sat on the floor in silence, he listened to his heart speak with every beat. *Get Lena. Want Lena. Want Lena. Want. Lena. Only want Lena. It's Lena. Lena.* He was better with Lena. She pushed him. He accomplished more. He believed in himself more. He was more positive. His mom loved her. She felt good. She smelled good. Their bodies fit perfectly. She had her own life, yet he always felt needed. She cooked. She kissed him in the morning before he brushed his teeth. She stroked his ego. She wasn't weak. She had taken him back once for inappropriate interactions with Tiffany. She wouldn't take him back again for the same offense. He got up and sat on his couch. He called Tiffany.

"What?" she yelled into the phone.

"Look. I'm really sorry, but can you let me know when you get home? Okay?"

"Fuck you!" She hung up in his face.

He lay back on his couch. He could still taste Tiffany's lips on his tongue. He got up, maybe a little too fast because he suddenly felt dizzy. He went to his bathroom and brushed his teeth, then looked in the mirror at his red eyes. *Second time this month, Zo. Women hate me. First "kick rocks," now "fuck you." I don't even know what the next woman will say. I gotta fix this. What did she do to me? Fuck. I love you, Lena.*

Chapter

Lena rolled over. Winston's cologne was bold. *Damn, you smell good.* He pulled her closer. He whispered in her ear with a morning-raspy voice. "You taste exactly how you look." They folded their shoulders toward each other and she cuddled under him. *What a night!* Startled by a sharp, high-pitched sound, she jumped. She briefly opened her eyes and Winston disappeared. *It was all a dream . . . Ugh, my head!* She turned her head slowly to face her nightstand. Her phone continued to ring. *What do you want?* She scrambled for it for a second, and then grabbed it. It was Sheree. She smiled. "Hello?"

Sheree was undergoing the same struggle. "Morning, sunshine."

"Girl. It would've been a great morning if you didn't wake me from my dream with Winston." Lena laughed.

"Hold on." Lena heard Sheree moving and scurrying to get out of bed, and then she heard a door close. "I had to go into the bathroom so Tony wouldn't hear. Girl! Why didn't you tell me he was that fine? Now I see what the fuss is about!"

"Yes. He's suave, too. I think I might really like him."

"What are you going to do?"

"About what?"

"These guys."

Lena laughed. "Nothing. Enjoy their company."

"Okay, girl. Be careful. I was just calling to check on you. I didn't know if you were going to survive that last round of shots they got."

"My head is killing me. I'm going to be in bed all day. I'm too old for this!"

"Okay. Me too probably. Tony is in there snoring. I think he took Alonzo out last night. I'm going to get some details later." She laughed.

"Well, don't tell me."

Sheree laughed. "Yes ma'am."

"All right, girl. Back to sleep."

"Okay. Bye."

Lena pulled up her calendar on her phone. September 13. *Two more weeks until I'm at the beach.* She laid her head back and went back to sleep. She slept until two o' clock. She could barely get out of bed. She dragged herself to her bathroom, used it, and got into the shower. Feeling weak and dehydrated, she sat on her tub floor and let the shower water fall onto her. *C'mon, Lena. Shake it off. You only have two more weeks of work. You can't call out.* She felt her stomach stir. She leaned her head on the side of the tub. Her stomach swirled and she felt dizzy. *Oh shit.* She stepped out of the shower as quick as she could and lifted the toilet seat. She got on her knees in front of the toilet and let all of her drinks and tequila rise and escape her body. She stopped long enough to turn her shower water off and went back to the toilet for round two. *Ugh . . .* She grabbed her towel from the hook on the wall and wiped her mouth with it. She slowly stood up and walked back to her bed, taking her bathroom trash can with her, then collapsed on her bed with a wet body and closed her eyes. Her head was swimming.

Her phone vibrated next to her. She felt it with every inch of her body, which made her head hurt worse. She picked it up and read the incoming text.

Winston: *Hey. How are you recovering today?*

She smiled as she squinted from reading Winston's text.

She held her phone over her face and texted him back. She almost dropped it on her face.

Lena: *Horribly.*

Winston: *I can imagine. You went in pretty hard . . . Poor thing. Want me to bring you anything?*

She thought about his question. She felt like she could barely get up to put on clothes. She thought about how rough she looked. She didn't want him to see her that way, so she went over her options. *I can't call Alonzo. There's no telling what he did out with Tony last night anyway. Danen is too far away. Sheree is with Tony. Winston it is.* She responded ten minutes after his text.

Lena: *That would be great. I'd really appreciate it.*

Winston: *Cool. I'll be over with my hangover kit. Send me your address.*

Lena: *Thank you.*

She sent him her address. She lay there for about fifteen more minutes before barely making it to her dresser to throw on some sweats and a T-shirt. She went to the bathroom and brushed her teeth. Her eyes were super dark, and her hair was damp and frizzy. She looked as tired as she felt. She went to her living room and balled up on the couch under a blanket while she waited for Winston.

Her doorbell rang. She stumbled, but made her way to the door. When she opened it, she saw Winston standing there with a big, brown paper bag. "What's up, candy?"

She laughed. "Come in." He walked in and went straight to the kitchen to put the bag on the counter. She went back to the couch. "Umm . . . the bathroom is the first door on the right."

"Okay." He came from the kitchen and patted her head.

"Yeah, it's rough. Don't judge me."

"I'm not." He laughed. "I like it. I'll be in the kitchen if you need me. I'm going to take care of you."

She smiled and he went back to the kitchen. She lay back on the couch and looked up at the ceiling. She heard Winston closing drawers and cabinet doors. He didn't know his way around her kitchen, but he figured it out without asking any questions. He actually didn't say anything to her. She lay there listening to him hum. She liked Winston's vibe. He was easygoing, he didn't try hard, and he just went with the flow. She thought about pushing up against him in the club and how he had kissed her neck. *Now he's taking care of my hangover.*

Even though he had helped cause it. She laughed to herself. *Winston is definitely in the running. Maybe I should give him a chance. Those other two had their chance.* She peeped over the couch. He was stirring a pot on her stove. His shoulders looked like they could rip through his black T-shirt. She bit her lip and lay back down. *Dang, that man is fine.* Alonzo could cook, but was often too tired to. The sight of Winston in her kitchen cooking was turning her on. She turned on her side and watched her TV. She needed it to distract her from her imagination because she all of sudden wanted to know how he looked outside of his shirt. Thirty minutes later he was in the living room, tapping her on the shoulder.

"Do you have a tray?"

She sat up. "Yeah. It's under the counter in the cabinet to the right of the sink."

"Okay." He gave her a smirk, then came back in with a tray loaded with the sustenance that he felt she needed to recover. "You ready?"

"Yeah." She sat up and scooted to the end of the sofa. He sat the tray in her lap.

"It smells good." She looked over her tray. He had prepared a bowl of chicken-noodle soup. It looked like it had come from a restaurant, complete with a parsley leaf as garnish. Next to the soup was a huge, golden, buttery, soft crescent roll. She also had a glass of ginger ale, and her napkin was folded neatly with her spoon sitting on top of it. In the corner of the tray two Aleve sat in a small ramekin. "This looks really good!"

"Thanks. I like to cook." He sat next to her on the couch. "The soup is pretty hot."

"Okay. I'll be careful." She held up the ramekin containing the pills. "You aren't trying to drug me, are you?"

His smile faded. "No. It's just part of my remedy. Soup, ginger ale, and something for the headache. I'll get yours if you have some."

She patted his leg. "No. I was only joking." Something about him told her that he only meant her well.

"Oh." He held his hand to his chest. "I didn't want you to think anything like that."

"No. It's fine. Thank you. I really appreciate this."

"No problem, Lena." He grabbed her hand and kissed it. "I just want you to feel better."

"I think I feel better already." She smiled, and he matched it.

They talked while she ate. He told her what he and Eric had done after they left, and how he had wanted to call her, but hadn't wanted to come off like some drunk guy trying to get the girl after the club. "So I just texted you to make sure you got home okay."

"It's cool." She laughed.

"I really didn't want the night to end, Lena."

"Yeah, it was a good time. That Eric is funny!"

"Yeah, I've known him for over four years now. I actually met him at my bar. He told me he was about to buy a place, and I offered him some pointers. Next thing I know, he was inviting me go look at venues and stuff. We started hanging out. He's like my best boy. He understands the pressure and stress from owning a business, especially a club or bar. You know?"

"Yeah. So, did you know Sheree? They seemed to know each other very well."

"I know! But no, I'd never heard of her." He laughed.

"Yeah, I had never heard her say anything about an Eric before." *Guess me keeping secrets is okay after all. She's certainly been doing it.*

"Anyway, I'm so glad that you're not feeling good."

She finished eating and attempted to put her tray on the coffee table. "What?"

He laughed. "I got it." He took her glass of ginger ale and put it on the end table next to her. Then he took the tray and dishes to the kitchen and put them in the sink. He came back and sat next to her. "I'm just glad that I could come take care of you. It gave me a chance to spend some time with you. You feeling any better?"

"I am, surprisingly." She smiled. "What was in the soup?"

"That answer comes with a ring."

"Huh?"

He pointed to her ring finger. "Oh, stop!" She waved him off.

He grabbed and unfolded her leg that was tucked under her and stretched it across his lap. The other leg followed. He sat back, slouching, and rubbed her legs and feet while they watched a movie on TV. Each time his hand grazed her skin, she tingled on the inside. There was an attraction between them that grew with each meeting. She shifted her legs and rearranged herself to get a brief break from her arousal. He shifted as well and scooted closer to her. She let out a heavy breath. *Sheesh. Can't you see I'm trying to get away?*

"Something wrong?"

"No. I'm just sleepy." *And aroused.*

He moved her legs from his lap and pulled her to him. He arranged her so that her head was on his shoulder. She tucked her legs back under herself. "Are you good now?"

Lena sat there with her eyes closed.

"Lena, you asleep?"

Lena found herself back in the club. The trigger was the cologne she had dreamed about. She let the smell of his cologne take her. She was back in the club sweating with him, rocking and grinding, the lights flashing on their faces. Blinking. Black. Winston. Blinking. Black. His smile. Blinking. Black. His eyes. She was back to feeling his short, prickly beard rub across her face as he smelled her. She was back, breathing hard and wondering how good he was in bed. She was back, lusting. She was back. *I'm back.*

"Lena . . ."

"Huh?"

"Did you fall asleep that fast?" He laughed.

She lied. "Yeah, I dozed off."

"My apologies. Go back."

She went back to the club in her head and then fell asleep. Winston fell asleep, too. His phone rang and woke them up. It was nine o' clock p.m. He had spent half the day with her. She got up and went to the bathroom, and when she came back, he was standing in the kitchen putting the leftover soup in her fridge. "Are you heading out?"

"Yeah. I know you have to get up pretty early."

"Yeah, I do." She hugged him. "Thanks so much for coming over."

He kissed her on the forehead. "Anytime. It was my pleasure."

She walked him to the door, and he left. She thought about the moments they shared as she locked the door. He brought a feeling with him when he came around. She couldn't put her finger on it. He felt warm and welcoming, but the feeling was not complete.

Chapter 30

Lena was standing in her closet. She had pulled out four pairs of shoes that she knew she wanted to take with her. "Tan, strappy sandals . . . They go with everything. Teal flats for my sundress, red heels with jeans, and black heels for my shorts . . . Yes!" She was so anxious. It was Wednesday the twenty-third, and she was only one week away from Virginia Beach. Danen planned to pick her up the following Wednesday and take her away for four nights and five days of total, worry-free bliss. *Worry-free until I think of Alonzo, that is.* Her week could not go by fast enough. She wanted to hit a button and transport herself to September 30, but she couldn't. Patience, after all, was a virtue. She sighed.

As she browsed through all of her hanging garments, she imagined Danen's face. She could so clearly see him and her at the poolside with drinks in hand, soaking up rays. Him in his shades, with his glowing white teeth, smiling at her and sitting next to her. It was funny, because just a week or two earlier she had been thinking about Winston. He was really giving Danen a run for his money, but she considered her and Danen's history and decided that her old flame could be trusted more with her emotions and maybe even her heart again one day. That was, if she felt like sharing it. She hadn't heard from Alonzo. However, she had heard from Sheree that he and Tony saw Tiffany in the club. *I bet she was all over him.* She shook the thought away and got back to picking clothes to pack. *Focus on your secret getaway. Focus on Danen.*

She walked to her bed and sat down with her cell. She texted the guy who was *currently* occupying her mind space.

Lena: *Have you started packing?*

She scrolled through their conversation while she waited for his response. The last thing he had sent her was a photo of himself with the caption "How I look when the name Lena Harris pops up on my phone." He smiled so hard in the photo that you couldn't see his eyes. She laughed out loud at it. *Ugh, he looks the same.* Yes, Danen had filled out some, but he still had his same old baby face. It was covered in a beard and well-manicured mustache. She lay across her bed and closed her eyes, wishing she could open them and already be at the beach. Her phone rang, and she sat up quickly to grab and answer it, thinking it was Danen, but it wasn't. "Hello."

"Hey, sugar. How are you?"

Lena's face was quizzical. She scooted to the head of her bed and leaned against her headboard. "I'm fine. How are you today, Ms. Ray?"

"I know you're probably wondering why I called you."

"Umm . . ." Lena laughed.

Ms. Ray laughed with her. "Don't start worrying now. It's not about my son. I just wanted your permission to go to court with Dougie on Friday."

"Oh." Her phone beeped. *Bet that's Danen's text coming in.*

"Now, you let me know if I'm overstepping my boundaries. I know about you and Alonzo, and you would probably expect me to not be involved, but it doesn't work like that with me, and I didn't want him to have to go by himself. I know you have to work."

"Yeah, I will be working. I thought about taking off, but I really felt like Dougie needed to go by himself. Dougie has some major growing up to do and I can't hold his hand through life. I've supported him all through this even though I believe he thought this was something I had to do. I didn't have to. I chose to 'cause he's my little brother, but he's so entitled."

"I understand, sugar."

"But if you'd like to accompany him, that's fine."

"I would, and thank you."

"No, thank you for everything. He'd be in far hotter water without your referral. I told Alonzo to tell you for me. I don't know if you ever got the message."

"I did, and you're welcome. This will be an open-and-shut case for Mr. Howell. He does this all the time."

"Good."

"Well, I will let you go."

Finally. "Okay."

"Wait!"

And here it comes. "Yes ma'am?"

"While I have you on the line, I wanted to tell you that I have always thought you were a brilliant woman."

Shocked and flattered at her statement, Lena could find only one word. "Thanks."

"I have. And I was so proud when my baby brought you home."

"Oh . . . Ms. Ray." Lena sat up and dropped her head.

"Let me finish now."

"Yes ma'am." She sat back.

"Alonzo is a man, and he made a dumb choice. There ain't no way around that. I hit him over the head when I saw him after he told me."

Lena laughed, imagining her hitting him. Ms. Ray laughed, too.

"I'm not making excuses for him. Alonzo was raised by me alone, and I taught my son to go after the things he wants by any means necessary. My son loves you. I hear it in his voice and see it in his face. He will not stop until he gets you back. He's sore now, but he will come to his senses. When he does, he will be a force to be reckoned with. Being the brilliant woman that you are, I know there are probably plenty of guys after you, but I also know that you love my son. Y'all will have your fun, but just know that there will be a day that you will have to make a choice. Just take your time out there, sugar."

"Yes ma'am."

"Okay. That was all. Bye, sugar."

Lena hung up the phone and dropped it in her lap. *"You love my son."* *How do you figure?* She looked over to the pile of clothes sitting on top of her suitcase—the suitcase that Alonzo got for her when he took her to Florida. She sighed, picturing them on the boardwalk. *NO!* Again, she shook the thought away. *I've got to be in more control of my emotions!* But the fact of the matter was she and Alonzo had a lot of good memories. *We seemed so happy back then. We were. But I'm not happy with him now.* She still loved Alonzo, a lot, but every thought of her love for him was somehow tainted with Tiffany and the pain he had caused her. Lena refused to allow Ms. Ray's comments to trigger an Alonzo-themed trip down memory lane. She checked her text messages to escape her thoughts. Danen had responded to her text.

Danen: *I packed Monday, lol. I can't wait to see you . . . I have so much to tell you.*

Chapter 31

Tammy tapped on Lena's open door and walked into her office. She sat down. "Hey, Lena."

"Hey there." Lena smiled. She missed Tammy and was elated that she was back working and almost back to her normal self. "Close the door so we can talk privately."

"Okay." Tammy went back to the door and closed it. She went to her chair and scooted it closer to Lena's desk.

"So, what's going on? Everything still okay?"

"I mean, if 'okay' is staying at an extended-stay hotel with my daughter at the cost of my parents, then yeah."

"'Okay' is you not fearing for you or your daughter's safety in your own home."

Tammy sighed. "Everything is okay, Lena."

"Things will get better, Tammy. They will."

"I know." Tammy perked up. "Anyway, are you ready for your vacation? Only two days left!"

Lena smiled. "Do you really have to ask?"

Tammy laughed. "No! You deserve this. Especially with that little brother of yours."

"Tell me about it! I'm so glad that this court stuff is behind us. He had a hefty fine. I helped him with it, but he's hit my pockets hard in the last month! As far as the suspended license, he's on his own." Ms. Ray had called Lena as soon as the judge made his orders. Dougie, however, hadn't called until that night. He hadn't been expecting his license to be suspended.

"Lena, you're so sweet to do what you did for him, and I've been meaning to thank you for my card. You really didn't have to give—"

"Don't. I'm here for you."

Tammy blushed. "Okay. I'll change the subject. I still can't believe you're going by yourself on vacation."

"Oh, I'll be fine!"

"I know you will. I meant to ask you. Does Lonnie know that you're going?"

Lena winced a little. Tammy was almost the only other person that called Alonzo "Lonnie." It was because Lena always referred to him as that whenever they talked. It reminded her of how hard she tried to avoid calling him that after they broke up. Lena looked down at her fingernails. It made her nervous thinking that he could possibly know that she was going with Danen. *No one knows, Lena.* "I don't know. He could, but I didn't tell him."

"Oh, I'm sorry. I guess that's still a sore spot."

Feeling a little tense from the thought of Alonzo, Lena wrapped up their conversation by alluding to work. Tammy returned to her desk. Lena went back to her e-mails. She was getting everything squared away. She needed her department to run smoothly in her absence. She had a list of assignments for everyone to take on and have completed. It was nothing major, just a few things to keep them on task. Kalvin had proved himself to be a leader, so she was leaving him in charge. Tammy had also missed a heap of new updates while out handling her family matters. She made sure to set up her autoresponse for her e-mail and voicemail. The work day droned on for hours. She was thankful when four thirty rolled around.

Lena got off and rode around looking for a nail shop that was nice enough for her to try. She rarely had them done. She would go with her mom or Sheree if they asked, but she wouldn't go on her own. She found one in a shopping center near her house, where she splurged on a manicure and deluxe pedicure. She felt fancy as she walked out of the shop with her pink fingernails and toes. *I have to do this more often*, she thought. While she was in the shopping center, she also went into a small boutique to look around. She came out with two bathing-suit covers. Her stomach growled when she got in her car. Lena had eaten a light lunch, as she was still trying to tone up for her trip. Along with eating lighter, she walked a few nights a week. She had lost almost six pounds in two and a half weeks. She stopped by a Mexican restaurant and ordered some food to go. She rode home, trying her best not to open her food and nibble while she drove. Her car smelled exactly like the Mexican restaurant. *Oh my gosh, I'm so hungry*. She pulled up to her apartment and maneuvered holding her workbag, purse, clothes bag, and food without messing up her fresh nails. As she approached her door, she saw a rectangular package sitting outside of her door. She fumbled and dropped her food while opening her door. *Damn. Hope it didn't spill.*

She flung her door open, stepped in, and dropped her bags on the floor by her door. She stepped back out and grabbed the food and the package. She closed her door and locked it, and set her package and food on the table. After washing her hands in the kitchen sink, Lena stood at her table and opened her food. While untying the plastic bag, she looked over the package. There was no postage label on it anywhere. She removed the paper cover off of the foil tin that her food was in and started digging in with the plastic cutlery that came with it. After three bites, she sat down and picked up the package. She moved the food and bag around on the table until she found her keys, and then proceeded to use them to open the box. Once she tore the tape with her car key, she lifted the box's flap to see another box with a clear, plastic front. Someone had sent her flowers. She cheesed. Who had sent these? She pulled the box containing the flowers out. She then opened the inner box up from its bottom and pulled the flowers out by their stem. She had a dozen red roses with baby's breath. They were beautiful! But there was no card. She retrieved a vase from under her sink and filled it with water, then placed the roses in it. She sat it in the center of her table. She admired the flowers as she ate. Once she was done, she gathered all of her trash. Before she discarded the flowers' box, she shook it in hopes that a card would fall out. Nothing fell out. She went back into her living room and picked up her bags from off the floor, then set them on the table.

Lena hopped in the shower, then lay in her bed. She wanted to make sure she was on time to work the next morning and figured she'd get her shower out of the way tonight. *All I have to do in the morning is put on my clothes and finish one more day! Yes!* She hadn't heard from Danen all day and was just about to call when he called her.

She rolled over on her side. "I was just thinking about you."

"I can tell."

"How?"

"I can hear your smile through the phone. Just like I could in high school."

"No, you can't." Lena thought about the many late-night phone conversations that they had. He was the main reason why she would be grounded or on phone punishment . . . calling her house after nine. Her dad did not play that. She yawned.

"Long day today, Ms. Harris?"

"Yeah, I'm pretty sleepy."

"Okay. You all set for Wednesday?"

"You know it!"

"All right, baby. I'm going let you rest. I really called to see if you got my pre-trip surprise."

"Oh! Yes, I did!"

"You like?"

"I love!"

He chuckled. "I love you. See you two days from now."

"Okay. Good night, Danen. See you Wednesday."

"Still not saying you love me?"

"Danen . . ."

"It's all right. I guess you need time."

"Good night." She hung up the phone and shook her head as she sat on her bed. *Love you?* Danen had triggered a short trip to the Lena Zone.

Love . . . is such a strong emotion. She lay back thinking of what *love* looked like. She could only imagine smiling faces, kissing at a wedding, or moonlit dates, honeymoons, vacations, sitting on the couch snuggled up, sex . . . everything she had seen in any sitcom or read in a book. Images that she now felt were so superficial. Like it wasn't enough. *He loves me? What does that mean? This is a very intimate trip. Maybe I'm sending the wrong message. I shouldn't go. I should call him and tell him that I changed my mind. I can pay him back.*

"Don't go." She heard her voice in her head.

I'm not going. She picked up her phone, and hesitated. She dialed his number, then she quickly hung up before the call connected. *What am I doing? I've been waiting for this!* She imagined him invading her space, moving in closer to her, and kissing her. She searched her memories for the feelings he'd given her in the past. She thought of anything she could instead of talking herself out of going on the trip.

Chapter 32

Tuesday came and went. It was Wednesday morning. Lena, too anxious to sleep, woke up to a text from her mom. "Bon voyage, baby. Let me know you get there." Lena had showered, gotten dressed, ate, and was sitting on go by nine thirty a.m. She was cleaning off her bathroom counter. Her living room, kitchen, and bedroom were spotless. Her bathroom was clean too until she took everything out of her drawers and put it on the counter looking for one of her makeup brushes. *Hurry up and clean this mess. I probably won't even need this brush. I'd need it if I left it. Danen will be here any minute.* She hurried and swiped everything in the drawers without organizing it. She took a paper towel and the bathroom-cleaning spray from under the counter and wiped her counter off. Nice and spotless. Not wanting to put anything in her recently emptied bathroom trash, she walked to the kitchen and tossed the dirty paper towel in her kitchen trash can, then washed her hands in the sink. She did a walk-through around her apartment to see if she was leaving anything. *I am set!* There was a knock on her door as she set her last bag by the door. *He's here.*

Lena reached to open the door, but hesitated long enough to allow her nerves to set in. He hadn't seen her in person in a long time. She looked to her right to the mirror on her wall to check herself out. She took a step to walk over to it, but it was on the other side of her kitchen table, and she didn't want to keep him waiting. Lena smoothed her brown tube sundress over with her hands, then pushed the loose strands of her bun behind her ear. She turned the knob. *It's just Danen. He thinks I'm beautiful. I'm his Lena Harris.* She smiled, then opened the door.

Danen stood there, tall and built, in khaki cargo shorts, a white wife-beater, white sneakers, and a black bucket hat. You could barely see his eyes under the shadow of his hat. His beard was freshly trimmed. His smile was beaming. She could've sworn music started playing. Or maybe it was in her head.

"Lena Harris." She smiled.

"What's up?"

"Sooo . . . are you going to let me in?"

"Oh. Yeah! Sorry." Lena stepped back.

Danen laughed at her. He closed the door behind him, and set the huge department-store bag that he was holding on the floor. Lena hadn't even noticed it before. He walked to her and embraced her. He felt warm, and his body felt firm, but his skin against hers felt soft. All of his coaching had kept him on track with his fitness. His physique was something like a professional football player's. His cologne filled her nostrils. She took a deep breath of him, and as she exhaled she leaned her head on his arm. He lifted his arm to move her head closer to his. *He feels so good. I might melt now.* He kissed her on the cheek. *I can't take this.* She slowly broke their embrace. His arms went from wrapped around her to his hands just holding hers. She had escaped the hug, but the feeling he gave her lingered.

"You look . . . incredible."

"You do too, Danen." *Like really incredible. Like damn! Mmm-mmm-mmm.*

He smiled at her. "So, are you ready to come away with me?"

She blushed. *Too ready.* "Yes."

He walked to her table and set his keys down. "Nice. I see someone sent you flowers." He raised his eyebrow.

"I thought you did."

He made a confused face. "No. That wasn't me. What made you think that?"

"You said you sent me a pre-trip surprise."

"Yeah. This." He picked up the bag that he brought in and pulled out a big hat box. He handed it to her. "You didn't get my e-mail?"

"No." She opened it. In the box was a huge, tan, floppy hat. There was a long, black scarf tied around the band.

"Wow! I love it! This will look awesome with my bathing suit!"

"I saw it online and thought you'd look great in it. So . . . the flowers?"

"I don't know. There was no note or card. They came Monday."

"It was probably your punk-ass ex. Where does he live?"

She sucked her teeth. "Come on, Danen. Stop."

He wrapped an arm around her shoulder. "Stop what? Tell him it's too late. You're with me now."

"I'm single."

"Excuse me." He gave her playful push.

"You're excused." She laughed.

"It's okay. You can only play hard-to-get for so long . . ." He pointed to her bags by the door. "Is this all of your stuff?"

"Yep."

"Well, let's get this car loaded. It is eleven and we have about a six-hour drive ahead of us." Danen loaded all of her bags into his black Camaro in two trips. He walked back into her living room. "You sure you have everything?"

"Yes."

"Okay. Bathroom?"

"I'm good. You?"

"Nope." He looked at the roses on her table again and shook his head.

She laughed. "Don't be so jealous. I'm going to check all the rooms again."

"Okay. I'm in the car." He walked outside.

Lena checked her bathrooms and bedroom again. All of the lights were off, and her big electronics were unplugged. She walked outside. As she closed her front door to lock it, she stared at the roses on her table through her closing view. Who had sent them?

Chapter 33

Alonzo came in from the garage. *It's warm. Come on, fall. I could use a breeze today.* He wiped the sweat from his forehead as he walked into the shop. "Mr. Wilson!"

"Hey, Alonzo. Is my darling ready?"

"Yes sir. She's purring like a kitty." Alonzo laughed.

"And the shakes?"

"They are gone. Come follow me to my office." They walked to his office. "Have a seat. I'm going to wash some of this oil off of my hands."

Alonzo looked at himself in the mirror as he washed his hands. He was looking better. He had gone to the barbershop after work the day before. A fresh haircut and trim always boosted his swag. He returned to his office to talk with Mr. Wilson. They chitchatted. Mr. Wilson went on and on about his upcoming trip to Myrtle Beach. Alonzo assured him that his car would be running much better and ready for their trip from its maintenance.

"You taking the missus?" Alonzo asked as they walked to the waiting area.

"Oh yes. Wouldn't leave home without her."

"Sounds like the life, man." Alonzo handed Ms. Susan the work order. He shook Mr. Wilson's hand. "Have fun on your trip. See you in a few months."

"Okay, Alonzo. Have a good one!"

Alonzo walked around the other side of Ms. Susan's desk to the hall where Mike's office was located. He heard Mike on the phone as he closed in on his office. He stuck his head in. Mike lifted his head up. He pointed to the phone, and made a talking hand gesture while rolling his eyes. Alonzo laughed at him. He went back to his office. He pulled up his e-mails, then pulled up his regular customer accounts. Everything looked well. Last week's meeting with Mike and Ms. Susan had been working. She was being more attentive now and made fewer mistakes. She would have to be more attentive if she wasn't going to retire.

Alonzo crossed his hands behind his head and leaned back. He wondered about Lena. Tony informed him the week before of her going on vacation . . . by herself. *I'm supposed to be with her. This would've been the perfect time to propose. Gotta give her time. That's all she asked for.* He opened his eyes, sat up, and sipped some water from his water bottle, then went back to his accounts. Two more days until Friday. His phone buzzed. He checked his messages.

Dougie: *Yo! Thanks for the package, Alonzo. Good looking out!*

Hmph. He smirked and replied.

Alonzo: *No prob. You're fam. I got your back.*

Alonzo had been sending Lena's little brother money here and there. He couldn't be there for Lena in the forefront, but that wouldn't stop him from being there for her in the background. He knew Dougie wasn't making real money, and he also knew that Lena couldn't afford to send all of her money to her little brother. Dougie wasn't in the position to hit his parents up for money while trying to keep his secret. So Alonzo had become the buffer. The more he assisted, the less Lena would have to.

Dougie: *I don't know how I'm going to pay you back, but I will!*

Alonzo: *Don't sweat it, Doug. Hey, I'm coming to Greensboro this weekend to visit my ma. I'm taking her out to eat. You should come.*

Dougie: *I'll be there*

Alonzo: *All right. I'll hit you up.*

Dougie: *Cool.*

Mike stuck his head in. "I don't know why I pay you."

Alonzo laughed. "'Cause I run shit!"

"No. It's 'cause you charm all of our lady customers into getting extra shit done!" He laughed. "Who were you texting? Bet it was a lady!"

Alonzo mimicked a buzzer going off, then laughed. "Wrong. That was Dougie."

"What's going on with him?"

"Nothing. Just poor." He laughed. "I've been helping him out."

"Does Lena know?"

Alonzo shrugged. "I don't know."

Mike gave an approving nod and sat down. "What'd you need, man? The oil vendor was talking my head off."

"To give you this." Alonzo pulled an attaché case from under his desk. He pulled out the contract for the shop expansion, set it on his desk, then slid it to Mike.

A huge grinned spread across Mike's face. "Is that what I think it is?"

"Yep. Our divorce is final."

"Aww, shut up! You in?"

"Of course I'm in!"

Mike rose from his seat, shook Alonzo's hand, and pulled him in for a hug. "Looks like I have a partner!"

"Looks like it."

"We have to make an announcement. Yes. Let's do it at the fall picnic in Greensboro!"

The fall picnic . . . that's late October. That will be perfect. Momma won't have to drive out of town, and Sherman and Dougie will be there too. I want Lena there. I have to get Lena back on my arm. I want her there when the announcement is made. I have a month to prove my love to her. I know she still loves me. She has to. That's it. I'm buying a ring. This is going to work out.

Chapter 34

The coast was warm during the day and cool during the night, but it wasn't cool enough to keep vacationers and locals inside of their homes and hotels. Lena could smell the salt in the warm breezes. The sun peaked around the high-rise hotels that lined the beach and warmed her. She enjoyed the tropical landscape. The palm trees swayed as if they were welcoming her to the city. Their first day in Virginia flew by, and they were fully rested and ready to be out and about. It was close to sunset when Danen and Lena got to the strip, and the strip was packed. People were everywhere getting their last summer flings in before fall really made its presence known.

"What's up with that grin?" Danen held Lena steady with his hand on her lower back as they walked through the crowds on the sidewalk.

"I can't smile?" Lena was feeling her last mixed drink.

"I wouldn't have you any other way."

"So, why do you ask?"

"Because it almost looks evil. What are you plotting?"

"Oh, nothing." She gave him a flirtatious look.

"Are you sneaking into my room tonight?"

"I bet you'd like that." She laughed. "I guess you'll have to find out."

Lena and Danen had spent their first day there unpacking, eating and drinking at a bistro across the street from the hotel, strolling the beach, and sitting by the pool. They made friends with Jeff, the hotel's poolside bartender. He had kept their drinks coming. Afterward, they'd stumbled to their rooms after one a.m. Danen had made the "mistake" of walking to Lena's room, but she kindly directed him to the next door over. Lena had lain in her bed that first night wondering what Danen had on as he slept. Boxers or naked? She'd wanted him to come knocking at her door. She'd stayed up and waited for an hour, but he never had.

Danen and Lena continued to walk alongside all of the summer lovers. He slowed her down by clutching her waist, then directed her toward a bar with an open patio. There was a band playing live jazz on the outside, and he spotted an open table. "Let's go in here." Danen led her into the open door of the bar. She immediately felt the calm and peaceful vibe of the place. It was dimly lit with candles flickering on each table. It had a combined feel of fêng shui mixed with new age. Servers came from the kitchen carrying sizzling dishes. She didn't know what they served there, but the food smelled divine. She watched Danen talk with the hostess and point to the patio. She overheard the hostess say, "Sure, I can seat you two out there. Do you need menus?"

"Yes, we do." He walked back over to Lena. "C'mon."
He held out his hand.

She looked at his hand hanging there, waiting for hers.
The veins in it were so defined. *A man who takes charge*, she
thought. She grabbed his hand, and they walked to the
patio. He pulled out her chair for her. They were seated at
a brown, wrought-iron table with a stone top. The chairs
were wide with navy-blue cushions. Their table was in a
corner adjacent to the band. Lena noticed that they were
directly under an outer-lighting fixture. It looked like a
lantern. It was cute, but she worried that it would attract
insects. "Are there any other tables?" she asked as she
opened the menu.

Danen looked around. "I didn't see any others out here,
unless you want to sit inside. What's wrong with this one?"

She pointed to the light above them. "We're going to
have bugs."

Danen sighed. "Aw, girl. Man up!"

She laughed.

"There are bug zappers all around here. We'll be fine."

"Okay!" She laughed some more.

He stopped flipping through his menu and looked up
at her.

"As much as we used to sit outside on your porch growing up. You weren't worried about bugs then."

She looked in his eyes and saw the same eyes that sev-
enteen-year-old Lena got lost in on her front porch. *And
that's why I never worried.* "You're right. We'll be fine." She
smiled. *Yeah, we will be fine. This is fun. Now, aren't you glad
you came on this trip?* Lena spoke to herself.

A short woman with a toned, athletic shape in tight jeans and a tank approached their table. She had long, wavy hair that passed her shoulders and hot, red lips. Lena admired her shape, then looked at Danen to see if he admired her too. Danen was still flipping through his menu. She walked up to their table and smiled at Lena. "Hi, I'm Tina. What can I get you guys?" Lena smiled back, then looked at Danen.

Danen looked *up* at their server, but looked unbothered. "Hey, Tina. She'd like a top-shelf margarita with sugar instead of salt, and I'd like a top-shelf Long Island. I'd also like to get the appetizer sampler with shrimp, calamari, and stuffed mushrooms. It will all be on one check."

"Oookay. I like a table that's prepared," she joked, jotting everything down. Lena laughed. Tina winked at Lena, then walked to one of her other tables before walking back into the restaurant.

"Well, she was really pretty, and who told you to order for me?" Lena raised her eyebrow.

"I didn't notice, and did you want something different? You've been drinking them all day." He raised his eyebrow back at her.

"Whatever." She laughed. "How could you not notice?"

He pulled her chair closer to his so that both of their chairs were next to each other rather than across from each other. With their backs to the building, they had a full view of the band. He grazed her arm with his fingertips. "You know I only have eyes for you, Lena."

"Yeah, right!" She looked away from him and toward the band. He seemed like he was exaggerating to her.

He needs to prove it . . . Feeling appreciated feels nice either way, though. The band was covering various songs. She hummed along to the songs that she recognized, one of which was Maxwell's "Sumthin' Sumthin'." The guys in the band were very energetic and looked like they were having a great time.

The sun was setting. Lena sipped her drink and took it all in. Danen, the drink, the smell of the beach, the music, and the commotion of everyone else chatting and enjoying themselves. She felt at ease. There were no thoughts of Alonzo, Dougie, or Tammy. She kept her mind and eyes fixed on Danen. He was her great *escape*, and some part of her still couldn't believe that she was there at that table with him. She looked at him while he wasn't looking. Her eyes couldn't get enough of him. His facial hair was already growing in, and looked fuller than what it was the day before. He had a prominent chin, and the curves of his lips enticed her. Everything about Danen exuded power. Before she knew it, she had drunk all of her margarita while Danen-gazing and made a loud and empty slurping sound while sucking her straw. "I'm sure that means it's gone, Lena."

Embarrassed, she giggled. "Yeah, it is."

He put his hand on her knee under the table and patted it. "I'll tell Tina to get you another one when she comes back. Do you want to order anything?"

"No, I'm still pretty stuffed from earlier. The appetizer will suffice."

Danen ordered them another round of drinks when Tina came back. They sat, drank, and enjoyed the band.

Lena became really tipsy and snacked on the food at their table. It was cold and Danen offered to order her something else, but she declined. He was pretty observant. She wondered how it was so easy for him to pick up from where they left off. They'd had conversations about the period after their relationship. Danen had had a few girlfriends. Lena had only had one other boyfriend, Alonzo. Maybe the distance was the only thing holding him back. She watched him. He was into his phone. Lena reached in her purse for hers, but forgot that she had accidentally left it in the room. Then, it happened. She thought about Alonzo. *What if he tried to call me while I was here?* She was somewhat shocked at herself for feeling anxious to get back to her phone to see if Alonzo had tried to reach her. She hadn't been worried before, or had she?

Chapter 35

The restaurant's staff were shuffling around. As the night grew older, the tables closest to the stage were cleared and moved closer to the building as their occupants left. They were creating small dance floor. Danen leaned in and put his arm around Lena's shoulder. "Let me know when you're ready to go."

"You keep hinting. Are you ready?" Lena laughed. She was still really enjoying the band, and even thought about asking Danen to dance. The band had slowed it down a bit, and their tempo meshed well with the way the margarita flowed through her system. Danen had been done drinking an hour before her since he was driving them back to the hotel. He looked sort of bored.

"I am. The younger crowd is coming in, and Color Me Bad won't be here for long. I see you're feeling them. They're probably about to bring a DJ in."

She laughed hard. "Why'd you call them that?" She laughed again then pushed his arm off of her shoulder. "You're getting old. Let's go."

He put his arm around her and slowly led her past all of the guys that were standing around. They walked to his car. He held her hand, but she barely held it back. Lena was thinking. The swirls of happy that were now residing inside of Lena's body were causing her to crave Danen's touch more, but the thought of the last person she intimately touched, Alonzo, made her withdraw. She didn't want to think about him. She wanted to think about Danen.

"What's wrong, Lena?"

"Nothing. Guess I'm tired."

"Well, we'll be back to your room in no time."

She looked at him and smirked. "Our rooms."

"Lena, I want to lie next to you."

"But you paid for two rooms."

"I don't give a damn about what I paid for. I want to be with you."

"Danen, I don't know."

"You don't know what?" They were back to his car. He opened the door for her, but Lena looked reluctant. "C'mon, Lena, don't look at me like that." He shut her door, walked around to the driver's side, and got in. He cranked up the car and sat there for a minute in silence. He grabbed her hand and looked into her eyes. "Lena, we are both two grown adults. I'm single. You're single. I play a lot, but I won't rush you into anything. I just want to be next to you, that's all. I mean, can you blame me? Look at you. You're so beautiful. You're so damn sexy."

Lena blushed. She liked having her ego stroked. *He's right.* "I want to lie next to you, too."

Danen laughed. "You are so difficult. You've been feeling this way this whole time and still made me confess myself and do a whole spiel." He shook his head. "Women."

Lena laughed. Danen leaned over the center console and kissed her on the cheek. "Let me get you back to your precious room." He pulled off. The ride back to the hotel was quiet. Only his Silk CD played. They were at the hotel in less than twenty minutes. They walked in and waited for an elevator. Danen looked her over. He wasn't inconspicuous about it. He wanted her to see him checking her out. They stepped into the elevator and he pressed the fourth-floor button. "So, when can I come over? I know you want to get all primped up." Lena raised an eyebrow. "You brought some lingerie? Are you going to seduce me?"

"Oh, stop! You're so full of it."

"Full of love for you." He grabbed her and hugged her tight.

She looked up at him. "Is that why your eyes are so brown?"

He chuckled then kissed her. It was the first time she had been kissed on the lips since Alonzo. She hesitated for a second, then kissed him back. His lips were so soft against hers. In that moment, her lips remembered all of the other times that they had kissed; she felt herself slipping away into Danen's allurement before the elevator dinged, signaling that they had reached their floor.

They got off of the elevator and took a right to their hall. "Sooo . . . I'm going to take a shower, then I'll be over. Is that cool?"

"Yeah." They unlocked their doors and stepped into their rooms almost simultaneously. Lena walked into her bathroom and turned on her shower. *He's freshening up. I'd better, too.* She took off her black halter dress and heels. She went to the dresser and pulled out a pair of cotton shorts and a camisole. While closing the drawer, she saw her phone sitting by the TV with its notification light blinking. Still rocky from her drink, she sat on the bed and put her nightclothes down beside her. She unlocked her phone and saw two missed calls; there was one from her mom and one from Dougie. Why would both of them call? Oh no! It was too late to call either of them back, so she moved on to her text messages. There were three of those.

Sheree: *Hey, girl! How's it going in Virginia?!?*

Mom: *Hey, baby. Just checking on you. Call me.*

Alonzo: *Hey, Lena. Hope all is well. Can we talk when you get back?*

Whew! Lena was relieved to see her mom's text. Her suspicion of her mom knowing about Dougie blew away, but Alonzo's text remained with her. *This is it. This is what Ms. Ray told me was going to happen.* She composed a text back to Alonzo.

Lena: *Talk about what?*

I'll send it tomorrow. As she stood and gathered her clothes, her phone slipped from her hands. In an attempt to catch it, her thumb hit send, but Lena didn't notice. She continued to the shower and prepared for Danen's sleepover.

Lena had just finished showering when she heard Danen knocking on her room door. *Damn, that was quick.* She quickly wrapped a towel around herself and let him in. Danen looked mesmerized as he walked in. There was still steam rising from her body. Her reddish-brown skin was accented with warm water droplets that rolled down her flesh, leaving glistening trails. The towel wrapped around her was barely hanging on, but she held it tightly under her arms and scurried back into the bathroom.

"Sorry. I'll be out in a sec."

Danen watched her return to the steam of the bathroom.

Lena looked in the mirror. *That probably wasn't a good idea.* The look in Danen's eyes conveyed desire, but she had every hope to keep her legs closed. This would be a difficult task. She heard Danen turn the TV on. The thought of them kissing in the elevator trickled back to the forefront of her thoughts. She thought of all of the nights they shared as she put on her shorts. *Just keep your clothes on, Lena. Self-control!* All the nights they'd lain together became active memories. The rolling around, the rubbing, and kissing. Everything came back at once. *What the heck? These are the thoughts opposite of what I need right now! Stop it, brain!* She pulled on her camisole and hung her towel on the rack. She tied a satin scarf around her hair and stepped out of the bathroom.

"Took you long enough." Danen was lying on the bed with one leg flat and the other propped up. He had on black basketball shorts and a white T-shirt.

She sat on the bed beside him and leaned back on the headboard. With her eyes closed, she told him, "Be quiet." Sitting on the bed brought to her attention how much more relaxed she was after her shower. They'd been up all day walking around, drinking, and in the sun; her body was still in workday mode and was used to being shut down before nine.

Danen looked up at her and saw her dozing off sitting up. He tugged at her waist. "Come here." He pulled her down to him and lay behind her. "You don't have to be all awkward. You can lie with me without me trying you, although you tried to seduce me with your wet body."

Lena sleepily laughed. "I did not."

"Mmmhm." Danen put an arm around her while he watched TV. Lena tried to keep her eyes open, but dozed off in his arms. Her comfort level was at a full 90 percent.

Either way, it was high enough for her to fall into a deep sleep.

Buzz. Buzz. Lena's phone vibrated, then started to ring.

Danen's eyes went to Lena's phone. "Who's calling you at two a.m.?"

Lena slowly sat up as her phone continued to ring. "I don't know." She rubbed her eyes and grabbed her phone off of the nightstand. Danen sat up and looked over her shoulder. Alonzo's face and name flashed on her phone for all of three seconds before it went black. She had meant to go and delete his contact photo. *What? Why is he calling me now?* She opened her messages to see what else he had sent and saw her accidental response, followed by him asking, *You're up pretty late. You okay?* Damn. She returned her phone to the nightstand and lay back down. Danen continued sitting up.

"Why's he calling you so late? Are y'all back together, Lena?"

"No. You know that."

"He sent you flowers."

Lena fluffed her pillow and scooted away from him. "I don't know who those flowers are from. I told you that there was no card."

"You should ask him if he sent them."

She turned her head toward him and said, "No! What if *he* didn't?" Then she turned back away. "Why are you questioning me?"

"Well, who else would've?"

"You know what? You're acting like him right now. Like you don't trust me. Good night."

Danen sighed. He cut off the television and then lay back down and scooted right behind her. He tried to lift her arm to slide his underneath, but she was resistant. "Lena Harris."

"What?"

"All I'm saying is let me know if that's where you want to be. Will you? No secrets."

"Yeah."

"Okay . . ." He put his face next to her ear. "Can I hold you now?"

Chapter 36

Waking up in a man's arms felt great. Lena opened her eyes to the sun shining in their room. She moved carefully so as to not wake Danen and got out of the bed. She walked to her balcony and looked out of the window. There were people already out enjoying the Atlantic Ocean. Four or five families and about six couples were scattered along the beach. She stepped outside and took in the air. She turned around and looked at Danen. He was still asleep in the bed. Her stomach growled. *Mmph. Time to eat. I'll wait for him . . . No, I think I'll eat.* Breakfast would be over in forty-five minutes. She laughed to herself as she tiptoed around the room. She put on some tights and a light athletic jacket, brushed her teeth, washed her face, and went downstairs. She greeted a couple in the elevator as they went down. The woman was holding a toddler on her hips. She checked both the mom's and dad's hands for rings. No rings, but that didn't stop them from smiling from ear to ear. She felt their love and smiled right along with them. Plus, the little one kept waving at her. *How sweet.* The breakfast smelled yummy. She fixed two plates, one with only meat and scrambled eggs, including sausage links, bacon, and ham; the other plate included grits, two biscuits, a yogurt, and fruit. Some of the other people in line watched her pile up the plates, and she returned their stares. Unaffected by her onlookers, she grabbed two sets of utensils, stacked the plates with the meat plate on the bottom, and managed to hold a cup of orange juice. *Now, back to my room without making a mess. I don't know how I'm going to open the door.*

She got back to the room and set the plates on the floor. As she unlocked the door, Danen opened it. "Good morning. I don't need room service today."

Lena picked the plates up and smiled. "Okay." She pretended to walk off, and he caught the bottom of her jacket. Lena laughed.

"Girl, if you don't bring your ass . . ." He pulled her into the room.

"Careful!" Some of her juice spilled on the floor.

"I was wondering where you disappeared off to."

"Food!" Lena set the food on the coffee table and sat on the couch. "I think I have enough for the both of us." They ate the food and left the paper plates empty.

Danen rubbed his stomach. "That hit the spot. What do you want to do next? My plans for us won't be until tonight."

"Okay. Let's hit the beach, then!"

"We can make that happen." Danen stretched and got up. He put the plates in the trash and looked out the window. "I'm going to go put on my speedo."

Lena leaned over and laughed.

He laughed and walked to his room. Lena got out her black bathing suit and set it on the bed. Then she pulled the hat Danen bought her out of the room's closet and set it next to her suit. *Perfect. What's not perfect is this full little belly of mine.* She patted her stomach. She went to the bathroom and pulled her hair out of its bun, then combed it down. She glossed her lips, put on deodorant, and applied sunscreen. Finally, she slid into her black bathing suit. It was low cut in the back and had slits that exposed her sides and stomach. She turned around back and forth and checked herself out in the mirror. She put on her hat and flip-flops and threw her beach towel across her shoulder. *Hmm . . . no need for a suit cover.* She put on her sunglasses and waited on her balcony for Danen.

Danen knocked on her door, and when she opened it he bit his lip at the sight of her. "Took you long enough," she mimicked him.

"I'm going to let you slide with that 'cause you're so damn sexy." He shook his head. "Lena Harris, you ain't missed a step, girl!"

"I know." She looked at him over her sunglasses.

"Shut up." He laughed and nudged her. He held out his hand. "C'mon." Danen was so proud to have her on his arm. Lena was smart, fine, and a good woman—a triple threat.

They stopped at the bar by the pool. Jeff was on duty and smiled hard when he saw them. It must've been the tips Danen had left. "D! Lena!"

"What's up, man?" Danen gave him dap. Lena smiled at him.

"I see you two are heading to the beach! I have just the drinks!"

"Okay! I'm game. Are you?" Jeff and Danen watched Lena as they awaited her response.

"Let's do it!"

Jeff went to work. He pulled two huge, topless coconuts from under the bar. Lena's eyes lit up in wonderment, and Danen laughed at her. He made what looked to be a flavored, top-shelf margarita for Lena and a top-shelf Long Island for Danen, but he added some extra ingredients such as strawberries, mangos, more liquor, and an umbrella each. He sat the gigantic tropical beverages on the bar. "Taste them!"

Lena and Danen both took a sip. Danen nodded his head. "This is good, man."

"Yeah, it's delicious, Jeff." Lena beamed. Danen eyed her.

"Great! Glad y'all like it. We're promoting a new coconut vodka. I added two shots to the both of yours, so this may be the only drink you need." He laughed.

"That's what's up. We may still come pay you a visit." Danen handed him the payment and tip. "How long are you here?"

"All day, man! All day! Let me know if you need anything." Jeff walked over to his next customer.

Danen nodded. Lena waved bye, and they were off to the beach. The sand was hot, the sun was warm, the sky was blue, and the ocean was singing and crashing. All was well. Lena's world was at peace. Danen talked to the rental guy and talked him down on the rental umbrella.

He set up their umbrella away from everyone else. They had a longer distance to walk, but the privacy was worth it. He laid his beach mat under the umbrella's shade and sat down. He patted the space beside him. "Sit your fine ass right here, girl!"

"Hahaha! You're so corny." She smiled and sat next to him. Their spot on the beach was perfect. It was quiet. The only thing they heard was the ocean, each other's voices, and them sipping from their coconuts. *I needed this*. Lena was in a no-daydream zone. She was already living out a fantasy. They lay on the beach in each other's arms, hiding from the sunrays. Jeff was right about their drinks. There was no need for another. Their bodies were tingling as their blood-alcohol levels increased. Danen smiled so hard. *He must be living out a fantasy, too*. The rays from his smile warmed her even deeper. They sat out there for hours before Lena got up to put her feet in the water. She walked around, bending over to pick up seashells every now and then. Danen watched.

Drained by the sun plus their alcoholic beverages, they brainstormed their next move and decided they'd return to the room. They waved at Jeff as they passed the pool. Once in Lena's room, they took a few sodas from her mini fridge and mixed them with a bottle of rum. They moved the party to her balcony. After ten minutes in separate chairs, Danen pulled her out of her chair and into his lap. She leaned back on him, and he rubbed her sun-warmed legs. Her insides throbbed. His breaths were controlled, but deeper. They both knew what was coming soon, but neither of them said it. *Shit! Why is he touching me like that?*

"I'm hot." Lena abruptly got up. She slowly walked into the room toward the bed, strutting in her one-piece bathing suit. It was cut in so many ways that enough skin was showing for his seed to take root in her garden. She sat on the foot of the bed with her legs parted and let the chilled, air-conditioned draft cool her. Danen walked past her toward the TV stand as if he saw something on the TV's screen, but it wasn't on. He was trying to avoid her. She pulled him to her anyway. He was standing between her legs with his back to her. His hands were back on her thighs, but closer to her knees. They just sat there silently. Maybe they were breathing somewhat harder. The room was getting warmer. Lena laid her forehead on his back. *Lust, let me be. Please. I'm losing it!* She placed a kiss on his spine. Danen's hands immediately gripped her legs harder.

She knelt on the bed to move her kisses up toward his shoulders. Before she could get to his neck, he turned around and looked at her. She froze. "What?"

He kept staring.

"Why are you looking at me like that?"

"There are so many things I've been wanting to do to you. I don't know where to start."

"Start here." She patted her lips.

Danen Wimbush kissed her so intensely that she thought she'd collapse. She was on her knees trying to stay balanced. His hands were on her hips while he was kissing her; he lost control and pushed her over. She was now on her back, and he was steadily kissing and thrusting so that she could feel his boulder. She thought she'd knock out just then. His passion and his intensity were mind boggling, but she had to hold on. He patted her neck with the tip of his tongue, and she moaned so hard. He couldn't hold in his groans any longer. They escaped him. His tongue slithered down her chest. He slowly opened his mouth to her breast. She opened her eyes and looked down at him. His head bobbed with each lick. *Oh my goodness.* She laid her head back and closed her eyes, letting out a loud moan. His kisses trailed to her love below, and she was singing tunes for him. Every time he kissed it, she shifted and moaned. She tried to get away, but an orgasmic wave was upon her. "Danen. I'm ready."

Danen lifted up his head from between her thighs. "Whatever you want, Lena Harris." He hopped off of the bed, stroking himself. She lay there covering what was between her legs.

He grabbed a condom and watched her as he put it on. He placed his free hand on hers and balled it up, causing her to insert two of her fingers. She gasped. He pulled them out and put them on his tongue. "Mmmm . . ."

He climbed onto the bed and lay on top of her. His mouth met hers, then he pushed himself in. She savored the feeling so much that every time he pulled out she'd meet his strokes. She pushed her pelvis up to him. *Too good. He feels too good.*

They locked eyes for a minute. Then he flipped her over on her stomach. She felt his pressure. He pushed in her harder. His right hand gripped her waist and pressed her down at the same time. The left was under her holding her breast. His mouth was open and breathing hard on her neck. "Oh!" She inhaled.

He dug his teeth into her, then whispered, "You taste like the beach, and you feel like the ocean, Lena."

She gasped. He sucked her earlobe, and she gave in. He felt her wave. He flipped her over again, sat up on his knees, and wrapped her legs around him. She lay flat. He stroked long, then hard, and then harder. She quivered as her body curled up. His last jab was the trigger to her second release. He heard her juices squish from her to him. They were everywhere. "Damn, Lena!" He let out a deep breath and then became still. Then he fell on top of her, and put his mouth on hers.

Chapter 37

There was sex. There was sweat. There was sleep. Then there was hunger, piercing hunger. Danen rolled over and got out of the bed. He took two waters from the fridge. He stood at the fridge and drank his, and tossed the other on the bed. *Okay . . . not very gentlemanly.* Lena sat up and drank hers. She watched him stand in his boxers. *Damn. I should hire him as my trainer.* It was six thirteen and almost dark out. Danen finished his bottle. "So, are you trying to get out tonight?"

"It doesn't matter." Lena sat back against the head-board. "What time are your plans?"

"We slept through them." Danen grabbed another bottle of water and opened it.

"Oh," she said slowly. His vibe felt a little different.

"Yeah." He drank the second bottle down.

"What do you want to do?"

"I wouldn't mind staying here. We can order in, find a movie, and talk. You know I've been wanting to talk to you."

Lena was still drained from their first round and was pretty lethargic. She was okay with anything that kept her in the same room with the bed. "Sounds good to me."

"Cool." Danen grabbed a few menus from by the room's phone and sat on the bed next to her. He flipped through the menus and asked her what she wanted to eat. She told him that it didn't matter and asked him what he had a taste for.

"You."

Lena laughed. "You're gonna pass out. Pick a place!"

Danen chuckled. "Don't be scared. Round two is coming . . . Let's get pizza for now, though."

"Okay. No fruit or mushrooms or olives. I'm good with anything else." She leaned back. "Oh, and no anchovies."

"I'm getting a pizza with all of that on it!"

"Then go eat it in your room."

"Ha-ha! Damn, Selena. It's like that?"

"Yep."

"Whatever." Danen order the pizza, and Lena checked her phone. She had another missed call from her mom and Alonzo. She wanted to call her mom back, but didn't want her to hear Danen in the background. *Great, now I'm keeping two secrets.*

"You calling your boy back?"

"Danen. That's getting old."

"Whatever." He walked onto the balcony and stretched.

Lena shook her head. *Men are so jealous. It's irritating.* She went to the bathroom and took her phone with her. She texted her mom.

Lena: *Hey, Mom.*

It took her mom a few minutes to respond.

Mom: *Hey, Selena. You must be having fun. Alone.*

Alone? Why'd she add that? Lena thought.

Lena: *I am. How's everything?*

Mom: *Fine. You can't talk?*

Lena: *I'm in a restaurant.*

Mom: *With who? Danen?*

Lena felt like the whole room disappeared, and her vision zoomed in on her phone. Danen knocked on the door.

"You okay in there?"

"Huh? Yeah!"

"Okay. Well, don't forget to spray." He laughed. "I'm going to my room to get some money."

"Okay." She looked back at her phone. *She's just guessing; she doesn't know.* She sent back, *What, Mom?* Her mom called. She waited a few seconds and called her back.

"Hello."

"Oh, hey, darling. You left the restaurant?"

"No."

"I saw Ronda today. We talked for a long time in the mall. She told me Danen was in Virginia on vacation."

He told his mom. Lena's heart skipped a beat. "Look, I didn't plan—"

"I knew something was fishy about you going on vacation by yourself for *four* days." Her mom laughed.

"I planned to come by myself, but . . ." Lena stopped herself before she mentioned not having the money because she had paid for Dougie's lawyer. "But he said he'd been planning a vacation too, and decided to come Virginia. We've been hanging out."

"Mmhmm."

"It wasn't the plan in the beginning, Mom. I promise. I was going to come alone."

"If you say so, baby girl."

Lena rolled her eyes at her mom's sarcasm. "It's not a big deal."

"I hear you, baby. You still could've told me."

"I'm sorry."

"I know. You are since I caught you." She laughed. "Ronda showed me picture of that baby of his. She's a cutie."

"Baby?" Lena blurted it out before she could catch herself.

"Yeah. He didn't tell you? His mom was gushing about it. I thought you knew."

Lena dropped her phone and left it there for a few seconds.

"Lena . . . Selena!"

She heard her mom yelling from the phone on the floor. "Yeah, I'm here. What baby, Mom?"

"You're on vacation with the man and don't know about his baby? I figured I was just finding out."

"Mom. Stop playing."

"Look. You're in a 'restaurant.' I'm going to let you go. Call me when you get back, baby, and we can talk. I don't want to interrupt. Love you."

"Love you. Bye." Lena sat there with her eyes closed and pretended that she hadn't heard what her mom had just said. She heard her room door close. Danen was back with the money.

Her phone buzzed in her hand. Her mom sent another text.

Mom: *I'm so sorry, baby. I should've waited to talk to you when you got back.*

He knocked on the door again. In a singsong voice, Danen asked, "Lennnnaa . . . What are you doing?"

Lena looked at the door. She felt like she stared a hole through it. Then, she snatched it open. Danen stood there and looked a bit rattled. Lena was red. Her eyes were glistening. "Danen, do you have something to tell me?"

He backed up. Lena stepped closer to him. He grabbed her shoulder and held her away. "What's wrong with you? What are you talking about?"

Look at this. Hours ago, he wanted to be close. Now, he's pushing me away. "Do you have a baby?"

He dropped his arms, tilted his head, and looked at her. He held his hands up; his palms were facing Lena. "Before you attack me, remember the pizza man is on the way."

"I don't give a damn about a pizza-delivery boy! Answer me!"

"Who told you?"

Lena stepped closer again. "Who told me? So the answer is yes?"

"Shit!" He slapped his hand to his side. "Yes."

She backed up and leaned up against the bed. "Danen. Stop joking."

"I'm not. Who told you?"

She stared at him. "This isn't a joke? You're serious?"

He walked to her. "I know I should've told you before, but I was still processing it myself . . . I told you we needed to talk." He reached for her.

"This is absurd. I thought my biggest worry on this trip was us making a baby, not finding out that you have one!" She slapped his hand away.

"Lena . . ."

"No! Why didn't you tell me? Why would you bring me here to tell me this?"

"I brought you here because you needed a break. You wanted to come here."

"Not if I knew about your baby! What kind of break is this? This is stress! You are a liar!"

"So, you wouldn't have come, Selena? And I didn't lie!"

"No, I wouldn't have! I am not your main concern. Hell, you aren't your main concern anymore. Your baby is! And you did lie! You lied by withholding details—big-ass details!"

There was a knock at the door. Danen turned around and looked at the door, then back at Lena. The delivery guy knocked again. "Well, go get the door! Damn!"

He sucked his teeth and walked off. "Thanks, man." He paid the delivery guy. He came back in and set the pizza on the coffee table and sat on the couch. "Look. I just found out a few weeks ago. I can't become a dad over-night. Me and her mom have been talking. This is a big step, and we're coming up with a plan."

Lena walked to the side of the bed closest to the table. "I can't believe this . . ."

"Lena, with how we are . . ." Lena eyed him. "Well, with where I thought we were going, I thought you'd be by my side in this."

What the f— "I didn't know the baby existed. What kind of rationale is that?"

"Lena. You're angry. You don't mean that."

Forgetting if her mom mentioned the sex, she asked, "Yes, I do. How old is it?"

"*She* is six months."

"I want to cry, but I'm so damn mad that I can't. You have said nothing about a child. Danen, you take the damn cake! This is the worst by far."

He stood up. "You're not giving me a chance, Selena!"

"Damn sure I'm not! Leave! Take your pizza with you, and take me home in the morning."

"C'mon, Lena!"

"I will take a cab if you won't!"

"You have to let me explain!" He grabbed her arm and pulled her to the couch. She stood there, looking down at him as he sat. "Sit, Lena." She folded her arms. "Selena Harris. Sit." She plopped down next to him. "I've wanted to tell you so many times, but couldn't find the right moment."

"Any time before this trip would've been the right moment! Just last night"—she pointed at him—"*you* questioned me about my ex and told me 'no secrets,' and you've been keeping one this entire time!"

"No moment was right to hurt you, Lena. I thought I really had a chance at winning you back, then Lauren," he paused, "her mom, really threw a monkey wrench in my plans. I was in shock. I promise I had no idea. I wasn't trying to keep my daughter a secret. I was looking for the right time to break it to you."

"What's her name?"

"Mya." He pulled his phone out of his pocket and showed her a picture. Lena looked at him after staring at Mya's picture.

"She looks just like you. She's gorgeous." She got up and walked to the balcony window. *Don't cry.* She held her face.

Danen looked at his daughter's photo. "Thanks," he whispered to himself.

Lena went and stood on the balcony. She let the salty night air whisk away her worries. She held on to the balcony's rail and took a few deep breaths. Danen joined her. He sat in a chair behind her.

"I dated Mya's mom for a few months when I moved back to NC. She was cool, but she wasn't girlfriend material to me.

"We kept in touch, talked on a daily basis, and kind of messed around on and off. In March, she told me she met a guy and that she was really into him. So after a while, I fell back. I heard she was pregnant, but figured it was by the other guy. I had my suspicions, but she never said anything to me about a baby. The guy asked her to marry him recently and wanted a paternity test; the results came back, and she wasn't his. She called me, and asked me to be tested, and Mya . . . was mine."

Lena sat down in the chair next to him. "Are they still getting married?"

"Yeah, the wedding is still on. Sometime next year."

He must really love her. "Every time we've talked, you made it seem like you've been missing me so much."

"I have, but you were with someone, Lena. Was I supposed to wait for you and hope it didn't work out? I mean, if that guy was making you happy, truly happy, then I was all for it . . . but *you* started hitting me up."

"Yeah. I did." *And look at the mess I got myself into.* "I'll be packed by morning, Danen."

"Please just stay."

"I can't." She walked back into the room.

Chapter 38

The ride home with Danen was unbearable. She felt humiliated. Her mom knew an important detail about the man whom she'd slept with that she didn't even know. *Why did I sleep with him?* Lena punished herself. Lena was still too exasperated. She could not think straight. She'd balled all of her clothes up and thrown them in her suitcase when she packed. She had not eaten and felt a tad woozy, so she just laid the seat back and drowned in her thoughts. *I wish I had taken a cab.* She remembered her mom saying, "His baby is a cutie . . ." *No, I wish I had never come. Something told me not to come. I said no, I can't let him take me to Virginia. I should've stayed my butt home.* She looked at him. He looked at her, frowned, and then looked away. Danen was upset that she didn't want to stay their last day, but Lena didn't care. She kept her eyes fixed on him. Danen was sexy. He was cute. He was the coach that all his players' moms probably wanted. *I knew you, but I don't know you. You have as much credibility as some guy I meet in the club. History doesn't prevent you from hurting me. I can't trust anyone. A six-month-old . . . Oh my God.*

Once again, her phone started vibrating. *I should turn this thing off!* She looked at it and saw that it was her dad calling her. *Why's Dad calling? I know Mom didn't tell him about Danen.*

"Hello?"

"Good afternoon, Selena."

"Good afternoon, Dad." Danen looked down at her lying in the seat. She turned her head away from him.

"When are you coming back from out of town?"

"I'm on my way back now."

"Well, I don't want you driving and on the phone, but I just got off the phone with the insurance company . . . and Doug Junior. You need to call me when you get home."

Lena covered her face as it warmed. The tears were on their way. "Does Mom know?"

"Not yet. She's at the shop. I didn't want to bother her while she was there, but she will be informed tonight."

"Okay. I'll call you."

Lena turned her back to Danen. It was all too much. Her dad's call dismayed her. She was crushed. Alonzo had let her down, Dougie had let her down, and Danen had let her down. A fierce headache came over her. She had no energy, and her hunger made her feel sick. Tears begin to escape.

"Lena. Please stop."

She continued and balled up in the reclined seat.

"Lena you're going to make yourself sick. You need to eat. I'm pulling over." He pulled over to a random restaurant. They were an hour away from her apartment. He unbuckled his and her seat belts and rubbed her back. "Lena."

She sobbed.

"Lena, talk to me, please." He watched her cry. "Look, I'm going into the restaurant to get you some soup and something to drink, okay?" She said nothing. He got out of the car and opened her door. He stooped down on the ground and told her to open her eyes. They were fire red. He grabbed his towel from the back seat and wiped off her face. "I know I fucked up, Lena, but I'm still your friend. It may take a while for you to forgive me. I don't blame you, but you need to talk to me right now, and you need to listen. You have to eat! Will you eat the soup?"

She nodded yes.

"Okay. I'll be right back." Danen looked disturbed. He walked off and disappeared into the restaurant. Thirty minutes later he was walking out with a to-go bag and two cups. He got back in the driver's seat. "Sit up. Please, Lena." She sat up slowly. He unwrapped her soup and bread and sat it in her lap. "I got you the chicken-and-dumplings soup. It's hot."

He knows I love chicken and dumplings. He knows me well. Why would he lie? I can't eat. She took the cover off, and the soup's smell filled the car. She looked down at it and started crying.

"Lena, talk to me."

She took a sip of the soup after she blew on it to cool it off.

"My world is coming down, Danen."

"What happened?"

"Besides your baby news?" She looked up at him with red eyes. "My dad knows about Dougie."

He shook his head at her baby-news comment. "Shit."

"I know." She tried to get down another spoonful.

Danen cranked up the car and continued the trip to her apartment. "He's young. They'll forgive him."

"What about me?"

"You too."

"I don't think it will be that easy." Lena felt like a kid or a teenager awaiting her punishment. Her mental state was overwrought.

When they arrived to her apartment, Danen unpacked all of her things and took them inside. Lena sat at her kitchen table as he brought her things in and took them to her room. Her eyes followed him making his trips, then they drifted to the roses in the center of the table. They were faded, brittle, and drooping. Their stems were curved near their sepals, just as a person's neck looks when their head hangs low. Poor flowers. She felt the same way they did. Neglected.

"Lena."

Lena had her head lying on her folded arms on the table. He patted her back and bent down so that he was eye to eye with her. She wasn't crying anymore, but her eyes were puffy and red. "Lena, I'm heading out, but I will stay if you want. I don't know if me being here will upset you more. I'd like to stay just to make sure you're okay."

Her mouth was on her arm. "No. You can go," she mumbled as she looked at him through half-open eyes. She lifted her head and sat slouched. "Thank you, Danen, but I need to be alone."

"Okay." He stood up. "I know the trip didn't turn out like we wanted, but you need to know that I meant it every time I said I love you."

And I meant it every time I didn't say it. Lena didn't have the energy to be angry and respond. "Thank you. Be safe, Danen."

He hugged her one last time. "Just call me. Please." He walked out of her apartment without looking back.

Lena lay on her bed. The wells of her eyes overflowed repeatedly. She tried to remember the peace she'd had at the bar and on the beach, but it was shattered by her mom's phone call every time. It wasn't real peace. *I need real peace. Oh God.* Her tears soaked her pillow. She screamed in it. *I can't bear anything else going wrong in my life right now. I just can't.* She finally stopped after an hour and went to the kitchen for water. Her phone sat on the table. *Might as well get this over with.* She set her water on the table, picked up her phone, and dialed her dad.

"You made it back okay, Selena?" Lena's dad was stern. He never called her Lena. He always thought nicknames were an excuse to be lazy. He didn't take shit from his students when he was a professor, nor did he take it from his children. He rarely called and checked on her because his reports came from her mom.

"Yes, Dad."

"Good. How was it? I thought your mom said you'd be there until tomorrow."

"I came back early."

"Well, I hope it wasn't on account of me . . . I suspect a little break was needed with you dealing with Dougie on top of that breakup."

"Have you told Mom?"

He cleared his throat. "Yeah. We had a talk with Junior."

"I guess I need to call her."

"You might want to give her some time. She's pretty upset."

"Okay." She laid her head on the back of the chair. It was hard and uncomfortable, but she felt like she couldn't hold it up herself any longer.

"I must admit, Selena. I'm upset with you, too. Maybe I expected this type of behavior from your brother, but you're almost thirty. You should've called us . . . At least I know you two are loyal to each other. Not everybody can say that."

"I wanted to tell you guys, but he begged me! I didn't know what to do. So I didn't say anything."

"He's on my insurance, Selena. I was going to find out, and when the bill came, I did."

"I didn't know that."

"The truth always comes out, sweetie. You should know that by now. Well, I know my son is good at putting people in binds. So, how much did you dish out?"

"Close to three hundred for his bail. Fourteen hundred dollars for his lawyer, and so far, two hundred to help with his fine."

"The lawyer fees sound cheaper than what I've heard in some other cases, but I guess that's thanks to Ms. Ray. It's a shame that she knew and I didn't, but I'm happy she was there to help." Lena sighed.

"I'm going to give you that money back. You should have it by next week. He's my son. Thanks for taking care of your brother. Let this be a lesson. You can always come to us. Your mom and I should be the first place you go for help until you get married."

"Yes sir."

"Take care, Selena."

She ended the call and sighed. *That wasn't terrible. I'll call Mom tomorrow.* She dialed Dougie.

Dougie answered casually, "What's up?"

"Don't 'what's up' me!" *Guess you don't have a care in the world!*

"I tried to call you. You weren't answering your phone!"

"Dougie! I thought you said you paid for your insurance." Her phone beeped. Someone was calling on her other line. She didn't stop to check it.

"I do. I pay Dad!"

"Boy! Oh, I can't with you! You should've told me that! Common sense should've told you that they would find out if you're on their insurance!"

"I didn't think about it. They don't even seem that mad."

"Yeah, not with you!"

"Well, you don't have to worry about it anymore, so you can stop calling me with the attitude!"

Lena exhaled sharply. "Doug, I will—" She hung up the phone before she said something that she'd regret. She picked up her water and went back to her bed, then lay down and closed her eyes. She needed to vent. There was too much on her chest and she needed to take the weight off. *I can't call Sheree. She'll kill me. Well, she didn't tell me about Eric . . . She can't be mad about Danen.* Lena unlocked her phone and went to her call log. Alonzo had called her while she was on the phone with Dougie. *Definitely not calling him.*

Chapter 39

Lena woke up Sunday afternoon with a banging headache. She sighed and rolled over. *I don't even know what the point is. I should stay in this bed.* She forced herself up and into the shower. After her shower, she sat on her bed wrapped in a towel. She dialed her mom. She should be out of church. No answer. *Okay. I'll try her later.* She went in the kitchen and took out the soup that Danen had bought her and warmed it. She stood at the counter and ate the remnants. Winston called her as she ate, and she didn't answer.

Oh, I'm not ready to go back to work tomorrow. I need a vacation from my vacation . . . Worst vacation ever. I can't believe Danen. Doesn't matter now. She contemplated calling Alonzo back, but she didn't really know what to say to him. *I slept with Danen. We're even. You gonna take me back? Hell no.* She went to her room and put on a long-sleeved shirt and shorts. No panties. No brassier. Sluggishly, she went into the kitchen and took two aspirin. Finally, she retired to her couch and called Sheree.

"Hey, stranger!" Sheree was thrilled to her hear Lena's voice. "How was the vacay?"

Horrible! Lena heard people in the background. "Okay. What are you doing? I need to meet."

"I'm in Greensboro with Tony. Just okay? Why just okay?"

"I need you, Sheree . . . to explain why it was just okay. What's in Greensboro?"

"Umm . . ." Sheree was hesitant to answer. "Alonzo is taking his mom out for her birthday and invited Tony, who invited me. Dougie is here."

"Oh. Wow. Okay."

"You all right?"

"No! I'll just say it. Something happened between me and Danen in Virginia, and I regret it big time, and my parents know about Dougie."

"Lena—what? Hold on." Sheree stepped outside. Lena could hear Ms. Ray's screen door slam. "We're at Ms. Ray's house and Tony was looking at me funny. You went to Virginia with Danen?"

Unfortunately. "Yes."

"So, you lied to me?"

"It's not like that. I didn't want to put you in an awkward situation with Tony anyway."

"Lena, that's no excuse. You lied to my face in the club when I asked you."

"Sheree, right now is not the time to point out old stuff. I need you right now. Everything is falling apart!"

"Well, I'm in Greensboro. I didn't drive. I can't come! And I told you not to talk to him. You don't listen!" Tony stuck his head outside and asked if everything was okay. Sheree told him yeah.

"God! Sheree, please. Just talk to me."

"Yeah, God is who you need to talk to! This is your mess. Alonzo cares about you so much. So what if he made a mistake?"

"I don't need you judging me, Sheree. I need a friend."

"I can't talk about all of this right now. My boyfriend is best friends with Alon—your ex. Don't put me in this position."

"The position of my friend? Are you serious, Sheree?"

"Yeah, I am. I'll talk to you later, Lena." Sheree hung up.

Lena tried her mom again. No answer. She tried her parents' house number. No answer. *Damn. Mom won't talk to me either.* Lena was distraught. She lay there and squeezed her eyes closed. She wished everything would stop and go away. Suddenly, she found herself in her grandma's living room. She was five. The trigger: feeling alone.

Her grandma was sitting on her sofa ironing her grand-dad's clothes. She lowered the ironing board until it was to her knees. Lena sat on the floor watching her. Her grandma pressed a white, collared shirt and hung it on a hanger.

"What are you thinking about, Selena?" Grandma Ethel patted her head as she walked into the kitchen to check dinner.

"I don't know, Grandma."

"You do know. What's grinding your gears?"

"Is my dad okay?"

"Yeah, he's fine. Your mom and his doctors are taking good care of him, Selena."

"I'm always by myself. I hate it, Grandma!"

"You're never by yourself, Selena."

"Yes, I am."

"What about God? You forget about him?"

"I can't see God!"

"That doesn't mean he's not there, and when you feel lonely you can talk to him. It's called praying. You know how to pray, girl! In fact, we can do it now." She sat on the floor next to little Lena. "Say this when you feel alone. You listening?"

"Yes ma'am."

"God, as you watch over me, remind me of your presence. Send me your grace and mercy, and watch over my family. Send me your love so I can share. Keep me in your hands and sacred care. Thank you for showing me that I cannot be broken. Bless me, oh Lord, as these words are spoken. Amen." She hugged Lena. "Now, I want you to remember that, sugar. Okay?"

Lena smiled. "Yes ma'am."

Lena was back in her apartment. She fell to the floor. On her knees and slumped over, she buried her forehead in her hands. She wiped the tears from her face as she knelt on her floor. She closed her eyes and held both of her hands at her chest. *I'm not alone. I am not alone. I have God. God, please show me that I'm not alone.*

Her phone rang. She stayed on the floor with her eyes closed. The caller called right back. She looked up, took the phone off of the couch, and answered without checking the ID.

"Hello?"

"Lena. You all right?" Alonzo questioned. He'd found out from Tony that Sheree was on the phone with an upset Lena.

"No."

"Lena. *Baby*. What's wrong?"

"I made a mistake."

"I made a mistake first, but none of that matters. I'm coming to you. Just hold tight tonight. I promised my mom that I'd stay, but I'm off tomorrow. I'll be there first thing in the morning."

She sighed.

"I promise I'll be there. I talked to Dougie. I know your parents know. That's part of why I was trying to reach you . . . to warn you."

Lena wished she had answered his call. Alonzo was only trying to help her. They hung up after he reassured her that he was coming to be with her.

Chapter

Lena woke up and called in first thing in the morning. She had sick days that needed to be used. October 5 would be used as a personal day. She could not go to work looking like she walked fresh off of the set of *The Walking Dead*. Kalvin assured her that the HR department at Powers Communications was functioning and efficient. *Good.* Selena Harris was feeling a hell of a lot better than the day before, thanks to her grandma and Alonzo. She longed for her grandma. *Maybe that was her who told me to talk with God yesterday . . .*

Alonzo called. "Good morning." Lena was brushing her teeth.

"Morning! I'm on the way."

"Okay. I'm here." She said between brushing and spitting.

"I'm glad you're handling that. Wouldn't want you to melt my face when you see me."

"Whatever, Lonnie." Lena looked up and at herself in the mirror. *Lonnie? That slipped.*

Alonzo chuckled. "It's nice to see you're adjusting. I'll see you in a few with brunch . . . and more roses. I'm sure the others are dead."

"They are. You sent those?"

"I did. Who else would it have been?"

"No one."

Alonzo chuckled. "I'll call when I get there."

Lena smiled. "Okay."

Lena fixed her face and dressed. She tried her mom's cell again. Still no answer. She sighed. *I should've gone with my gut and told her.* She went into her bedroom and started unpacking her suitcase. She'd avoided even looking at her bags because they reminded her of Virginia with Danen, the baby daddy. Clothes were flying into different piles. Dark colors, whites, light colors, and dry-clean only. She emptied the rest of her luggage and put them in her hall closet. As she stacked them in the closet, her phone rang in her room. She ran to it, hoping it was her mom, but it wasn't. It was Tammy. She laughed before she answered. *I bet she wants to know why I didn't come in.* "Hello, Tammy?"

"Lena, I need your help!"

"What? What's going on?"

"Can you meet me? Now?"

Not again. I should just call the police. I don't need to be involved in this. Shit. "I'm at home. Just come here. I'll text you my address."

"Just tell me where to go. I'm driving now!"

Lena gave her directions and remained on the phone. Loudly knocking on the door, Tammy arrived frantically. Her hair was disheveled. She looked like she had been running for dear life. Lena opened her door, and Tammy walked in sobbing. She took a few steps in and collapsed near Lena's table, just missing the leg of a chair. Lena closed the door, locked it, and ran to the bruised and battered Tammy. Tammy covered her face, but there was no hiding her blackish-purple right cheek. She had a swollen lip and another black eye. Lena's eyes watered at the sight. She could feel her blood pressure rise. All of the peaceful energy that she collected the day before was being sucked away with each heave of Tammy's chest.

"Tammy, I'm calling the police." Tammy said nothing. She lay there on the floor clutching her purse. Lena dialed 911 while she walked to the bathroom to grab some damp towels. She reported that her coworker had been attacked and needed medical attention, and gave them her address. "Tammy, where's Lisa?" Tammy made no attempt at making any words. Then there was a knock on the door.

Tammy jumped up suddenly, leaving Lena's consoling hug. "Who is that?"

Lena, just as confused as Tammy, answered, "I'm sure it's just the police." But only a few minutes had passed since she had called them, and Tammy's paranoia was rubbing off on Lena. *Too soon to be Alonzo, unless he left sooner than what I thought.*

"That's not the police! Oh my God! He was watching me. He followed me!"

Lena patted Tammy on the back. "Tammy, calm down. That could be anyone. It's not him." The visitor knocked again. She started to walk toward the door.

Tammy grabbed Lena's arm tightly. "Whoever that is got here too quickly to be the police. I didn't hear any sirens."

Amazed at how quickly Tammy had come out of her crying spell, Lena snatched her arm away and continued to the door.

"Stop!"

Lena, startled from Tammy's yell, turned around to tell her to stop yelling, but found herself focusing on a barrel of a .38-caliber revolver. Tammy was about a foot and a half away, standing with unsteady hands. Lena put her hands in the air.

"Tammy, put the gun down."

"He's not coming in here! He's not hitting me!" Tammy was screaming and crying again.

Lena blew up. "This is bullshit! You are not in my house with a gun pointed at me! I didn't do this to you! What the fuck!" Lena was breathing hard and tried to calm herself down. "Tammy, I'm your friend. Put the gun down, please."

The knocking grew louder. Whoever it was, was really trying to get in. Tammy motioned for Lena to come to where she was. Lena walked toward the table, while Tammy, keeping the gun on Lena, traded places with her and walked toward the door.

Lena was furious. She was being held hostage in her home by a battered woman with a gun. Her cell phone was ringing off the hook, and Tammy was now mumbling "This is it" repeatedly like a crazy woman. She wanted to block it all out, but the banging on the door continued and the person was now shouting something.

Faintly, she heard them say, "Open the door!" She heard that maybe twice, but couldn't hear what they had been saying before that.

Lena contemplated walking to her ringing phone that she left in the bathroom, but didn't want to take her eyes off of Tammy. "Tammy, just check to see who it is! It's not your husband." Tammy didn't acknowledge Lena at all. Lena watched as Tammy unlocked the door with one hand and held her gun toward the door in the other. As the door opened she finally heard the first word of the shouter opposite her front door.

"Lena, open the door!" It was Alonzo. *Alonzo. Oh my God. She'll shoot him!*

The police were there. She could hear a siren. What seemed like a lifetime passing by was only about twelve minutes, but now it was fight or flight. Lena's protective instincts kicked in. She had spent too much time, even in their separation, loving Alonzo too much for him to go out like that—at the hands of a momentarily insane woman.

While Tammy opened the door with her eyes closed and pointed her gun out of it, Lena ran up behind her and grabbed her by the back of her neck. She caught a glimpse of Alonzo. His eyes widened at the unexpected sight. She squeezed as hard as she could, trying to restrict Tammy's oxygen flow. In that moment, she left her body. That release that she depended on had finally arrived, but this time it wasn't just some fantasy. This time it was her current scene. She saw her neighbors outside watching the dramatic scene unfold. She saw the cops, one on the radio in the car and the other running to her door and unholstering his weapon. She saw Tammy, whose hand was growing tighter around her gun, and she saw Alonzo. Sweet Alonzo, with his hands up trying to take a step back. Two guns pointed at him. All the sounds faded back in a flash, and the commotion came back to life. In a whisper to God, while holding Tammy's neck, she pleaded, "Please don't pull the trigger."

Chapter 41

How is he so cool right now? If I were him, I'd be flipping out. "You're taking this pretty well." Lena sat next to Alonzo on his couch.

"Well, there's no need in crying over spilled milk." He sat next to her, but he felt so far away.

"I know, but—"

"But what? Clean the milk and move on. That's what we have do in life, Lena." He scrolled through the cable menu searching for the game.

"So, what do you want to do?"

He turned the TV off and faced her. "It's not what I want to do. That's how we got into this situation in the first place. It's what you want to do. Are you going to stare at this puddle of milk on the table or clean up your mess? It's me or him! Alonzo or Danen! You take so much time wallowing in mess when you can just make a decision and move on. Damn, Lena."

"Lonnie, you know I love you."

"I love you too. You know that, but I don't think it will be enough. Will my love for you be enough to make you forget about my mistake?" He stood up and looked down at her.

"Lonnie." She reached for him. "Come sit back down."

He stepped away from her. "Will it?"

"I don't know. I need to think about it!"

He walked toward the door. "Nah, Lena. You do too much thinking. You overthink. What's your heart say? You know what you want."

"I don't want to say."

"You got me, Lena, and you know it. As long as I'm in your grasp, you never have to decide." He stood at the door.

Lena wanted to stop him. She tried to get up from the couch. She tried to stand. She couldn't move. She felt stuck to the couch. "Lonnie. I don't want to be without you."

"But does that mean you want to be with me?" He opened the door. It was black inside of it. Fear took over Lena's eyes. The blackness entered the room. It engulfed him. He was surrounded by it. The door closed behind him, then the whole doorframe disappeared.

"Lonnie!" The panic that stretched across her face was unsightly. The blackness spread across the room, sucking up everything in its path. The walls, the appliances, the furniture; everything was disappearing into the blackness. She tried to move from the couch, but she was still stuck. The blackness crawled under her feet. The floor disappeared from beneath her. She covered her face with her hands and prayed it would go away. She opened her eyes after a gust of wind brushed her, and then there was nothing. There were no remnants of Alonzo or his apartment.

She heard a loud crash that snapped her out of the blackness. The trigger to her ghastly nightmare was Alonzo standing at gunpoint. She heard her heartbeat. *Thump. Thump.* It was slow. The room blinked out. She felt something wet on her face. She wiped it off. The room blinked out again. She looked down at her hands and saw blood.

Her body was sprawled across the floor near her table. *Blood. There's blood everywhere.* She looked around. It was on her hands, shirts, pants, and floor. Everything was black. *What's going on? Alonzo . . . Alonzo! Alonzo! Alonzo! Alonzo!* Her voice echoed. *Where are you?* She stood in blackness. She was locked away. Overloaded. *Lonnie!* She sat on the floor in the black room; she chose Indian style as her position. *Don't leave me now. Don't go . . .*

"Please don't pull the trigger. Please don't pull the trigger." She heard her voice over and over. She saw Alonzo's eyes. She had never seen him so afraid. The cop was closing in and Tammy was squeezing the gun's trigger tighter; the reel stopped and replayed every time she heard the gunshot. *Oh my God. Was he hit? Is Alonzo okay? God, tell me!* She sat there for what seemed like hours covered in blood. *Is it my blood? What happened?* She felt a sharp sting in the back of her head and became dizzy. *Please wake me. I was only trying to help. How could she turn on me?* She held the back of her head. It was throbbing. She wondered if she would see her mom, father, and Dougie again. *Maybe I was too hard on him. He made a mistake. He's so young.* Her anger for Sheree and Danen left her. Her only concern was leaving the dark room and making sure Alonzo was safe. With no other option, she closed her eyes. The gunshot continued to echo. *I'm alone again, Grandma. Maybe I'm on the way to see you.*

Chapter

"Let me through!" Alonzo jerked his arm away from the police officer. Sirens were wailing in the background. An ambulance and second police car were pulling into the parking lot.

"Listen, sir. My partner is clearing the scene. Just hold on a second!" The officer could barely keep him restrained. He tussled with Alonzo, then finally put him in a controlled hold to keep him still.

Alonzo watched as the other two officers approached them and calmed down a bit as he didn't want to be arrested *or shot* for anything. He quickly refocused on Lena's doorway. He was steps away and his heart was beating so fast that he started to hyperventilate. He could see her toes pointing toward the ceiling. She was lying on her back on the floor. There was blood on her white carpet. He knew that she would be pissed if she saw the mess. The officer in her apartment was crouched on the ground in between her and Tammy. Tammy was lying on the ground, too. Lena was so still. Her arm was by her side. He looked at her hand. It was so slender and dainty. Lena looked so fragile, and she was. *If I had gotten here quicker, this wouldn't have happened. She's so fragile, and I didn't take care of her.* He said a prayer to himself as the other officers and EMTs entered Lena's apartment.

"Sir. I'm Officer White. Calm down before you make yourself sick. Okay?" The officer loosened his grip from across Alonzo's chest.

"I just need to get in there. That's my girl on the floor!"

"Which one? We were called here about a domestic disturbance. One of the young ladies in there was attacked earlier today. What's your name, son?"

"I'm not your son!"

"Just tell me your name, and I'll let you go, but you can't go in there until it's clear."

"My name is Alonzo, and I haven't attacked anyone. I just got here from Greensboro to see the woman that lives here! And she's lying in blood!" One of the EMTs had knelt down beside Lena and was leaning over her. Alonzo couldn't see her face. He stretched his neck, but couldn't see her. "Fuck!"

"I'm sure she's okay. Just calm down! I need to see your ID." The officer released him and held out his hand and waited.

"My girl might be shot, and you're out here IDing me? Man!" Alonzo bogarted Officer White and tried to get in, but another officer in the doorway stopped him. Both officers grabbed him. They tussled until he was pinned to the ground with his hands behind his back. He winced.

One of the officers had his knee in his back. The other was pressing down with his elbow. Alonzo didn't know his brute strength until that instant. He strained while lifting his head and looked into her apartment. Lena was still lying still. He could see her face. There was splattered blood across her cheeks. Her eyes were closed. He tried to concentrate and look harder. He wanted to see her chest inflate, but the officers were pressing down on him so hard that he dropped his head. With his face lying on the concrete, he looked. The EMTs were checking her pulse. *Shit, Lena. Hold on!* He closed his eyes.

"I tried to warn you, Alonzo." Officer White was huffing and out of breath. "I'm going to have to put you in cuffs for your protection. I don't want to have to take you downtown. I know you're worried. They're almost done in there."

The other officer searched Alonzo's pockets while he was down and removed his wallet from his back pocket. "The ID says Alonzo Thompson. This isn't our guy." The two officers stood Alonzo up and walked him to the door. His face stung and had small pebbles and dirt falling off. Alonzo watched an officer and EMT roll Tammy over onto a stretcher. Her shirt was cut off and her arm was wrapped in gauze, although blood was seeping through. He then knew whose blood it was all over Lena's carpet. Tammy was asleep, or at least she looked like it. He overheard the EMT tell the cop that he had to sedate her as they rolled Tammy's stretcher to the ambulance.

"Hey what's your name?" Officer White called to the other EMT that stayed with Lena.

"Mark."

"What are her stats, Mark?" Officer White nodded toward Lena.

Alonzo gazed at Lena. He wanted to touch her. He remembered the last time that he did. *The last time I touched her she walking away from me. She brushed my hand away and walked off. That can't be the last time. I want our last time to be loving. I want our last time to be unforgettable. I want our last time to be . . . I don't want us to have a last time.*

Mark yelled back, "Her vitals are fine."

"You hear that?" Officer White nudged Alonzo.

"Huh?" Alonzo asked.

"I told you she was okay."

"Lena!" Alonzo called out for her.

Chapter

Lena could hear voices. She heard her name. She heard Alonzo. There was mumbling and shuffling going on around her. *Help . . . I'm in here.* She stood up in the middle of the black room's floor. No one came. *I know this isn't the end. I wasn't even happy. Would God allow me to die unhappy? I was alone. I hated my job. I wanted to quit . . . I should've quit. If I get out of here, I will. I'll enjoy myself. I'll go out and travel! I'll love without fear.*

Outside of Lena's head, the EMT was flashing a light in her eyes. She wasn't responding or moving. He pulled an ammonia inhalant from his shirt pocket and held it under her nose. She took a sharp breath. She looked totally out of it as she came to. She moved her arm, but the EMT told her to be still. "Just calm down, miss."

"Her name is Lena!" Alonzo yelled out while watching intently.

"Don't move, Lena." He finished checking her out. Lena looked woozy.

"Owww!" she screamed loudly as the EMT grabbed her arm to help her up.

"What are you doing to her?" Alonzo took a step toward the door, pulling away from Officer White.

"Hold on, Alonzo." Officer White uncuffed him. "Go." Alonzo rubbed his stinging wrists and walked into her apartment. He could finally see her, and he wouldn't leave her side.

Lena lost her footing and almost fell over while the EMT attempted to help her stand. "Okay, Lena. Take it slow." He and another officer helped her to a chair at her table.

Two officers went over to Lena as she sat at the table. She was slumped over and breathing heavily. They questioned her and took her statement as the EMTs checked her arm. She had been holding it since she sat in the chair. Mark, the EMT that checked her out, pulled one of the officers to the side and told him that it was urgent that they get her to the ER. The officers wrapped up their questioning. Mark and his partner put her on a stretcher and rolled her to the ambulance. Lena looked at the faces of all of her neighbors standing outside of their apartments as she rolled down the sidewalk. She wished they would go back in while she thought of all the awkward stares she would come back to when she was back home from the hospital.

Alonzo grabbed her hand as he walked beside her stretcher. "Don't worry, Lena. You're safe now." The

EMTs lifted her up. Alonzo let go of her hand as they rolled her into the ambulance. Mark climbed in the back with Lena while the other EMT hopped in the driver's seat. He turned on the vehicle, and the lights on top of the ambulance began to flash. Mark began to close the doors. "I'm right behind you, Lena. I'll see you at the hospital."

Mark closed the doors. Lena closed her eyes as she prepared for her ride.

Chapter 44

"Lena Harris . . ." Danen called Lena as he walked into her hospital room.

She looked at him and smiled. "Hey, Danen."

Danen didn't smile back. He frowned instead.

"I'm okay, Danen. Has word circulated back home already?" It was her third day in the hospital, and she was ready to be back home.

"No." He set a rolled-up, brown paper bag on her food stand, and set the fresh flowers he brought in the window. "I saw your aunt at the game last night and asked her where your mom was. They *always* come to the games together to see Monty play." He started smiling. "By the way, your little cousin is going to take us to state . . . but anyway, your aunt told me she was up here with you at the hospital." He sat in the chair next to her bed. "She said a woman almost shot you, and something about a domestic situation."

Lena let out an uneasy "Yeah."

Danen continued. "Then I remembered what you told me about your coworker. I couldn't believe any of it. I was thinking . . . I was just *with* her." He shook his head and placed a hand on her arm that was in the sling. "How'd this happen?"

Lena explained all the events that led up to Tammy pulling the gun on her. She heard the gunshot and blacked out soon after it. According to the arresting officer's statement, he saw them tussling and ordered Tammy to drop her gun, but she wouldn't. He saw a clear shot and shot Tammy in her left arm. Lena fainted at the sight of Tammy's blood splattering on her. Tammy dropped her gun near Lena, who was out cold. She walked over to retrieve her weapon, and the officer went to restrain her. Their scuffle ended with them both landing on Lena, resulting in her broken arm and minor concussion. The doctors told her that she would have to stay at least three days to make sure there wasn't any serious head trauma.

"I don't know what to say. I'm just sorry this happened to you."

"Yeah, it could've been worse. I could've been shot, but I wasn't, and I'm thankful." Lena stared at the muted TV. "I've definitely learned my lesson about getting into people's domestic situations."

"I don't know what I would've done if you were shot . . . Man, I'm just so sorry. About everything, Lena. I should've told you earlier. We would've still been in Virginia if I had told you before, and you wouldn't be here."

"You don't know that." She patted his hand with her free hand. "Seriously. I forgive you."

He held her hand. "You were so angry before."

"I know, but I didn't know if I was going to wake up. I was so afraid." She squeezed his hand. "I'm not mad at you anymore, but I do think that we should be friends only."

He dropped his head in discontent. "Damn. I mean . . . I think we could at least try—"

"To be just friends?"

He chuckled. "You don't want to give us a chance, Lena?"

"Danen . . . I . . . ." She let go of his hand and sat it in her lap. She stared at the off-white walls to find the words that she was looking for.

"Lena, you can't quit on me," Danen begged.

Danen's statement triggered a free flow of words from Lena. Everything that she felt and needed to say escaped her like a bird gliding through the sky after being released from its cage.

"Danen, I have to *quit* lying to you. I knew all along that this was not meant to be." By the look on Danen's face, Lena knew that her statement left him stunned.

"I don't mean to hurt you, but everything in me told me not to go." She remembered every instance she told herself not to proceed with him, from telling herself not to let him book the trip to her almost backing out the day before they left.

"I even talked myself out of calling you the night before we left. I was going to tell you that I changed my mind." She looked at Danen and waited for him to say something.

He paused. "Well, then, why didn't you go through with it?"

Lena sighed at her predicament. His questioning called for her to be brutally honest. Not only to him, but to herself as well. "Danen, you were my great escape. There were times before the trip when I would think about Alonzo, and I tried not to. I would force myself to think of you instead, but I couldn't shake him. I was running away from my problems with him by going on the trip with you."

Danen sighed. "*He* doesn't deserve you. You still love this man? C'mon, Lena! We spent so many years together! All of that time . . . you're going to throw it away?" He grabbed her hand again and looked into her eyes.

She looked back. "All the time we spent together has passed. It's gone. All we have is now, and I think you need to be catching up with your daughter. She *deserves* all of your time . . . To get to know you."

Danen became quiet. He squeezed her hand, put it to his lips, and kissed it. Then, he placed it back in her lap. He sat quietly for a few seconds. He looked at the TV screen, then out of the window. They both scanned the room whenever they had something hard to say. "You're right. Absolutely right. My baby needs me."

He told her that she'd always have a special place in his heart and that he'd always be here for her. She said that she felt the same way. Danen smiled, stood up, and kissed her on the cheek. He told her that he had brought her something special. He pulled the food stand closer to them, unrolled the brown paper bag, pulled out a plastic storage container, and handed it to her.

She sat it in her lap. "Is this what I think it is?" She tried to pry the lid off with her free hand, but struggled. "Damn." *I'm not looking forward to operating with one hand.*

"Let me help." He picked up the container and pulled the lid off. The container made a loud, suction-release sound. He sat the dish back in her lap.

"Chicken and dumplings! Did your mom make these?"

He crossed his arms and smiled as if he felt accomplished from bringing some excitement into the dreary hospital room. "Yep. Special request . . . and on short notice."

Lena asked him to relay her thanks to his mom. He told her that he would when they met for dinner later, and that she wanted to accompany him on his visit, but could not take off of work early. He had plans to take her out to eat within the hour. They talked a little while longer. Lena unmuted the TV and flipped through the channels. She asked questions about his plans for his daddy-daughter time. He told her about all of the research he had been doing to prepare for Mya's first weekend with him. There wasn't one sentence where his mom wasn't mentioned. Lena figured his mom would be doing all of the legwork, but Danen was a good guy. He'd for sure do some of it. *He'll be the father Mya needs.* She imagined him holding Mya and smiled.

"Well, I need to be heading out. Do you want me to get this warmed for you or anything?" Danen pointed to the container.

"No, I'm not hungry. I'll get my mom to do it later."

Danen set it on the table. "Where is she, by the way?"

Lena tried to sit up on her own, but Danen hurried to her side to assist her.

"I got it. I have to try to do it myself." She rearranged herself. "She went to the cafeteria. She should be walking in soon. Sheree is actually on the way here, too."

He sat with her and they talked for a few more minutes. He showed her some new pictures of Mya that Lauren sent. "Well, tell your mom I said hey. I'll probably see her around town when she comes back. I hate that I'm missing Sheree. I haven't seen her in years!"

"I know! Thanks for coming to see me." Lena held out her arm for a half hug.

He leaned in and wrapped his arms around her. "Don't thank me. If you need anything, Selena Harris . . . Don't hesitate to call. Okay?"

"Okay, Danen." She smiled. She still liked to hear him say her name.

He kissed her on the cheek again and walked out. She watched him disappear into the hallway as her room door crept closed. Lena looked out of her window at the sky. It was blue and clear. There wasn't a dark cloud present. She briefly felt the ocean air caressing her skin. She closed her eyes and saw the waves crashing. The vacation was just another memory for her now. After thinking about the water and waves, she felt the urge to relieve herself. She removed the covers from her legs with her free hand and inched herself to the edge of the bed. Her stomach growled and she began to wonder where her mom was. *Maybe she ran into Danen.* Her phone rang as her feet touched the cold hospital floor. The cold startled her. She felt around the floor for her slippers and slid her feet in them before she reached across the bed to look for her ringing phone. After flipping the sheets around and working up a small sweat, Lena retrieved her phone and answered it just before it went to voicemail. Her dad called to check on her and her mom. She gave him a report on their day and assured him that she would be leaving soon so he wouldn't have to make another visit. Her dad hated hospitals. He had spent so much time in them when she was a child. She didn't think he needed the extra stress on top of his worrying about her. Her dad kept her on the phone longer than she intended. Another ten minutes went by. He normally wasn't so talkative, and she hated to rush him off the phone, but Dougie and his court business could wait because she had to go. She placed her phone on the food tray and stepped in the direction of the bathroom. She found herself being yanked back to the bed. A cord had somehow become tangled with her sling. *Shit!* She held her knees together to relieve the pressure. *I'm not going to make it!* Her phone vibrated. She ignored it and pulled the cord through the loop of her sling and untangled herself. *Damn. Finally!* She went to the bathroom. As she walked back to her bed, she saw the notification light on her phone flashing. She remembered that she had gotten a text. Lena sat on the edge of the bed and unlocked her phone. She flipped down the notification panel on her phone and read that Sheree had sent her a message.

Sheree: *Your boyfriends are about to fight!*

Chapter 45

Alonzo walked into the hospital. He had been thinking about Lena all day. He called and checked on her that morning and during his lunch break. Mike tried to convince him to take off twice, but he insisted on staying on the clock. He knew that Ms. Vivian would fuss at him if he walked in at any time before he normally got off. He spent the first two days there with her, and her mom made him promise to go back to work on the third day. She had walked him out of Lena's room past the crowded nurse's station. She waited at the elevator with him and told him, "I'm here with her. Go to work. She won't be alone." She gave him a hug when the elevator reached their floor. She squeezed him tight and said, "Thank you for being there for my baby."

He greeted a custodian who was sweeping the floor as he walked toward the first-floor elevators. He and a nurse reached the elevators at the same time. She quickly stepped up to press the "up" button once she noticed his hands were full. Alonzo thanked her.

"Looks like someone is tired of hospital food." She laughed.

He laughed with her. "Yeah, I brought something just in case."

The elevator dinged. He and the nurse stepped in. He was careful not to drop his large pizza and two-liter soda. The nurse got off on the floor before Lena's. She smiled and told him to have a good evening. He did the same. He hummed the song that was playing in his car as he ascended to Lena's floor. The closer he was to her, the happier he felt. He stepped off and saw Ms. Vivian, Sheree, and a man that he didn't recognize standing by the wall across from the elevators. Sheree was hugging the guy while Ms. Vivian stood smiling with her arms crossed. Must be a family friend. Ms. Vivian caught his eye as he walked toward them. Her smile quickly began to fade.

She stepped away from Sheree and the man and met him halfway. She placed a hand on Alonzo's back. "Oh, hi! Off already?"

Her tone seemed awkward to him. "Yeah, I brought food. Didn't know if you or Lena had eaten."

"Okay. Lena will love that. Hurry on down there. I know you can't wait to see her."

He turned his head to face Sheree and the guy, who were now both looking at him. Sheree had the same awkward look that Lena's mom had, and he thought it was a little suspicious that she had not come to speak to him. The man stood with his arms crossed. He had a look of disappointment on his face as he glared back at Alonzo. *What's his fuckin' problem?*

Alonzo turned his head back to Ms. Vivian. "Who's that?" He said it loud enough for both Sheree and the guy to hear.

Ms. Vivian forced a smile on her face. "That's Mr. Wimbush. He's a family friend."

Sheree walked over to Alonzo. She tried to lighten the mood by laughing. "You know I love some drama, but don't do this here. Let's go to Lena." She kept her voice low as she grabbed the pizza and drink, freeing his hands.

Alonzo turned his head at an angle and looked at her. All the anger that he had was rising to the top of his body. It was in his head and taking over his brain. He felt his blood pressure increasing as the blood rushed through his veins. He remembered being in that hotel parking lot with Lena. He remembered asking her who it was that was stealing her away. He remembered her yelling "Danen."

"Sheree, there won't be any—"

"You're a grown man. If you want to know who I am, then ask me." Danen had stepped up behind Alonzo. "I'm standing right here."

Ms. Vivian's eyes widened. Alonzo was still facing Sheree. He clenched his fists, then lifted his head in the air and took a deep breath. He didn't know if he should tell himself to calm down or to turn around swinging. Sheree quickly handed Ms. Vivian the food and took her phone from her purse.

Alonzo began to turn around.

"Alonzo!" Ms. Vivian shouted. Sheree quickly hushed her, and whispered, "Don't bring any more attention to them!" She whispered that as if no one else could sense the major amount of testosterone in the hall, and maybe no one could except for them.

Alonzo's phone began ringing in his pocket. He ignored it and looked at Danen. "Who the fuck are you talking to?"

"I'm talking to you! You're asking questions. I have answers. I'm Danen." He rubbed his hands together. "What's up?"

Alonzo took another deep breath. He tried to silence the rage inside of him, but it kept screaming, "Finish him!" His phone began to ring in the background as he attempted to calm himself down. The anger was in control. They may have been something in the past, but now Lena was his, and Danen was trespassing on his territory.

Ms. Vivian whispered his name loudly, still trying to get his attention. "Alonzo!"

"Please get the fuck out my face." He pointed his finger in Danen's face. "You're old news, man."

Alonzo began to walk back to Sheree and Ms. Vivian when Danen said, "Not too old," then laughed.

Alonzo clenched his fist again. His face tightened. He turned back around and walked toward Danen again. By this point, Danen had uncrossed his arms. He motioned for Alonzo to come to him. "C'mon. Let's talk."

"What?" *I'm about to let these fists do the talking.*

Sheree looked around. There were no security guards around. There was a couple waiting for the elevators who were peeping at the two and clearly trying to figure out what was going on between Danen and Alonzo.

She whispered to Ms. Vivian, "Shit. They're gonna go to jail."

Ms. Vivian stared at the two men in fear. She didn't even respond to Sheree.

"Shit!" Sheree handed the food to Ms. Vivian and walked over to them. Alonzo was just walking up to Danen when she jumped between them. "Neither one of y'all better hit me!" Danen had a bright smile on his face. Alonzo had tight lips. His teeth were clenched.

"Move, Sheree!" Alonzo snapped at her while still looking Danen in the eyes. Danen chuckled.

"No, I can't. Lena needs you. Please, Alonzo. You're going to go to jail!"

Danen's smile disappeared. "Selena doesn't need this fool."

It was at that point that Alonzo realized that Sheree was right. *Lena needs me.* Danen had already lost, and he was taking his anger out on him, but Alonzo was too prideful. *I still ought to fuck him up for trying me.* "So, that's what this is about? Lena not choosing you?" Alonzo shook his head.

Sheree hit Alonzo on the chest. "Stop it!" She turned around to Danen. "They will call the cops if you two do this here. Danen, just go home! Think about Mya!"

Danen huffed and looked down at Sheree. He grabbed her by her shoulders and stepped away. "You know I'd fuck him up, right? You know it." She nodded her head yes. "Just go. Please."

Danen looked at Alonzo one last time. He walked to the empty elevator. Alonzo's eyes followed him as he entered it. Danen's smile crept back on his face once he stepped in. He yelled, "Old news, my ass. We had a great vacation!"

He leaned to press the floor button on the panel and stared at Alonzo until the elevator doors closed.

Vacation? Alonzo stormed away. He left Sheree and Ms. Vivian by the elevators as he briskly walked to Lena's room. He got to her room and stood outside of her door. *I was worrying my ass off over here and she was going on secret getaways and shit. Why do I even bother?* He slowly paced in front of her door. He was trying to calm himself down as much as he possibly could, but it was hard with all of the adrenaline being pumped from his recent altercation. *I can't go in there yelling. She's in the hospital.* He looked down the hall to see if Ms. Vivian and Sheree were coming. He didn't see them. Alonzo took a few deep breaths before he knocked on her door and entered.

"Are you okay?" Lena exclaimed as he walked in.

Alonzo was taken aback. *How does she know?* He walked over to the bed. Lena sat up as he got closer and moved to the edge of the bed. Her feet were dangling off the side of the bed and were almost touching the floor. He got to her before she stood up. He put his hands up and motioned for her to stay seated. "Don't get up."

Lena froze. Her free hand was pressed down on the mattress for support. She looked worried. "I called you. I called you twice. What happened?"

Alonzo vaguely remembered his phone ringing. He stepped away from the bed, and sat down in the chair next to the bed. Lena remained sitting on the edge of the bed. He rubbed his forehead with the palm of his clammy hand. He felt a headache coming on.

"Alonzo . . ." She began to stand up.

Alonzo stared at her. Lena stood up and walked to the chair. She stood in front of him. "Are you okay?"

Alonzo looked up at her silently. He stood up and towered over her. *You cause me so much trouble, Selena. I could've gone to jail.* He was so angry. He could see himself walking up to the wall and punching it. "I think I should go."

"No! Don't."

Alonzo stepped away from her.

"Oh my God. Just talk to me!" She grabbed the bottom of his T-shirt.

Alonzo stopped in his tracks when he felt her tugging his shirt. She was begging him, and he couldn't turn a blind eye to her concern for him as she stood there with her arm in a sling. He put his hands on her shoulders and lightly squeezed them. Lena looked at him with heavy-hearted eyes. He knew that she felt guilty. He sighed and dropped his head. He couldn't find the words. He was too hurt, too tired, too mad, too frustrated, and too confused. He backed her up to the bed. She sat down. He sat next to her.

"Lena." He looked down at the floor. "Did you go to Virginia with Danen?"

Chapter 46

Lena felt her stomach turn. As if her nerves weren't already out of order, Alonzo asking that question made her stomach churn. Lena quickly thought of what excuse she'd give him. *I was drunk. I didn't mean to . . . but I did. We just happened to pick the same vacation spot . . . shit! We wouldn't be here if you didn't sleep with Tiffany! That's an automatic win! But it's not true. I can't control what he did to me, but my reactions, I choose. I chose to seek refuge in pleasure and hurt you.* She knew that seeing Danen was detrimental to her relationship with Alonzo and she still did it. She did not want to be alone. She wanted to hide from her problems, but she was tired of hiding. She didn't know how Alonzo would react, but she had to present *her* truth, no matter how difficult it was. "I tried to tell you. I tried to tell you the day I got back." Lena's voice cracked.

Alonzo looked up at the ceiling. "So, when you said you made a mistake . . ."

"I was referring to him." She touched his hand.

Alonzo stood up, letting Lena's hand slide off of his and onto the bed. "You feel better now? You feel better since you got me back?"

"Alonzo, it wasn't like that!"

"Whatever, Lena." Alonzo walked to her door.

Lena yelled, "Where are you going?" She followed him to the door.

Alonzo put his hand on her shoulder and held her back. "Man, stop it." He held her off. "Go get back in the bed."

Lena couldn't feel him anymore. He felt emotionless. She needed to feel him again. "No. Come back. We need to talk."

"I don't want to talk. Your mom and Sheree will be in here in a minute. You can talk to them. They can tell you what happened."

"Alonzo, it's not like that. I wasn't retaliating."

"Is that why your mom wanted me to work today?"

"Lonnie, what are you talking about?" Lena looked confused.

"Don't 'Lonnie' me now. Did she ask me to go to work so Danen could come?" Alonzo stood with his back against the door.

"We didn't know he was coming. I promise. I haven't talked to him since—"

"Since y'all's vacation together. Right?"

Someone tried to open the door, and it bumped Alonzo in the back. Lena could hear Sheree calling her mom over. Alonzo opened the door and held it for her mom and Sheree to come in. They both walked in with the same look of confusion. Alonzo continued to stand by the door. Lena didn't go back to her bed. She stood there in her hospital gown and slippers. Her bare back and blue panties were showing through the opening of her gown. She had nothing to hide. No more secrets to hold on to.

"Is everything okay?" Sheree asked as she sat at the foot of the bed.

Alonzo answered quickly, "Yeah. I was just leaving."

"No, you aren't!" Lena exclaimed.

Lena's mom stood up from the chair that she had just sat down in. "Selena, you need to have a seat, honey."

An annoyed Sheree interjected, "Yeah, you need to rest. Let him go if he wants to leave. It's not that serious."

Alonzo sucked his teeth at her comment. "Why don't you hush for once?"

Ms. Vivian took Lena by the hand and pulled her to the bed, where she sat her down.

Sheree looked appalled. "Oh no. Don't be getting an attitude with me because you were scared to fight Danen."

"Scared?" Alonzo yelled.

Lena watched them go back and forth. She didn't have the energy to stop them. Her mom called Sheree's name, urging her to stop.

Sheree belittled him. "They don't do all of that talking where I'm from. One word and he would've been dropped."

"Her little ex-boyfriend didn't want to see me, and if he felt bold enough to hit me, then this was the perfect place for him to be."

"I hear you talking, Alonzo." Sheree rolled her eyes and started picking at her fingernails.

"There wasn't going to be any fight!" Lena's mom had had it. "It's getting late, and this is too much excitement for Lena. I can't believe you two right now!" She looked down at Lena. Lena's eyes were watering. "Lena should be going home tomorrow. I'll update you then, but she needs to rest."

Lena wanted him to stay, but she knew he wouldn't. He felt so cold. Every time she approached him, he pushed her away. It was such an agonizing feeling. She wondered if that's how he felt when she pushed him away in the parking lot of Tammy's hotel. *Why do we keep hurting each other?* She let the question bounce around the walls of her head. She hoped he would hear her. She hoped Alonzo would feel her.

Alonzo looked at Lena, then walked out of the door without saying another word.

Sheree shook her head. She grabbed her purse and hugged Lena. "I'll see you tomorrow, girl. Sorry . . . about all of this."

Her mom stood beside the bed with her hand resting on Lena's shoulder. She stayed there after her visitors had gone. Lena leaned into her mom's arm, her weight becoming heavier every time she inhaled. She was holding back tears. *I'm tired of crying.* Her mom sat down beside her and pulled her in closer. She sat and hugged her.

"Everything will work out the way it is supposed to. I know you may not understand it, but you will later." She rubbed Lena's cheek and kissed her on the forehead. "Lonnie . . . he is pretty heated. You should give him some time, baby."

Lena sat up and scooted back to the head of the bed. Her mom helped her. She sat there not saying anything. Her mom asked her to eat. She wouldn't. She hated how he walked out so angry. He didn't kiss her goodbye. He didn't say a word, and it was tearing her up inside. She imagined him in his truck fuming on the way home and prayed that he made it to his place safely. *How am I going to fix this?*

Lena sat back in her bed. Her mom had fallen asleep in the chair after telling her about Alonzo and Danen's altercation. Hearing about how Danen provoked Alonzo irritated her. It made her even more satisfied with her decision to leave him alone. *He clearly has more growing to do.* She listened as the heavy hospital doors on her hall opened and closed. The night-shift nurses were doing their rotations. Her nurse had already come in and informed her that she would be leaving the following day. She wouldn't miss the dreary beige walls or the generic painted, flower print. The news gave her something to look forward to. *I've got to make some changes. Anything. Anything to make my life better.* She contemplated how she went from her normal life to lying in a hospital bed calculating her love triangle. She couldn't even fathom going back to work. She didn't even know when she would be going back. Whenever she closed her eyes, the backs of her eyelids were covered with scenes of the police in her hospital room asking questions about Tammy, or doctors telling her, "You hit your head pretty hard," Danen giving her his most persuasive smile, or Alonzo looking at her with his most worrisome eyes. If her thoughts were a pool, then she was drowning in them. She lay there all night, barely sleeping, and waited for the morning to come.

Chapter 47

It had been a week since the hospital fiasco, and Alonzo was just calming down. Every time he tried to let it go, he thought of Danen in the elevator grinning. He would think of Danen holding Lena, touching her, and kissing her. He knew that something happened between them, or at least that was what he assumed that Danen was implying. He had not spoken to Lena, although she had called him several times. What she had done was unforgivable. It didn't matter that he cheated first. His situation was a mistake, but Lena's was deliberate. He would constantly tell himself, *She planned a vacation with him*, to justify his anger.

Alonzo sat on the side of his bed rubbing his head and the sleep out of his eyes. It was Saturday morning, and he needed to do something to get out of his bad mood. He looked over to his nightstand. Lena's face sat in a frame, smiling at him. Even though the past few months were filled with hurt and anger with her, he had not moved her photo. As angry as he was with her, he still wanted to feel her near him. He wanted to hear her voice, but he wanted her to feel his pain even more. He wanted to punish her. So, he wouldn't return any of her calls, and then she stopped calling. Alonzo called her one time to check on her. His ego made him feel weak for calling. So, he made sure their conversation was short. He didn't answer anyone's calls. Tony and his mom called him regularly still. He would only speak with Mike and the other people at his job because he had to.

He looked away from her photo, stood up, and stretched. He rubbed his bare stomach as he walked to his bathroom. His pants sagged down from his waist, exposing the band of his boxers and the curly hairs on his lower abdomen. He stood in his bathroom mirror and brushed his teeth. The whole time, he thought of his and Mike's conversation the day before. Mike suggested that Alonzo take some time off or get himself together over the weekend. Mike's voice rang in his head.

They were in his office when Mike told him, "I know you're going through some things and you're having a hard time with Lena, but you can't let that show here. I'm getting bombarded with questions from all of the other guys that you should be answering or tending to, but hell, they're afraid to talk to you. You walk around looking mean all day and avoiding people. You can't run a business that way, man!" The conversation reminded Alonzo that although he and Mike were friends, Mike would always be his boss first . . . or at least until he became his own boss. *I'm supposed to be running a shop. I have to get myself together. I'm letting this bullshit bring me down. Lena just isn't the person I thought she was, and I need to move on. I need to talk to her and let her know that I'm done. I'm going to see her. We should just end this once for all and she can go be with that other dude.*

He went back in his room and picked up the picture frame from his nightstand. He walked into his nearly empty guest bedroom, past his computer desk, and went straight to the closet. In the closet was a box he labeled "junk." It was filled with little knickknacks that he never unpacked, but didn't want to throw away. He looked at her picture one more time before placing it in the box and refolding the flaps. *I can't believe I thought about buying a ring. I'm fucking making plans for our future while she was making plans with another man. A lame, at that.* He closed the closet doors and shook his head as he left the room. He showered and finished getting ready. He walked into his living room and stood in the middle of the floor facing the windows. The noon sun was peeking through his half-closed blinds. Something about his apartment felt empty and hollow. He plopped down on his couch and took out his phone to call Lena, but he couldn't. He wasn't ready to talk to her and end it, but he'd say anything to convince himself that he was. *She cheated on me with her first love. Shit, and Sheree told Tony she was talking to the white boy from the bar. You don't need her in your life!* He stood up, grabbed his keys from his coffee table, and left his apartment. *I need to talk to her in person. I just need to clear the air.* He made his way to her apartment with the goal to permanently end their relationship. He wouldn't fall second to any man.

Chapter 48

This feels so good. Hot water surrounded Lena's body. Her oversized tub was more than halfway full. She extended her legs so that her knees would go below the surface of the water. She let her shoulders sink into the water. Her straight hair was down and the ends were curling back up to their natural state. Her hair was broken and damaged from wearing it in a ponytail, especially as she slept during the last week or two. *I should cut it . . . Nah, Alonzo would hate that.* She scrunched her face at the thought of not cutting her hair because of someone else's preference. *I can cut my hair if I want.* She let her hair be totally submerged. She could sleep in the water. It felt so good to her, but every time her arm slipped down from the tub's side, she'd get up. She had tied a plastic bag around her cast, but she was very worried that it would still get wet. She sat up, letting the water drip from her hair onto her shoulders. Water rolled down her face. She closed her eyes and wiped it away. With her arms propped around the tub, she thought about her lost love. They had talked only once, and it was two days previous. Their conversation was short. He asked her how she was feeling, and she gave him a generic report. She asked how work was, and he said, "Same old, same old." Both of them had a lot to say, but neither of them knew how to say it. And even in their disconnect, she felt him. She could not shake him. *Obviously, he feels the same or he wouldn't keep calling me.* She drifted away to another place. The trigger, a song titled "Callin' Me."

Lena was in Dougie's car. She had gone to visit him. It was also during the time frame that she found out about Alonzo and Tiffany. He was driving them to a restaurant and was excited that she was treating. The song was blaring from his speakers. She reached over to his dashboard and turned it down. "Who is this?"

"Don't be turning down my music. That's Boosie." He laughed. "You like it?"

She smacked her teeth. "It's nasty." Although she did think the song was vulgar, she really didn't want to hear it because it made her think of Alonzo. He kept calling her. He had already called her three times, and it was only noon.

"That's life, though." He smirked and looked at her. She rolled her eyes, and he burst out laughing.

He's grown now, but he's still my irritating little brother. "I don't need to hear all of that. Mom did tell me that you have a li'l girlfriend." She smiled at him as he tried to keep a straight face. She missed her little brother. *I should call him more. He probably won't answer, but at least he'll know I'm thinking about him.*

He sucked his teeth. "Mom told you wrong."

She laughed and teased him. She told him to show her a picture. He kept denying having one. "Whatever, you'll slip up and she'll tag you in a picture one day."

Dougie turned into a steak house–restaurant parking lot. She looked up at the sign as they pulled in. *Of course he wants steak on me.* She laughed to herself. Dougie fixed his collar in his mirror. He pulled out his brush and went over his head a couple of times. He rubbed his hand over his hair. They got out of his car. Lena fixed her skirt and rubbed out the wrinkles. They were definitely Doug and Vivian's children, checking themselves out before they entered the place. They walked to the restaurant. Dougie made a big gap between them as they walked.

Lena looked over. "Why are you all the way over there?"

"I don't want anyone to think I'm *with* you." He smiled and opened the door for her.

"Anyone like who?" she asked as she walked through.

"I don't know. Anybody . . ."

The hostess seated them in a booth by a window and took their drink orders. The sun was setting and shining through the open blinds. Her last outing to a restaurant was with Alonzo. She sighed as she opened the menu.

"This isn't too expensive, is it? I have some money."

"Oh no. This is fine. I'm just tired."

"Oh. Well, I already know what I want." He laid down his menu, sipped his drink, and looked around.

I bet. She skimmed the menu and settled on a grilled-chicken dinner. She placed her menu on the table. Her brother made a face at her. "What are you doing?" She laughed.

He laughed. "I don't know." He looked around the restaurant. "I have a friend that works here. I don't see him, though." Lena looked around, too. "So, uhh . . . while you're asking me about my imaginary girlfriend . . . what's up with you? When are you getting married?"

Never. She thought about Alonzo and Tiffany and sighed.

"Now you want to get quiet." Dougie chuckled. The waiter came to their table and took their orders. As soon as he had gone, Dougie persisted to question his big sister. "So . . ."

"I don't know." She sipped her drink.

"What do you mean? You've been with Alonzo forever. You don't want to get married?"

Lena shrugged. "I don't know." It wasn't such an easy question to answer. She had to consider his recent actions. She didn't know if he was a cheater or if he had made a mistake. As far as she knew, she'd never answer the phone again, but she missed him a lot.

"What's the point of dating him so long if you don't want to marry him?"

"Love is complicated."

"Well, you need to uncomplicate it. You're getting old, Lena. You're like forty now, right? You're going to be sagging soon if you aren't already." He laughed and Lena shot him a bird.

Lena stepped out of her bathtub and onto her microfiber floor mat. She dried off her back and shoulders, then bent over to get her legs. Drying off took much longer with a cast on her arm. Everything did. *How do I uncomplicate love?* She didn't want to let go of Alonzo, and she thought she wanted to move forward with him, but she knew she hadn't forgiven him for his infidelity. They were both suffering because of it.

Weary of brainstorming ways of trying to solve her Alonzo problem, she climbed in her bed with her laptop. It powered back on to her Internet browser. The last window opened was her e-mail account. All new e-mails filled her screen. She scanned the subject lines. Many e-mails were from work. Some were just conversations that she was cc'd on. Others were from coworkers sending their support and prayers. There were a couple from her boss regarding her return, and one from Tammy. Her eyes froze when she read Tammy's name. *Fuck.*

She let her mouse pointer hover over it. The subject line read, "Please don't delete this . . ." *Bitch, you almost killed me.* She right-clicked on the e-mail and slid her finger down her touch pad until "Delete" was highlighted on the pop-up menu. Lena knew that Tammy wasn't coming back to Powers, and she was happy with the idea of never having to see or talk to her again. She thought, *There's something about having a gun pointed to your face that makes you reconsider forgiveness.* She would try to forget, but forgiving was not an option for her. She clicked off of the e-mail, causing the pop-up menu to disappear. *I mean, what could she really have to say to me? Sorry won't cut it.* Lena pictured her living room. There was a rug covering where most of the blood was on her carpet. Her dad found a CTS decon service and had her place cleaned up before she left the hospital. Lena had no idea that crime and trauma decontamination services existed. To her, crime scenes were just magically cleaned later. *Her crazy ass messed up my carpet.* Lena's curiosity irked her. She opened the e-mail and began reading.

Tammy: *Dear Lena, I hope you that you are doing okay . . .*

She skimmed over the letter. Tammy mentioned getting out on bail and seeing a therapist. She and her daughter moved in with her parents. She was looking for a job and trying to move on. "I'm very sorry about the whole gun thing. It was a horrible mistake. I put you in danger of almost being shot. You didn't deserve that. You were one of the only people trying to help me. I've been praying to God that you have forgiven me, and not for me, but for you. So you can get back to your happy, normal life. I'm so sorry for bringing you into my mess."

Lena shook her head as she read over some of the last lines. *Shot? Don't you mean* killed? *My skin makes me an automatic target.* She closed the e-mail without reading it to the end. She had seen enough. Just looking at all of the e-mails from her job made her anxious. She could feel herself becoming tense. She thought that maybe she should attempt to reply to some of them so that she could have a head start when she returned. *I really don't want to go back there.* And then it hit her—she didn't have to.

Those bare, mahogany walls of her office didn't have to see her anymore unless she was packing up her stuff. She opened her word processor and began writing her resignation letter to Mr. Edwards. She felt a burst of energy fill her as she wrote. She explained that there was too much mental turmoil caused by the relationship she formed with Tammy, and although Tammy would no longer be working there, the memories of the incident would cause her too much anxiety. She closed out by telling him how much she learned there and thanking him for the opportunity to work at Powers Communications. She read over her letter twice, double-checking her grammar and spelling. She printed it and signed it. As she looked around her corner desk for her envelopes, she felt empowered. It was the first time that she had felt that way in a very long time. *Why haven't I done this sooner?* The pay wasn't bad, but it wasn't the best. She was sure she could've been making more elsewhere. She signed the letter and placed it in an envelope. She was supposed to return to work the following week. She didn't want to go back before she had to, so she decided to mail it off. She set the letter on her kitchen table and put on her jacket and shoes. It took her longer to complete simple tasks, but she did them a little faster than she did when she was in the hospital. She smiled at her progress. For the first time, she was focusing on the good things that were happening to her.

It was cool and sunny outside. Someone close by was grilling, and she could smell the food charring in the air.

She walked to the mailboxes. *This fresh air will be good for me.* The farther she got from her apartment, the more she realized she had not done much walking over the past few weeks. She became a little short of breath, but she kept going, walking past the landscapers detailing the small, grassy lots of her apartment complex. She reached the mailboxes and slid her letter in the outgoing-mail box. She leaned on the mailboxes, catching her breath as she checked her box before starting her trek back to her apartment.

She was more than halfway back when a silver truck slowed down next to her. She looked over to it but continued to walk. Then, she stopped and tried to look into the tinted windows of the truck. *Alonzo?* The passenger window rolled down, and there she saw Alonzo smiling at her.

"What are you doing out here?" he asked as he pulled over to the sidewalk.

She opened the door to the truck. "Catching a ride." She climbed into the truck, struggling a little with her sling. She was breathing hard.

"You okay?" He drove to her apartment.

"Yeah, I haven't exercised in a while. I was getting the mail, and I just quit my job." She smiled.

Alonzo looked confused as he pulled into a spot in front of her place.

"Why did you quit? Do you have another job offer?"

They both got out of the truck and walked up to her apartment. "No I don't, but I have enough in my savings to hold me over until I do find something else. I was think-ing that I didn't want to go back. So, I quit."

She unlocked the door and tossed her keys on the table next to her laptop. "Anyway, how have you been? I called you a few times . . . Well, I'm sure you already know that."

Alonzo sat on her sofa. "That doesn't sound like you, Lena, quitting your job without a plan." He watched her as she fixed a glass of water and sat on the sofa cushion over from him.

She sipped some of the water. "Well, it is. What are you doing here?"

Chapter

"I wanted to come talk to you . . . to clear the air." He looked at her and rubbed his beard. He felt his plan crumbling. All of a sudden, he didn't know what to say. He hadn't planned to do anything but tell her about herself for cheating on him, but being in her presence messed all of that up. She was so beautiful to him. He found himself more wanting to kiss her than curse her. She leaned her head on the back of the sofa, still catching her breath from her walk, and closed her eyes. He watched her hair press into the sofa. It was curly. She normally straightened it out. It had been a long time since he had seen it that way. He missed her. "I like your hair."

"Thanks." She laughed and responded with her eyes still closed. "I look raggedy."

"Not to me." All of his anger was quickly disappearing. The atmosphere of the room was peaceful and quiet. She wasn't verbally attacking him as he thought she would. He didn't feel the need to defend himself. She seemed freer, and it radiated from her. He scooted over to the cushion next to her. He was enticed by her energy. Something was pulling him closer. Before he knew it, he cupped her face and lifted her head from the sofa. She looked at him but didn't stop him. He kissed her lips. Her posture began to slump under him. He pulled her closer, being careful to watch her arm in the sling. He moved to her neck. He felt her resist a little, and he bit her neck, causing her to moan. He pushed his hand down her lounge pants and felt in between her legs. It felt like she was melting. She rested her hand on his shoulders and squeezed every time he pushed his fingers inside.

She whimpered. "Alonzo, we shouldn't."

He didn't respond. He grabbed the waistband of her pants and pulled them down in one motion.

"Alonzo . . ."

He stood up from the sofa and got on his knees. He kissed up her leg to her thighs. She was breathing so heavily. *I know how to get you back. No one can make you feel better than I can.* It had been a few months since they touched, and he felt back at home between her legs. *Danen thought he had you, but you're mine.* He kissed her softly and didn't miss a spot. He knew all the right places on her body. He knew what made her squirm. He touched her like he had something to prove. He liked the control.

"Wait . . . Alonzo."

He looked up at her. "Just let me."

Chapter

Lena dropped her head back on the couch as Alonzo traced her thighs with his tongue. Her body responded to him in the most subdued manner. *Oh my God.* She squeezed his shoulder as he licked and moved his fingers in and out. He felt so good to her, but there was something that kept her from fully enjoying the moment. It just didn't seem right. She couldn't put her finger on it. She drifted into her head trying to define it. Alonzo flicked his tongue and jogged her back. *Shit.* She felt like Alonzo could hear her thoughts, because it seemed like he responded to her internal exclamation.

"Yeah, I know." He rubbed her and moved his hands up her shirt. His warm hands covered her stomach and moved to her breast.

She told herself to stop him so they could talk, but her body wanted differently. Her body wanted him to continue. She decided to let her body win. *Maybe next time.*

Alonzo started unfastening his belt. She watched him kneel between her legs.

He looked back at her and said, "You'll always be mine."

Breathing heavily, she sat up some. "What?"

He was pulling his pants down. "It doesn't matter. Nothing matters. You're mine."

She sat up all the way. He grabbed her waist. "What are you doing?"

"Give me my pants."

"Lena."

His love was tainted. It was poisoned with jealousy. She reached around him and picked up her pants from the floor. He removed his hands from her waist, and she stood up in front of him and pulled her pants back up. He stayed kneeling, looking up at her. "I'm mine, Lonnie. I belong to me. Not you. Not Danen. Me." She walked to the bathroom. She wanted to go back out there and let him finish what he started. Her knees felt weak. Her body was screaming for him. She looked in the mirror and cleaned herself up, shaking her head at how she almost let him take her power. The power she had recently gained. She heard him moving around in the living room. *I'm in control.* Lena walked back out. He was waiting for her outside of the bathroom. He put his hands around her waist again and asked her what was wrong.

"This isn't going to work. I've moved on."

He let her go. "You have someone else? Damn, Lena, you're all over the place. That's exactly why I came over here. To tell you we are done!"

She turned around to face him. He walked down the hall and into the front room where she was standing. "Really? Is that why you were on your knees? To tell me we are over?"

"I was on my knees 'cause I miss you, and I wanted to show you that. I mean . . . I thought we were over until I saw you. Maybe I should've stuck with my gut. Looks like you're on some other shit. I don't understand you. We were getting better before the hospital thing happened."

"There is a disconnect between us. You can't see it, but you know it's there, too."

He shook his head. "That doesn't make any sense, Lena."

"But that's faith. You believe in faith, right? Faith is the unseen that you believe in. Same thing."

"What?" He looked at her strangely. "This is different. This is negative." He walked up to her.

Lena didn't think it was negative. It was a positive thing that she was acknowledging the problem and was not ignoring it anymore. It was time that she be honest with herself. She knew that it was negative to him because he would not get what he wanted. They were addicted to each other, and Lena beat her addiction.

"This is positive. You shouldn't want to be with someone who hasn't forgiven you. I didn't forgive you when I took you back, and that made us worse."

Alonzo walked over to her sofa and leaned his back up against it. "Well, what about what you did with Danen?"

"I'm over here looking for clarity, and you want to play the blame game."

Alonzo patted his pockets for his keys. "I'm not playing games. You planned a vacation and slept with the man. That's clear! And you say you don't want to be with me, but you're melting in my hands. You let me in your house. You kissed me back. I don't know why you're acting so different, but whatever, Lena."

She could tell he was becoming frustrated. She couldn't think of a way to explain how she felt. She stood in the middle of her floor recalling everything that happened over the past few months. She looked down at her carpet. Just weeks ago, there was blood all over it. All of the events—picking up Dougie, their breakup, her vacation, the hospital—they were all becoming more distant to her. Time seemed less defined. The only thing that mattered was right now. How could she make her life better right now? What would make her permanently happy? She didn't want any more temporary fixes. Sex was definitely a temporary fix.

She looked up at him, then went to her kitchen table. She needed to sit down. Something had come over her. It was an overwhelming feeling that she couldn't control. Her soul felt lifted. Her eyes watered. Her voice cracked.

"Alonzo, I read a quote the other day. It said, 'Believe in yourself like you are a religion.' I need to put my faith in me. I need to rebuild. I have enough faith in me to quit my job and know that I will come out better, and the first thing you do is doubt me. We talked every day, you knew I disliked my job. I thought you would be excited for me . . . When I'm with you, I'm too busy questioning my decisions or wondering if I can trust you or if we are meant to be. That's wasted energy. We can pretend like everything is all right. But I want more out of life. I don't want to be a robot. Going to work at a job that bores me and coming home to someone that I don't truly trust . . . just to say I'm a part of something. I feel brainwashed. I let everyone else define everything for me. I listened to you, Sheree, and everyone else when it came to our relationship. Yet, always ignored myself."

She paused, thinking over everything. "Alonzo, there are levels to life, and we've only scratched the surface. I haven't been out of this country and I'm almost thirty! You keep asking what happened to me. I've changed. I'm different. I've been losing my life every second I didn't take or *create* an opportunity that *I* wanted. I wasted so much time trying to plan out my life when I should've been living. I finally did something about it. I did something that Tammy couldn't do that day. I pulled the trigger on the old Lena. She's gone."

Alonzo stood there, taking everything she said in. He slowly walked over to the table. Lena watched him as the space between them lessened with each step. His quietness moved her. His every move seemed calculated.

He slowly pulled out a chair and sat down. He leaned back and stretched one arm across the table. The other was in his lap. He looked over to the empty vase on her table. The vase that once held the roses that he'd sent her.

"I knew you hated your job." He tapped his index finger on the table. He looked up at her. His stare was captivating. They looked at each other. He let out a long, deep breath.

"Lena, I uhh . . . I wanted to propose." He paused. While he gathered his words, Lena interjected.

"But Lonnie—"

"No. It's my turn." He stretched his arms across the table. The backs of his hands were resting on the table and his palms were open.

She accepted his invitation and put her hands in his. He held them. "Here's my truth, Lena. I listen to you. I watch you. I know you like nice things. I know you are fed up with Powers. I *know you*. I know that I hurt you." He became quiet, and dropped his head.

Lena squeezed his hands. She had never seen him like that. So vulnerable. Although she could tell that he was uncomfortable in his vulnerability, she sat in silence until he finished.

"I'm a good man. To be honest, I'm a great man. I take care of people, my mom, my boys when they need me. I wanted to take care of you. I don't know . . . Seeing you work hard and hearing you complain about your job reminded me of my mother. Black women. Y'all just work so hard. And me, I'm a simple man. I have a nice truck and I splurge every now and then, but I'm all about the basics. I don't spend much. I've been saving. For me. For us, Lena. To build a home, to be married. I wanted to make you a stay-at-home mom like the families on TV. And with the offer from Mike, I really thought it would happen." He squeezed her hands.

"But you've created this image of me in your head. It seems like it doesn't matter that I do things for you daily. I'm automatically in the 'dog' category based off of my mistake. I *still* want a family. I want to settle down like many other men out there, but we get judged for our past. I work hard so we can have a home together in the future. I just try to be there whenever I can, Lena. Even with Dougie, and I did *one* thing out of character, and now that's me forever? That's not fair, Selena. I told you I had plans for us. I just needed time. I came here to tell you about yourself, but when I saw you . . ."

He shook his head. "I just love you so much. I felt like we could've made it, but you did what you did. The crazy thing is I can't even be mad, but I still get upset every time I think of him touching you. I just wish we could forgive each other and move past this."

He let go of both of her hands and picked up the hand in the cast. He carefully examined it and caressed her free fingers. Her hand looked tiny in his. She smiled at him. He smiled back, lifted her hand to his lips, and kissed it.

"I thought you looked different when I saw you walking. If it wasn't for the sling, I would've passed you. I may not be the man for the new Lena, but maybe the future me will be. I have to have that faith in me, but for now, I get it, I guess." He placed her hand on the table and patted it. He stood up and pushed his chair under the table. She did the same. She walked over to him and wrapped her arms around his waist. He held her closely as if he didn't want to let her go. He kissed her on her cheeks. She maneuvered her face so he could kiss her all over it. He placed his last kiss on her forehead. Lena rested her face on his chest. He was warm and his scent was nice and familiar. His arms wrapped around her and his hands rubbed her back. He rested his head on top of hers, his chin in her hair. "I really can't believe this shit, though. Damn."

She looked up at him. "I know."

He kissed her one more time and released her from their embrace. He walked over to her door, and she trailed behind him. As he opened the door, she called to him. "Lonnie, I'm sorry . . . for making you feel that way. I shouldn't have. You really are a great man. I'm proud of you. I love you."

"Thank you. Get better, Lena." He pulled her in for a brief hug, then closed the door behind him.

She opened it and stepped out. She watched him walk to his truck and drive off.

She took a long, deep breath and leaned up against her door. *That's it. It's done.* There had been that feeling that he was always there, but now it was gone. She felt like she had passed a test by not giving in. It had been so hard to let him go, and just like that it was over. She was amazed at her power. Yet, she stood confidently in it.

As she stood there, she swore that she would never settle or lose herself. She knew that there was something out there for her, and she was determined to get it. She didn't care if her mom and dad didn't approve or if her friends disagreed. She was living for Selena now, and Selena was living for herself. *I live for me now.*

She was triggered to live out her destiny.

Faith Underwood

At Least Love

I've come to the realization that love is differential.
We all receive differently.
We express differently.
But at least we took the opportunity . . .

To love.

At least we fell in love.

If I never had the chance to see you again,
At least I saw your eyes.
At least I looked deeply and tried to find the way to love you,
Even though I cried.
At least we tried.
At least we met. At least we connected.

If I never heard your voice again,
At least I made you smile.
Even when you were mad with me,
At least I drove you wild,
Then gave you the keys and let you freestyle.
At least I didn't mind,
And when the bells started ringing,
At least we read the signs, Yield and Stop,
But before that stop, we explored terrains.
At least we won't be the same.
At least it changed my brain.

If I never had another chance
To touch
On your . . .
Your . . .
Your body ever again.
At least I learned you were a lover and a friend.
At least I found out what love was all about.
At least we shared meals.
At least we met kin.
At least were real to each other,
Even if we can't mend.
I could never be mad at you . . .
Cause . . .
At least we made love.
Made sparkles.
Made magic.
Made a way to find love.
Brought to life what we imagined.

What's greater?
The quest to find love or the discovery?
The messages behind love and the recovery?
Maybe experiencing the love of others is what makes us
more rounded.
And we need these love experiences.
In love, we were founded.
The greatest disservice we could do to ourselves is not
love, or be loved.

At least love.

About the Author

Faith Underwood is a first-time author, freelance blog writer, and entrepreneur specializing in natural soaps and oils. She enjoys writing poetry and traveling. Faith lives in Georgia with her dog, Gianna.